Reynard's Fate

By Peter J. Blake

Copyright © 2013 Peter J. Blake

All Rights Reserved

To Cienna for showing me what love is

Thanks to the Wednesday Nighters: Alan, Andy, Delia, Luke, Mac and Rich who helped shape Lucarcia and all who live there.

Thanks to Lou and Luke for corrections, edits and ideas.

And the biggest thanks to my gorgeous wife, Lou, who encouraged, enthused and energised me, and made this possible.

Table of Contents

-Prologue-..7

-- PART ONE --..11

-Chapter One-...12

-Chapter Two-...25

-Chapter Three-..39

-Chapter Four-..46

-Chapter Five-...56

-Chapter Six-...69

-Chapter Seven-..80

-Chapter Eight-...92

-- PART TWO --...105

-Chapter Nine-...106

-Chapter Ten-..116

-Chapter Eleven-...131

-Chapter Twelve-..139

-Chapter Thirteen-..149

-Chapter Fourteen-...159

-Chapter Fifteen-..167

-Chapter Sixteen-..185

-Chapter Seventeen-...196

-Epilogue-..208

-Prologue-

Emperor Lucar stood on a high, wind-swept hill. The breeze ruffled his long blond hair and made his ceremonial robes whip around his legs. He shielded his eyes from the glare of the midday sun and looked out across the plains of the Rainbow Empire. The empire he ruled. The empire he was about to destroy.

Looking out across the open grassland, he saw dotted villages spread out across the lowlands, glinting in the summer sun. A well maintained road wound its way across the landscape from settlement to settlement, looking like a silver stream running through the countryside. The villages it connected were peaceful and prosperous, well maintained and cared for. Each was carrying on with life, completely unaware of the impending doom which crept and crawled from the Void in far off Granita. The Writhing Death was coming and they knew nothing about it.

Meanwhile, in the capital city of Antissa, the Conclave of High Magi was gathered. They were collected together in the fabulous white marble building of the University, which was the centre of scholarship and study in the whole empire, dressed in their rainbow coloured robes. Some of the Conclave were absent from the capital city. A group of High Magi had headed off to Granita where they were working to close the gate and stop the progress of the Writhing Death.

Months ago Magi from the noble houses of Granita had made a mistake in their research and had somehow opened a gate to the Void. Through that gate had come all manner of tiny, hideous creatures, a plague of writhing, crawling destruction. They had consumed everything in their path. Nothing could stop them and they were slowly and inexorably consuming the entire lands of Granita. The Magi had named the plague the Writhing Death, for it destroyed everything in its way.

Now Emperor Lucar had decreed that the Magi would stop them. No matter the cost.

Lucar looked down on the quiet and peaceful fields below him and felt a deep and overwhelming shame at what he had ordered. The farmers, weavers, potters, bakers and blacksmiths of the land had done nothing wrong. They had simply fulfilled their roles in the great machine of the empire. It was the Magi who had unleashed the Writhing Death but it was the common folk who would pay for that mistake with their lives. And he hadn't even told them.

Lucar pictured his capital, Antissa. Jewel in the crown of the Rainbow Empire. The City of Wonder. This place was the corner stone of his empire, the pinnacle of civilization. This place was where, at his command, the Conclave was currently working a terrible and powerful ritual to split the Rainbow Empire asunder. He had ordered the Magi to rip the lands apart.

As the emperor considered the fate of the lands before him, he felt a shudder in the very earth. The land gave a great quiver and far off in the distance he could hear a terrible roar. The roar grew and grew, getting louder and louder.

The ritual had begun.

Time seemed to stop and Lucar could not but help imagine the effects the Conclave's ritual was having on his beautiful city. He could almost feel the uncomprehending terror as the awesome power of all the High Magi working in unison ripped the city apart. He gave an involuntary shudder as the weight of guilt crashed into him. Thousands of people were about to die, all from his command.

As he watched, mystical light flashed and flickered across the far horizon. The terrible roaring sound stopped. A dull, far-off grinding noise, like the sound of two pieces of flint rubbing together very slowly, took its place. The grinding noise grew steadily louder as the mystical flashes of far-off light grew ever more intense.

The Magi had told the emperor what the great ritual would do. He knew what was going to be happening to his people in the city. He knew what evil fate faced the people living in the lowlands all around the city for miles and miles. He closed his eyes but his mind would not let him escape the pain of knowing he had doomed them all.

Lucar wished he could stop the catastrophe, but he knew it was too late. Even if he could somehow have sent a message to the Conclave from this far-off hill top, there was nothing they could do now. The ritual was in full flow and nothing could stop it. The majestic University, centre of the unimaginable power which drove the ritual, would have been the first thing destroyed. He knew it would already have been shaken to pieces like a dolls house in the hands of a child having a tantrum. He knew that the Conclave of High Magi, who had performed this catastrophic ritual at his command, would all be dead - ripped into little pieces by the unimaginable forces involved.

From the epicentre in Antissa the quake spread rapidly outwards. Like a sound wave, the explosion of power bubbled out, ripping apart everything in its wake. The quake smashed buildings to pieces, flattening them to rubble in seconds. The land itself split, terrible rents appearing everywhere, widening, ever widening. Where any buildings had somehow partially survived the initial quake, they quickly fell into the rapidly growing chasm which was appearing under and engulfing the city.

The chasm grew quickly, getting ever larger and ever deeper. Suddenly, the city of Antissa collapsed completely into the growing chasm which had formed underneath it. The small villages which lay around the city had moments of safety, seconds only perhaps, until the rapidly expanding chasm simply engulfed them too.

On the hilltop far from the epicentre of the cataclysm, Lucar heard the terrible grinding noise rise to an awful keen as the quake tore the ground apart. He felt the very rock shaking beneath his feet. Opening his eyes he watched as in the far-off distance the chasm became visible, rapidly approaching his position. He saw as it engulfed the once well maintained road which led from the capital to this far-off backwater of the Rainbow Empire. Village after village fell into the gaping earth. The noise grew till he had to hold his hands over his ears to shelter them. Moving at a pace which would catch even a man on horseback, the chasm grew. It was splitting the very land asunder.

The ritual had fractured the very centre of the Rainbow Empire. A giant crater ran in four directions from the site of the doomed capital of Antissa. The chasm was growing deeper and longer with every passing second, ripping the continent and the empire into four. Settlement after settlement, person after person, all was simply engulfed and lost in its depths.

The chasm reached the fields beneath the hill upon which the Conclave had told the emperor to stand. The quake had ripped apart the land below this high hill top and the chasm seemed about to swallow the hillside on which the emperor had taken refuge. Lucar prepared himself for death. Thousands of his people had died; it seemed only fair that he too should suffer the same fate for ordering the Magi to perform the ritual.

Then suddenly the ground shuddered and the splitting of the earth came to a grinding halt. The growing chasm had reached the edge of the continent. It had found its way to the sea. It had split the empire into four. The terrible grinding noise subsided as the crater stopped growing.

Lucar looked down and from his position on this high hillside. All before him was utter desolation. His hill top was right on the edge of the massive gulf the ritual had produced. Just as the Conclave had predicted, this hill top was to be the very edge of destruction. Hence this hilltop had been where he had gone before the ritual had begun – to a position of safety. Now he wished he had remained in his capital to suffer the same fate as his subjects.

Beneath him all was changed. Gone were the green fields, the orchards, the leafy woodlands. Gone were the villages, the blacksmiths, bakers and potters. Gone was the silver road, winding between them. All that was left was a gaping chasm which dropped deep into the ground, deeper than the eye could see.

For a moment there was calm and peace. The lands settled and a quiet silence covered the desolation. Then the sea rushed in.

Flowing into the space the chasm had created, the sea swept all before it. The sea flowed in like a cleansing draught and the raging torrent quickly covered up and hid the destruction and desolation left by the quake. Within moments the huge flood, which would soon form the Inner Sea, split the continent which had once been one land mass into four islands. Later, scribes would name these four islands Ursum, Manabas, Ibini and the cursed Granita where the Writhing Death had been let loose.

Far across the continent on the newly formed island of Granita, a group of High Magi had been hard at work. Pooling all their power and magical force together, they had managed to close the gate that other Magi had previously opened into the Void. The Magi had stopped the Writhing Death at source, but it was beyond even their ability to destroy what existed on Granita. The Magi were trying – throwing spell after destructive spell at the massive collection of creeping creatures as they advanced upon them – but there was no stopping the Writhing Death. There were just too many of them.

As the last of the High Magi was engulfed and devoured by the curse they had been sent to stop, a giant tidal wave, caused by the sundering of the empire, smashed into the land and rushed across the wasteland there, washing all before it. The wave swept up and simply washed the Writhing Death away into the sea. As the waters receded, they left the island of Granita bare, with no trace of the terrible scourge that had ravaged it before. The Writhing Death had been obliterated. The gate from which it had poured was closed.

Emperor Lucar looked down across the brand new Inner Sea before him from his position on the hill. He could not see the entire extent of the destruction he had ordered but he knew thousands upon thousands had died at his command. His order had destroyed towns, villages, and even the wondrous capital city of Antissa.

Emperor Lucar had stopped the Writhing Death. However, he had destroyed the Rainbow Empire to do it.

-- PART ONE --

-Chapter One-

Reynard pulled hard on the oar. His hands were beginning to blister and his shoulders were aching like nothing he had ever experienced in his twenty seven years. He pulled hard again and groaned as he felt the oar biting deep into the sea, the strain of rowing for hours upon unending hours continuing to take its toll on him. This was not what he had expected to be doing when he set out for a drink on the waterfront a few days ago.

He took a moment to look around the deck. He sat on a rough wooden bench, next to a huge hulking black-skinned fellow from some far-off land. There were six benches on this side of the deck and a like number on the far side where more rowers strained and laboured at the blades. Ahead of them all, next to a thick wooden pillar which supported the floor above, stood an obese Ibini, bald head dripping with sweat as he banged out a fast rhythm on his drum. He was responsible for making sure the ship moved at the speed the captain ordered. He had two guards to help make sure the oarsmen kept up the pace.

Behind the drummer, one ladder dropped into the dark depths of the hold where the rowers slept and another rose to the main deck above. Behind the benches of rowers another ladder dropped into the stern of the hold and beyond that, at the rear of the ship, were rooms where the ship's crew slept. Beside them a further two ladders rose up to the main deck above and daylight.

One of the guards noted Reynard's apparent lack of effort as he looked about him, and cracked a thin whip cord across his bare back, bringing up another welt. Reynard swore under his breath and pulled hard once again. There was no respite from these guards. Looking up at the one next to him from the corner of his eye he saw a Lucarcian, like him, with the blond hair typical of his people. This one kept his hair trimmed short and wore a few days' light stubble on his chin. He was dressed in simple leathers typical of his station and had a short sword strapped to his side. Leather sandals completed the uniform.

A few weeks ago Reynard would hardly have noticed a man like him. Now he and his fellow guards were the cause of all Reynard's pain and misery. They seemed to take great delight in striking the slaves, whether the cause was just or not, and the drum master did nothing to stop them.

The slave drivers appeared to take extra pleasure in striking a young woman pulling at an oar a couple of rows in front of him. With straight black hair and a light complexion, her slanted eyes proclaimed her as from the lands of Honshu across the sea. She was a slight figure and probably very pretty if Reynard was any judge but grime and filth made it hard to be certain. She wore the same rough sack smock as all the slaves, which hid her figure and did nothing to enhance her looks. She always bore the beatings with great stoicism, quite typical of her people Reynard thought, but her eyes shone blue murder to the guards every time their backs were turned.

Reynard felt a large elbow dig into his side and realised the huge black fellow sat next to him was nudging him. The guard was moving on and the giant grinned a smile of surprisingly straight, white teeth at him. "Time to stop daydreaming, little man," he whispered.

"Yes, I need to keep my wits about me if I'm ever to get off this damned ship," Reynard replied quietly.

"Get off the ship?" asked the towering man, raising a hairy black eyebrow at Reynard.

"Yes, of course get off the ship," Reynard repeated in a whisper, "You don't expect me to be happy spending the rest of my days chained to a slaver's oar, do you? There are far too many beautiful women in the world for that. I would hate to disappoint them." Reynard smiled his easy smile back at the man, taking a better look at him now he had the chance.

The man was tall: nearly seven feet tall, Reynard estimated, and was built like an ox. He had parallel scars across both cheeks. His skin was deep brown, the sort of skin which people in the Lucarcian Empire rarely saw. He had obviously come from a long way across the sea. Quite what he was doing here in a slave galley and how he got here was definitely a tale Reynard wanted to hear one day.

"What's your name?" he asked the giant, still speaking in a whisper. There was no talking allowed whilst rowing and Reynard had no desire to give the guard another excuse to whip him.

"Okoth," he replied, "from Nubia."

Reynard mentally scratched his head. Nubia. If memory served him right Nubia was two thousand miles and more away, right over the far side of the known world; a small country of farmers and villages and part of the most advanced empire in the world, the Rodinian Empire, yet subjugated and suppressed by the callous Rodinians. Reynard wondered again what had brought a man here to Lucarcia from that far-off place, and how he had ended up in a slave galley.

"I am Reynard," he said, "excuse me for not offering to shake your hand, but well met all the same."

Reynard had decided, soon after waking in the hold of this carrack and realising he was a slave, that he was best off not telling anyone his full name. If the slavers got wind that they had captured Reynard Ferrand, second son of Lord Caer Ferrand of the Iron House, they would likely kill him. If their captain was resourceful and brave he might consider trying to ransom him back to his father, the Earl of Providentia, but more likely he would see holding Reynard as a huge risk and simply have his throat slit and drop him overboard. No, whilst on board this slave ship he would simply be Reynard, another unfortunate drunk who ended up sleeping in the wrong alley on the waterfront, who slavers had picked up in the night and spirited aboard ship to a life of darkness, pain and labour.

Not for long though.

Reynard was not one to sit idle and had been busy planning since his capture some ten days or so ago. Was it ten? It was hard to remember. The slavers kept the slaves in the hold on the bottom deck of the ship, alongside the livestock and the less valuable cargo. It was almost permanently dark down there and time was difficult to mark. As slavery was technically illegal in the Lucarcian Empire they were shackled down there when not rowing, and when the ship pulled into port guards stood over them ready to silence any who tried to call for help. The cargo hold where the slavers kept the slaves was below sea level so there was virtually no hope of anyone on shore hearing them and, even if they did, who would be brave enough to accuse a ship's captain of slavery, especially one who probably had protection from the Guild?

The Guild of Master Merchants and Sea Farers, or the Guild, as people more commonly called it, was the organization that controlled all trade across the empire. Their power and influence in Lucarcia was considerable and growing. Headed by the mysterious Trade Lords, the Guild collected membership tithes from most sea captains and land based merchants across the whole empire. In exchange for this annual tithe and a small commission on all their profits, the Guild protected its members. They had all the benefits of powerful legal backing. They were able to call upon the huge financial power of the Guild if they had need of help with any outside influence that was disrupting their trade. Moreover, if the rumours were true, they were able to call on the Guild's aid for any nefarious activities they might be planning, as long as those activities furthered the Guild's goals.

It was well known that many of the Guild's sea captains used slaves. Of course, the Trade Lords refuted such claims and no ship captain ever openly admitted as much. Rare was the harbourmaster who insisted on a search for illegally held captives, or who questioned strange noises heard when in the depths of a ship inspecting cargo manifests – fear of the Guild kept them quiet. Therefore, Guild captains were able to continue this practice across much of the empire unhindered. Slaves cost nothing and the profit margins on a ship rowed by free labour was greater than that manned by a normal crew, so captains who used slaves would inevitably make more profit than those who didn't, and making profit was the Guild's main purpose.

"If you're serious, then I'm at your service," came back Okoth, unexpectedly. The black man pulled hard on their oar, making Reynard's job that bit easier.

"I am serious," confirmed Reynard, "and your help would be greatly appreciated. In fact I doubt I could escape alone. I've been giving it some thought and I believe there is an obvious time we could make our bid for freedom. The only thing is what do we do once we have overpowered the guards down here?"

"I'm the new one on board ship," said Okoth. "I do not know the routine yet." The Nubian had come aboard only yesterday, the most recent addition to the slaves.

"Indeed. We need to get out of here as soon as possible." Reynard was aware that before very long slaves could become resigned to their lot and the passion for escape could wane. He was determined to get out of this predicament before that happened to him.

Reynard considered his plan. The slaves spent much of their time manacled below decks in the slave pen. Only when the wind dropped would the captain order the oars put into use. The slaves would be unlocked, marched up to the oar deck and then manacled down to the benches where they would row until they were told to stop. Whilst they were rowing there were typically two guards and the drum master watching them. However, when the slavers were transferring them from the bottom deck to the oar deck there were usually three or four guards who would oversee their deployment. Reynard's simple plan was to attack the guards during this transfer – the only time they were out of their manacles. It was risky, he knew. The guards were armed with swords and would have no hesitation in killing a slave who was trying to escape. But he was willing to take that risk rather than languish in the bottom of an ocean going carrack until he died of scurvy or fatigue only for the guards to toss him overboard for the sharks.

"I'll explain all when we get back below decks," Reynard told the Nubian, putting his back into the rowing once more. The guard had reached the end of the row and had turned back to walk towards them. There was no more chance to talk now.

*

A couple of days later one of the slaves died. Daymon was a thin and feeble old man, his lank grey-blond hair revealing a liver spotted scalp beneath. He had been growing weaker for the last few days, and the guards had ignored his calls for more food. Reynard had tried to reason with them, to explain that more nutrition would enable Daymon to pull his weight at the oars more efficiently. He had explained that their master would surely be annoyed if a valuable slave was allowed to perish, but all that earned him were more welts on his back and neck. When the guards had brought breakfast that day, Daymon had not stirred from his sleep. It didn't take them long to figure out what had happened to him, and he was picked up and taken out of the hold, his destiny now that of shark fodder. This stirred Reynard to action.

"That's it," he whispered fiercely to Okoth, "The next time we get sent up to row we'll try it. Are you agreed?" Reynard was fuming now. His desire to gain revenge on the guards for the way they had treated him, for the way they beat the pretty girl from Honshu and for the way they had let Daymon die was threatening to overwhelm him.

"Only if there are three guards, not four or more," cautioned Okoth.

Reynard saw the sense in the reply and knew it was what they had agreed, but found it irksome all the same. Did the Nubian not understand that the guards needed to pay, and needed to pay now? He took a steadying deep breath, counted to five in his head and let it out slowly. "Yes, of course," he agreed, "Only if there are three guards."

The next day the winds dropped. The slaves could feel the effects of the wind on the carrack in the way the ship moved, even from below decks. It only took a couple of days on board to become accustomed to the movements of the ship and when the winds died and the ship floundered it was clear to those huddled in the cargo hold that they would soon be needed at the oars. Presently they heard the latch lift on the trap door to the oar deck above. Three guards climbed down the ladder.

Three guards: the escape was on.

Reynard and Okoth had no real plan. Reynard knew that you could make all the plans you wanted but when a fight actually broke out there was no point in trying to stick to any program. The chaos of combat made all that pointless. They had agreed that Okoth would wait for Reynard to make the first move and that the Nubian would then join in as best he could, but that was as far as their stratagem went. At least it was simple and easy to understand.

Reynard flexed his muscles, loosening up as best he could in the cramped and tight confines of their present accommodation. A few of the other slaves were doing the same – it was a sensible action when you were about to be rowing, potentially for hours on end. The guards moved through the deck, unlocking the manacles that chained the slaves to the deck. Reynard wondered where the best place to strike was. Down here, or wait until they reached the oar deck? Then he caught a glimpse of the Honshu girl out of the corner of his eye, her neck and face covered with the bruises inflicted on her by the slavers. His mind flashed briefly to the image of Daymon's body, being carried up the ladders by a laughing guard. His temper flared and he gave up planning and acted.

Reynard's elbow shot out, connecting squarely with the chin of the first slaver. Completely off guard and unprepared, the man dropped like a stone, unconscious and out of the fight before he even hit the deck. If Reynard's move surprised Okoth then his reactions were cat-like. He grabbed the second guard by the shoulders and planted a huge and powerful head butt into the man's face, smashing his nose like a melon. The slaver howled in pain and staggered. Okoth kept hold of him and wrapped huge hands around the guard's neck.

Reynard dived on the first guard he had taken out with his elbow, scrabbling for the man's sword. It was still in its scabbard and the unconscious guard was prostrate on top of it. Reynard looked up as he tried to recover it, watching almost in slow motion as the third guard drew his short blade and stuck it deep into Okoth's side. Okoth stiffened, dropped the guard he was about to throttle and slumped to the floor, eyes rolling up into his head. Recovering the short sword he had been scrambling for, Reynard stood, dropping into a fencer's stance. He faced two guards, one of whom had a smashed face and was looking concussed. The other had Okoth's blood all over his blade.

Reynard had faced two swordsmen before and knew that his chances now depended on his opponents to a large degree. If they had trained at fighting together he was dead. They would flank him, time their attacks and open him up like a fish on a fishmonger's skillet. However, if they had no formal training they might end up actually getting in each other's way and then he would have a chance. Looking at the two slavers he suspected and dearly hoped it was the latter, but either way he would have to be at his best to survive this encounter. And the more time he spent thinking about things the more time the stunned one had to recover. It was time to act.

Suddenly the Honshu girl appeared out of the shadows behind the two guards. Stepping from beyond a pillar she planted one foot squarely on the deck and spun in place, lightning quick, her other foot shooting out and smashing into the kidneys of the stunned guard. The force of the kick pushed him off his feet, throwing him forward out of control. Reynard took the chance and plunged his blade deep into the man's heart as he fell towards him. He groaned softly and slid off the sword onto the floor of the deck, blood oozing out of his chest to mingle with Okoth's.

The last guard, surprised by the attack from behind, recovered quickly. He realised the tables had been completely turned now and his thoughts turned to escape. Spinning sideways to remove himself from the middle of his two enemies he rushed for the ladder which led back up to the deck above. Reynard sprang after him and reached the guard just moments after he had got to the foot of the ladder. Figuring that to climb the ladder would mean a sword in the back, the slaver turned and faced Reynard, who slid to a halt and dropped into a comfortable stance, feet spread and weight on the balls of his feet. Reynard could feel the ship moving under his legs, gently rocking the deck below him. He studied the guard carefully, deciding to wait and let the slaver make the first attack. Reynard was more a counter attacker than an aggressive fighter, generally preferring to bide his time and block or dodge and strike when the aggressor was fully committed and off balance or open to a well-placed riposte.

As Reynard studied him the guard's eyes widened unexpectedly, his mouth opened and blood gurgled out of his mouth and down his neck. His legs went and he collapsed to the deck, revealing the Honshu girl hiding in the shadows of the ladder behind him, pulling a bloodied sword from the man's back as he toppled.

*

Reynard nodded his head in a silent thanks to the girl who had helped him and moved quickly past her to the middle of the deck where Okoth lay, still bleeding. He kneeled down next to the warrior and examined him. A very quick check revealed that the Nubian was still alive, if barely. His pulse was weak and he had lost a lot of blood. Reynard ripped some cloth from a slaver's tunic and quickly wrapped it around the warrior's side. The man didn't even stir. Blood was still oozing from the deep wound.

"He won't survive," said the girl, appearing at his side.

"You think I don't know that?" snapped Reynard.

"He was brave. He died well," she added simply.

"He's not dead yet," he came back.

Reynard turned to look at her. The girl had straight black hair and a pretty face, only slightly spoilt by the bruises the slavers had scattered across her cheek and neckline. She stood with arms folded across her chest and feet planted comfortably shoulder width apart, perfectly balanced on the gently rocking deck. She had tucked a short sword into the cloth belt which kept her rough smock tied about her waist. It looked like it belonged there.

"Thanks for your help," Reynard said, "I'm not sure I would have defeated all three of them without your help."

"No, you would not have," she came back.

Reynard bristled but realised the girl was only telling the truth. "I am Reynard, at your service," he smiled.

"Kita of Sapporo, student of the Niten dojo," she replied with a small but precise bow.

Looking back at Okoth laying on the deck in a pool of blood, Reynard grimaced. He felt helpless. He had become fond of Okoth in the few days he had known him. The huge man had always remained positive through their ordeal, able to smile his big white smile even when things looked grim. But they had never looked grimmer for the Nubian and Reynard felt like anything but smiling.

"I just wish there was something which could be done for him, but it is hopeless," he sighed.

"Always there is hope whilst the sun shines in the sky," came back a new voice from nearby. "May I look at him?"

Reynard and Kita looked up to see a dusky skinned man with black hair and a goatee standing close by looking down at Okoth.

"Is there anything you can do?" asked Reynard.

The newcomer stroked his goatee between thumb and forefinger. "Perhaps. His wounds look serious but he is a strong man. The Light has not yet departed from him. I am Mosi, Acolyte of the Light and whilst the Light remains with him there is still hope." Mosi knelt alongside Reynard and began to examine the fallen warrior. His hands moved expertly across his body, examining the wound and feeling for his pulse. He dropped his cheek to the Nubian's mouth and felt his breath, then listened to his heart beat through his huge barrel chest.

"I can save him, but I need my focus, "Mosi told them. "It is a small golden pendant in the form of a sun disk. Without that focus I will not be able to channel the Light's warmth into his body and restore him to health. With it, I can save his life. You must find my pendant, and soon, for his spirit is getting ready to depart his body and move on into the eternal Light."

Reynard looked sceptically at Mosi. "You're telling me you can heal him if I can find you a golden necklace? Is it really some sort of holy relic or are you just after treasure? Be honest with me or I will see you join him on his journey to the eternal Light you appear so fond of."

"Not just any golden necklace. The Haji of Shelech, High Priest of the Order of Light in my homeland of Hishan, gave me my focus. It is a holy artefact dedicated to the Light and I promise you with that artefact in hand I can help your friend. The Light is fading from him though, so you must hurry."

Reynard looked at Kita and she nodded briefly. Reynard turned back to the priest, "Okay, Mosi, I will find your pendant. The question is: where would they have stored it?" Reynard looked at Kita and Mosi and saw nothing but blank looks. Kita shrugged her shoulders, unmoving. Mosi shook his head, signalling that he too had no ideas. "There must be a store room here somewhere," thought Reynard aloud. "Unless they took your golden necklace and sold it, or the captain has it in his personal stash."

"I might be able to help," interjected a quiet voice from across the hold.

All eyes turned to look in the direction of this new, softly spoken man. The hold was silent, with most of the slaves now stood as far away from the fight as possible, wondering what was going to happen next and not wanting to be associated with the deaths of the guards. A space had naturally formed around the fallen Nubian and the people trying to save him. The voice had come from a striking figure that stood back with the rest of the slaves.

The man was slight of build, thin and short. His chin was pointed and he had a sharp hooked nose. None of that was the first thing Reynard noticed though, as the man had a shock of silver hair, even though he must have only been in his late twenties. But even more striking were the man's eyes. These were violet and somehow almost seemed to glow in the dim light of the cargo hold. Reynard thought that the man appeared Lucarcian like him, but he had never seen eyes or hair like those on one of his people. It was most unnerving.

"Who are you and what do you know?" inquired Reynard.

"I am Tanithil of Lucar and I overheard the slavers talking a few days ago," the silver haired man replied. "They talked about how the captain had put all the valuable items from the slaves they had captured into one big chest in his secure cargo hold. The secured room is almost certainly on this deck at the back of the ship – directly through that wooden bulkhead behind you, but to reach it you need to go up a level to the oar deck, cross that and then drop down a ladder into the aft compartment."

"How did you hear this and yet no one else knew about it?" asked Kita.

"They spoke in a rare dialect I suspect no one else here knows," came back the reply. "The slavers of the Inner Sea have long developed their own twist on basic Lucarcian," he continued. "It is a combination of slang words, apparent nonsense, made up phases and even gestures. It's not something that many people understand. You probably all heard them speaking but had no idea what they were discussing or that they were even having a proper conversation."

"Yet you understood?" asked Reynard.

"I have a rare gift for languages," the silver haired Lucarcian replied. "I have picked it up whilst on board the ship, listening and watching the slavers interact."

"You have been on this ship for how long?" Reynard queried.

"Thirty seven days," came the exact reply from Tanithil.

"And in thirty seven days, you have mastered a whole language?" Reynard asked, unsure if he was utterly impressed, suspicious, or a little of both.

"I only say that I have picked up a rough understanding of some of their brogue – and that it is not a language as such, merely a bastardized dialect - almost more a code than anything formal."

"And how do you know how to get to this store room?" continued Reynard, still suspicious.

"I know a bit about ships," said the silver haired man, quietly. "This is a three-masted carrack built on three levels: the main deck up top, the lower deck above us where the oars are located and the hold, down here where we are. There is usually a door which goes through that bulkhead behind you leading from this area into a separate compartment at the aft where captains typically keep a secure area. The brig is usually located there, alongside a secure store room and often a pantry. If you look carefully at the bulkhead you'll notice that someone has removed the door and has patched over the hole. Clearly the captain of this carrack did not want easy access from the cargo hold – where he keeps us slaves – to the secure aft compartment – where he keeps valuables like our possessions. The only way to reach that store room is up, across the oar deck and back down."

Reynard looked at Kita, "Are you up for a little foray onto the deck above?" he asked her.

She nodded in response, "Certainly. If there is a chest with our possessions in it then I wish to find it and recover my twin swords, my *daisho*. I have dishonoured myself by losing them and reclaiming them is my path to restoring my lost honour. I must do this."

Reynard shrugged, having no concerns for the strange values of the people of far-off Honshu, knowing only that in the chest might lay a golden pendant which could save Okoth's life – if Mosi was not some charlatan and truly had any powers of healing.

"Then let's go," he told her, taking a shortsword from a fallen guard and tucking it into his belt.

He knew they only had a short time in which to find the store room and reclaim their things. The captain had ordered the slaves onto the rowing deck which meant that the ship was going nowhere right now. The drum master would be on his way to the same deck from wherever on the ship his quarters lay. Sooner or later someone would notice that there were no slaves rowing the ship and they would send more guards to find out why. On top of that Okoth was lying in a pool of his own blood on the cargo deck and his only chance lay in the hands of a priest who claimed to have the power to save him.

Reynard had heard of the Light, the sun god who was worshipped across much of the world under different names. There was even a temple to this god in his home town of Providentia, although Reynard had never been inside – his father was not a great believer in the gods and that lack of faith had passed onto his sons. The priests at the temple there wore expensive robes of white, with gold threads running through them. They proudly displayed their golden symbols of the sun, showing off the great wealth the temple possessed. It was anything but holy as far as Reynard was concerned. But if Mosi could somehow save Okoth's life then he was not about to let the chance pass by just because Mosi might be a charlatan. Reynard knew that unless someone did something, Okoth would be dead within minutes.

He tucked his sword into his cloth belt and began to climb.

-Chapter Two-

Reynard climbed half-way up the ladder so that his head just reached the floor level of the deck above and peeked in. The oar deck was empty and quiet. Turning to look back down he saw Kita below him ready to climb and noticed she now had two short swords tucked into her belt. There was no point in leaving any below he agreed.

Climbing the last few steps he emerged onto the oar deck. Six rows of benches on each side greeted him and the smell of stale sweat and crusty salt filled his nostrils. Behind him he felt rather than heard Kita follow him up on to the deck. Reynard was well practiced at moving silently. Many nights returning from a long evening carousing in town had resulted in him learning to move quietly through his ancestral home without being heard by either his disapproving father, or any servants who might have given him away. He used those skills now, slipping quiet as a mouse across the floor boards towards the ladder which led down into the aft compartment, just as Tanithil had said it would. It was funny how he had not really noticed the hole at the back of the oar deck before. Kita ghosted along beside him, matching or even exceeding his silence. Reynard had no idea what they taught at this Niten dojo she proclaimed to be a student at, but she was clearly no ordinary slave.

They had nearly reached the ladder down when they heard movement ahead of them. Behind the oar benches towards the aft of this deck were the crew quarters. This was where the drum master had his bunk and he was on his way to the oar deck now. Coming out into the oar deck he spotted Reynard and Kita as they were making their way quietly past the benches towards the ladder down. He looked momentarily confused then realization clearly dawned on him as he saw the two slaves were armed and splattered with blood. Roaring in defiance the bald Ibini rushed forward, hefting the two heavy leather bound drum sticks he held as improvised weapons.

"Leave him to me. Find the chest and get that holy symbol," instructed Kita to Reynard, moving swiftly forward to put herself between the drum master and the ladder down. Drawing her two blades she dropped naturally into a fighting stance and waited for the huge drummer to reach her.

Deciding he had no choice as time was vital, Reynard rushed to the ladder and slid down it onto the darkness, landing in a crouch and letting his eyes adjust to the dark of the aft hold. To his left he saw the bars of the brig and beyond that the entrance to the secure cargo hold - a reinforced wooden door with a built in lock. A locked door and no key. Now what was he supposed to do?

*

Kita dropped into her favoured back stance, weight mostly onto the rear leg, low to the ground. She brought her two swords out and into position. Used to fighting with two blades she quickly mentally adjusted to the inferior balance of these weapons. Her own *daisho*, the twin long and short swords of the Niten style, were masterwork items, crafted by some of the best smiths in her homeland of Honshu. But the crew had taken them from her when the Ibini had tricked her into coming aboard the *Hammerhead*.

Kita's father, Heremod, had been born in the lands of Albion yet the Niten dojo in neighbouring Honshu had accepted him. There he had learnt the art of fighting with twin blades. He had been a gifted student and had risen to the rank of Master, becoming the first *gaijin* Master in the history of the dojo. Heremod had settled in Sapporo, the town where the dojo was located, and had married a local girl. They had one child – Kita.

When Kita was old enough to wield a blade, the dojo had accepted her too, allowing her to follow in her father's footsteps. She was the youngest student ever to be accepted and grew to become one of the school's best students.

A year ago, when Kita was approaching her tests to graduate from the school, Heremod had left suddenly, disappearing without the permission of his *sensei*. The school declared Heremod *ronin* – effectively a rogue, cast out of the school in disgrace. Kita had gone to her mother and asked where her father had gone, but all her mother knew or would tell her was that her father had travelled to Lucarcia.

Trying to complete her studies Kita had remained at the school, a shadow hanging over her. Eventually one of the other students cast aspersions on her and her father's honour and a duel ensued. The dojo strictly forbade duelling. To make matters worse Kita had lost her control and had killed her opponent. The school had no choice but to declare her *ronin* too and expel her from the dojo.

She had got on a ship to Lucarcia to try and find her father and discover the truth, hopefully to clear both their names. Kita had met the Ibini in a bar in a small port in Manabas. She was low on funds having spent most of her money travelling there from Honshu. She wanted to get to Ursum, where her father had last been seen, but she did not have enough money to do so. The Ibini offered her a deal. She thought she was going to be working passage from Manabas to Ursum and had agreed to travel for free in exchange for working on the oars when needed. As it turned out she was handing herself over to a slaver crew.

The moment she stepped aboard the *Hammerhead* with the fat Ibini she was grabbed, her *daisho* were taken and she was slapped in chains. She felt disgraced for being so naïve as to fall for such a deceit and would be unworthy of the Niten name until she could recover her two blades, the long *katana* and the short *wakizashi*. Then she would be a true student of Niten, the art of two blades, once more. The man who had conned her was the same man who faced her now. It was time for revenge.

The obese drum master rushed forward, a scream of rage bellowing from his mouth. Kita waited and watched. She prepared to slip sideways out of his reach and get behind him by virtue of his own speed and momentum. She was ready for the man to overreach himself, to overcommit, but surprisingly he did not. As he came rushing in he swung one drum stick in a wide clubbing arc blocking the way Kita had expected to move. His swing was faster and more accurate than she would have guessed and she was hard pressed just to duck under it and move sideways to safety as the other drum stick followed quickly on the first's tail. She re-evaluated her opponent instantly and chided herself for making assumptions. She had grown sloppy in her time in the hold and it had almost cost her life. Dropping back into stance she let her mind relax. She needed to let go of her rational thought and trust her instincts and her training. Her *sensei* would not be pleased if he found she had actually been planning her moves during a fight.

The drum master twirled the sticks in hand. The ends were cow leather wrapped tightly to make a heavy, hard ball and these were attached to the end of foot-long wooden sticks. Not intrinsically as deadly as a traditional weapon they could still be dangerous, and with the drum master's prodigious strength it would be fatal if he managed to land a blow to her head with one. Moving in towards her he swung the first drum stick laterally again. This time Kita parried the attack, using her first blade to deflect the attack past her safely; not trying to pit her strength against the drum master's and stop the attack dead, rather to redirect the power to her side. By doing so she was now inside his reach and she stabbed forward with the second blade aiming to gut the large man. But he was a canny warrior and in turn blocked her attack with his second stick – smashing downwards and being able to stop her attack with sheer power. He had less need of skill than she did, having a huge physical advantage over her.

The two pulled apart and circled one another their mutual respect growing.

"You realize I could call for the guards, pretty?" mocked the drum master. "They would be here within moments to overpower you and put you back in the hold where you belong. But I think I'd rather have you to myself for a while," he smiled a toothy smile, "and see how you fare with a real man."

Kita ignored him and concentrated on her technique. She was rusty but her skills were coming back to her. She was determined not to let the man's taunts and comments distract her.

The drum master, whose name was Bayo, was tall, bald and hugely fat. He was stripped to the waist as was usual when he was called upon to do his job. Bayo was a native of the island of Ibini, the second largest country in the empire of Lucarcia. Ibini was long and thin, occupying the eastern most edge of the continent of Lucarcia and was predominantly covered with jungle vegetation. It was home to a snake-venerating people ruled by the Verdant Queen, Lily Jade. The northern parts of the island were more fertile and agricultural and this was where the majority of the people lived but the Verdant Queen held court in her palace in the southern reaches of the island in the jungle lands.

Bayo had been drum master for Captain Waverly of the *Hammerhead* for three years. It was a position he thoroughly enjoyed. It gave him a strong sense of worth and empowerment when he was at the front of the oar deck, beating out a rhythm, knowing that the speed of the ship was totally under his control. The captain or first mate might call out the pace they wanted but it was his drum cadence which set the rowers to their tasks. He controlled the cadence of the oars and consequently the rapidity of the *Hammerhead* through the water.

He liked his job and his job relied on slaves. Sure, a normal crew could be made to row but there was nothing which formed a strong team like captivity. A slave team was far more motivated than a paid crew was – the threat of beatings, and even death, was far stronger motivation than mere gold. And now he was faced with a rebellion. It was maddening. The guards who had gone below were dead he was sure, after all the two escaped slaves had the guards' weapons and blood on their smocks. But the tall Lucarcian had disappeared for some reason, leaving just the young girl for him to play with.

Bayo licked his lips, tasting salt as sweat dripped down his face into his mouth. The young girl was skilled, he would give her that much. But she was no match for him – she was a mere slave and he was drum master of the *Hammerhead*, one of the Guild's favoured ships. Blinking sweat from his eyes he focused on the girl again. He should probably end this quickly and not toy with her too much, otherwise the crew above might hear and someone might come down to investigate, forcing him to stop. He launched a double attack, swinging both drum sticks at the same time, one from each side, one high, one low.

Kita saw the attack coming late. Her reactions were slow and she began to block, realizing too late that she needed to be avoiding this attack rather than trying to meet it. She parried one of the drum sticks but the other caught her in the midriff, knocking her to the floor and winding her. Struggling to gulp down a lungful of air she rolled to the side as Bayo smashed a club into the deck where she had been a moment before. Kita continued her roll and came to her feet instantly, both swords extended ready and poised in a defensive posture.

She realized that her time as a slave had taken its toll on her. Her reactions were slow and her instincts dulled. Add to that the badly balanced swords she was wielding and she understood that she was over matched. She needed to gain some sort of advantage. Moving easily across the decking, back into the main rowing area, she skipped nimbly up onto an oar bench – one of the ones she had spent many painful hours on, pulling an oar to the beat played out by the man in front of her. Bayo obediently followed her, twirling his sticks in his hands again, displaying remarkable dexterity for one with such fat fingers. In this position Kita had a slight edge – she was now above her opponent and that height advantage allowed her to attack from angles that the tall Ibini was not used to.

Kita turned her approach from defence into attack, deeming this to be a more effective tactic against this strong opponent. She began to probe his defences, using her fast swords in a series of strikes, cuts, pokes and slashes. Most of these were ineffective but the speed of her attacks was such that Bayo was not able to block every one. She began to get through his defences. Her hits were minor: a nick here, a scratch there. But they began to add up. Soon the bald drum master had blood running down his chest and huge belly from numerous little cuts across his body and shoulders. Blood ran down his arms to his hands, mingling with the sweat that was pouring from the hard-working drummer as he strove to keep his enemy at bay. Eventually the combination of blood and sweat proved too much and he lost his grip as he tried to change direction to block yet another attack. One of his sticks flew from his grasp and sailed across the deck to land near the ladder down to the slave pens.

Kita did not hesitate.

Using her left blade to catch and shift the remaining stick out wide she plunged her right blade into the bald Ibini's shoulder, next to the head, using her position above him to add her weight to the blow. The short sword drove deep into the neck and severed the cartiod artery. Blood fountained out of the drum master and he dropped to the floor, convulsing. Kita jumped down off the bench and stabbed both swords into his chest, to be certain. Bayo shuddered and lay still.

*

Reynard looked at the door. It was solid oak, reinforced with iron. The iron had rusted in places, the salt air doing what it does to ferrous metals. The door had a metal handle and, next to the handle, a built-in keyhole. His first reaction was despair: the door would be locked and he would be unable to get to the room beyond where he hoped he could recover his gear and, more importantly, Mosi's sun disk which Mosi could use to save Okoth. His second reaction was more pragmatic: he tried the door. The handle was stiff with rust and the door would not shift, no matter how hard he pulled. It was definitely locked.

Reynard racked his brains. He recognized that iron rusts, especially when exposed to sea air and it appeared that this door had a fair share of iron built into it. He also knew that rusty iron was brittle and prone to snapping if put under pressure. If there was this much iron in the door it stood to reason that the locking mechanism itself might well be iron. Perhaps if that was rusty, it too would be brittle and breakable. Placing the steel short sword he had taken from the guard into the gap between the door and the frame, Reynard applied his strength to the sword, using it as a lever to magnify his power. He strained and pulled, the motivation of a bloody Okoth lending him focus and strength. The last couple of weeks of hard work on an oar had hardened his body, removing the little fat he used to carry from days spent carousing and enjoying life. He was now as strong as he had ever been and he knew that this door could prove the difference between life and death, not only for Okoth but also, perhaps for himself and all the other slaves. He pulled at the sword with all his might, concentrating all his willpower.

The sword snapped.

Letting out a scream of frustration, Reynard inserted the snapped blade back into the gap. He focused his rage at being thwarted by the broken weapon, grasped the hilt with both hands, braced his foot on the wall next to him to add more leverage and pulled again.

This time the lock fractured.

Grasping the handle, Reynard pulled the door open and beheld a small cargo hold containing a large wooden chest.

*

Kita turned to see Reynard climbing back up out of the aft hold. In one hand he held a beautiful rapier, the weapon of choice for a master swordsman in Lucarcia. In the other hand he held a chain with a small golden disk, glinting dully in the dim light. He smiled at her and simply said, "I found it."

Kita nodded and told him she would meet him in the hold shortly. She moved swiftly past the Lucarcian and to the ladder he had just come up, quickly descending into the darkness of the lowest level of the ship. Reynard headed the other way, past the body of Bayo, noting the myriad of lacerations crisscrossing his body and the two shortswords impaled in his chest. He climbed down the other ladder and dropped back into the slave pen.

Mosi looked up and smiled as he saw his holy symbol. Taking it gratefully from Reynard he slipped it over his head and held it in one hand. He closed his eyes and began to speak soft words, hardly heard by those around him. His other hand hovered above the blood-soaked bandages covering the terrible wound Okoth had suffered where the blade had pierced his side. Reynard blinked in surprise as the dark hold was momentarily thrown into subtle shadows, as if a very soft but just discernible glimmer had become apparent in Okoth's side.

The huge Nubian groaned and opened his eyes.

Mosi continued to chant quietly and Okoth's face took on a look of extreme pain as consciousness hit him. As the priest from Hishan continued to pray the pain on the warrior's face subsided slowly. Mosi stopped chanting, removing his hand from the black man's side and the hold was thrown back into darkness.

Okoth blinked and sat up. "What happened?" he asked.

"You chose a bad time to take a nap," smiled Reynard.

*

Leading the three men up to the oar deck, Reynard looked behind him at his new companions. Mosi joined him, the Acolyte of the Light who, it appeared, had just healed Okoth from a potentially fatal wound. Behind the priest came Tanithil, silver haired and violet eyed. He had asked to come along, pointing out that it was his knowledge that had allowed them to find the secure cargo hold and saying he had no wish to remain with the other slaves below. Finally Okoth brought up the rear.

The giant Nubian was weak and ashen-faced but he was able to walk unaided. Reynard had seen the wound and it was ugly but it looked like a wound which had been inflicted weeks ago, not mere minutes before. It had definitely healed. Reynard could give no logical explanation for it, unless perhaps he had over-estimated the severity of the wound in the first place. That must be it, he reasoned, yet he had seen his fair share of sword wounds and this one did not look fresh. And he was certain it had been a fatal wound, or at least would have been, given a few minutes more. Was it possible that Mosi had actually healed him?

None of the other slaves had wanted any part in the escape. Reynard figured that they believed by not getting involved they would be spared any repercussions if things did not go well for the escapees, and he dearly hoped that would be true. Certainly he did not blame them for wanting to keep out of it.

Emerging onto the oar deck from the cargo hold Reynard stopped in place, amazed by what he saw before him. At the far side of the deck, standing near the ladder down into the aft hold, was Kita. Gone was the beaten up slave girl in hessian smock. In her place was a beautiful, poised, proud and deadly warrior from the lands of Honshu. She was wearing the traditional scarlet kimono of the Dragon Province, made from very valuable silks crafted in that region. She had wrapped it around her body in a way which Reynard found he liked, and had tied it with a silk obi. Embroidered across the back was the curled dragon emblem of the Niten dojo at which she was a student. Tucked into the obi around her waist were her *daisho* – the *katana* and *wakizashi* which were the signature weapons of the school. The Niten dojo taught the skill of fighting with two swords and its fame was such that warriors from across the whole of the Honshu Empire came there to learn from its masters.

"Wow," Reynard breathed, noting the way Kita stood, perfectly balanced with the gentle rolling of the ship in the swell.

"Ah, our little caterpillar has emerged a butterfly," observed Mosi, stroking his goatee between forefinger and thumb.

"Yes, yes," said Tanithil impatiently. "We had best get moving as the guards will be here soon."

Approaching the young warrior from Honshu, Reynard asked, "Will you wait here and look out for guards, Kita?"

"Certainly," she replied simply, a look of inner calm and confidence Reynard had not seen before now on her face. Was the recovery of her missing swords responsible for this transformation? It must have affected her more than he had appreciated.

Reynard led the men into the aft hold whilst Kita stayed aloft on guard. They entered the secure cargo room and opened the chest. Inside it was an assortment of items. The four men reached in, pulling various items of clothing and personal belongings from the chest.

Mosi pulled a simple white cloth robe and slipped it over his head. Unlike the gold threaded robes of the local priests, this one was plain and austere. He tied it with a white rope belt. He took open-toed sandals from the chest, put them on his feet and finally pulled out a wicked curved sword, known as a *kopesh,* which he tucked into his belt. When Reynard raised an eyebrow at the holy man and the long sword, Mosi merely shrugged.

Next to him Okoth had pulled out some simple leather garments, trappings of his homeland. He now wore long leather trousers and a pair of sturdy leather boots, both natural and uncoloured. Both were also well-worn and well cared for. He had not bothered to wear anything on his top half, other than the bandage covering the wound in his side. Okoth had used a strip of cloth, which he had ripped from his old slave smock, to hold the bandage in place. Held in his vice-like grip was a traditional *assegai* spear.

Okoth's people were mostly hunters. They were typically slim and fast. He was clearly an exception standing nearly seven feet tall and being built like a bull. The traditional weapon they used to hunt was the spear and the *assegai* was the spear of choice for most. It was long and thin, making an accurate throwing weapon. It could be hurled long distances and also used in close quarters if the need arose.

Standing behind Okoth, almost obscured by the great man, was Tanithil. He had recovered his simple clothes, typical of those worn by the men of Ursum. Tanithil's attire was a pair of dark cotton trousers, with short, soft black boots. He wore a green shirt and over that a brown waistcoat. His silver hair almost glowed in the dim light and his violet eyes were alert to everything, taking in all they saw.

"Ready?" Reynard asked the group, checking his own attire.

Reynard Ferrand was a tall Lucarcian. With shoulder length blond hair and steely blue eyes to match the colour of his House's standard he was a striking figure. His easy smile and angled jaw, plus the way he moved with grace and balance, made him a firm favourite with the ladies in his home town of Providentia on the south coast of the Spine of Ursum. Reynard was second son to Lord Caer Ferrand, the Earl of Providentia and a bit of a disappointment to his father. Where Reynard's older brother Maynard was always taking an interest in the family estate and affairs, Reynard preferred to spend his time carousing in the local drinking establishments on Providentia's water front. He was well known by the landlords, drinkers, gamblers and wenches of that disreputable district and reports of his son's actions regularly discomforted his father.

Reynard had a penchant for black and on the day he had been captured he was wearing one of his favourite outfits – head to toe in black. He matched comfortable black trousers with a loose fitting black cotton shirt. Over this was his favourite waistcoat of Honshu silk, black of course. Shiny knee high boots completed the ensemble. Strapped to his side was his rapier, the basket hilt made of silver and inlaid with a few jewels. It was a masterwork blade, finely balanced and sharp as a razor. The sword's creator had inscribed the words "Forged in the Iron House" down the length of the blade – the motto of the Ferrand family. Reynard had a throwing knife secreted in each boot and a third tucked into his trousers down the small of his back.

He was ready.

The others nodded and they climbed back up to the oar deck where Kita waited for them. As they moved up onto deck to join the woman from Honshu, half a dozen armed guards descended down from the main deck above. The captain was clearly wondering what was going on down in the hold and had sent them to find out.

*

The guards came down all three ladders from above simultaneously. They were performing a sweep of the ship, making sure no one could get past them. Seeing five slaves, fully armed and equipped, the guards paused looking momentarily surprised. Their leader was alert enough to react though, calling them to order, and the six of them drew weapons and moved into the oar deck cautiously, spreading out to surround the slaves.

Reynard, Kita and Okoth naturally split up to meet them, each one moving towards a pair of guards. They formed a defensive wall around Mosi and Tanithil who remained safely in the centre. As he moved forward Okoth stumbled slightly, obviously still weakened from the earlier wound. Then Mosi was by his side, *kopesh* in hand. Reynard faced two guards as did Kita. The slim girl from Honshu was completely unfazed by the situation, her face impassive, and balance perfect as usual. Her poise caused the two guards she faced to pause, unsure of themselves. She dropped into a defensive stance and waited for them to make the first move.

Reynard concentrated on his two guards. At least they should not be able to flank him if his new friends held their positions. One lunged and he parried easily, his rapier flashing to the side. The other guard stepped just out of his reach and moved in a circle, behind one of the pillars which supported the main deck above. As the second guard moved out of sight behind the pillar, the first launched a second attack, ferociously striking blow after blow. Reynard was hard pressed to parry and dodge each strike. With his attention fully focused on the first guard he didn't notice that the second guard had moved around the pillar and slipped past his position into the circle, until it was too late. The second slaver was now face to face with the weaponless and defenceless Tanithil. Reynard had to take a risk. He dropped his guard momentarily, but just enough for the first slaver he was fighting to spot the hole in his defences and lunge forward. Of course Reynard knew this would happen but still needed his timing to be right or the guard would skewer him.

His timing was perfect.

Reynard twisted sideways just enough for the sword to miss him by inches. Now alongside the guard and inside his reach Reynard then simply slipped his rapier into the man's ribs and pulled it cleanly out as the slaver collapsed to the floor, blood pumping from his chest.

Looking up and fearing the worst Reynard saw that the second guard was face to face with Tanithil. Tanithil's face was serene, no trace of fear or worry on it. His violet eyes seemed huge in his thin face and they were staring with great intensity at the guard who was looking to cut him down. Somehow the guard stopped in his tracks. Tanithil's eyes seemed to narrow, the burning look increasing further. His violet eyes seemed almost aglow such was the power of his gaze. The guard faltered and lowered his sword. Reynard didn't pause to think about what was going on, instead driving his rapier into the guard's back, through his heart and out the front of his chest. The guard dropped his sword from lifeless fingers and collapsed.

Reynard looked around. All six guards were dead and none of his new companions appeared harmed. He looked again at Tanithil, seeing the man quite composed, nothing like someone who had just been facing down certain death. Tanithil's violet eyes seemed to almost be alive with their own light, but as Reynard watched that light was gone and Tanithil looked his usual self.

Shaking his head to clear the strange image Reynard said, "We need to press on. There is only one thing to do now – take the fight to the main deck and the captain of the ship. If we can capture him we will be able to win our freedom. Who has been on the ship the longest?"

"I have," replied Tanithil simply.

"What can you tell us about it?" Reynard followed up.

"We are on the *Hammerhead*, a three masted carrack out of Selkie. Captain Anton Waverley, a merchant of high standing in the Guild, owns and captains the ship. He runs spices and drugs across the Inner Sea and the Straits of Lucarcia, taking his illegal cargo from Manabas in the north, to Ibini in the east and Ursum in the south. There is no port in Lucarcia he will not visit. He is a known drugs runner and slaver and a nasty piece of work.

"The first mate is a brutal man by the name of Scraggs. He is sadistic and the pure definition of evil. He has worked for Waverley for the last three years or so and is his main enforcer when it comes to collecting slave labour from the ports and secluded villages of the empire, and from further abroad. It is likely that many of you were captured and brought on board by Scraggs. Scraggs has a deep love of poker, at which he cheats, and has been known to gut a man if he loses money to him. He doesn't have many friends."

Reynard raised one blond eyebrow. "You seem to know rather a lot about Captain Waverley and his crew?" he enquired.

"I have a good memory," answered Tanithil evasively, not really answering the question.

"Okay, we can worry about that later, I guess," replied Reynard. "Right now we need to act. I suggest we split up and hit the main deck from all three ladders at once. Okoth and Tani, you take the aft port ladder, Mosi and Kita the aft starboard ladder and I'll take the fore ladder. Let's go."

Being the son of a noble, Reynard was used to being obeyed. He didn't even turn to check that his instructions were being followed. He moved off to the ladder leading up to the main deck near the forecastle. He grasped the ladder with both hands and scaled it with nimble ease. Behind him the others had instinctively split into the teams Reynard had suggested and they too were making their way up to the main deck.

It was time to take their freedom back.

-Chapter Three-

On the main deck of the *Hammerhead* the crew was hard at work. The ship was becalmed as the predominant westerlies had dropped off to a zephyr. They were a day out of their home port of Selkie on the northern tip of the Tail of Ursum and most of the men were looking forward to getting home to wives, families or the pleasures of the notorious Selkie waterfront. Captain Waverley had ordered the slaves into the oar deck, not keen to sit here stationary with a cargo hold full of valuable spices and other less savoury items.

Scraggs was on the warpath. Never a happy fellow, the first mate was in a bad mood today and his mood was made worse because the order to get under oar was taking ages to be obeyed. Standing at the wheel on the quarterdeck he had even sent six of his guards down to find out from Bayo, the drum master, what the holdup was all about. The crew was keen to make sure they didn't give the brutal first mate a reason to discipline them so they were all busy as bees and even those with little to do were finding tasks with which to look busy. No one wanted to be seen to be idle.

Bursting onto the main deck the five escapees blinked in the bright spring sunlight. It had been days since any of them had seen the sun and they were forced to shield their eyes against the glare. Those few moments of surprise they may have had over the crew were gone as they struggled to adjust to the brilliance.

A call went up from the quarterdeck as Scraggs spotted the escaping quintet. "Slaves! Get those landlubbers! A gold imperial to any man who fells one of the bastards!" Drawing his sword the first mate released his hold on the helm and dashed forward.

Reynard blinked back tears as the sunshine stung his eyes. Next to him were a couple of surprised crew men, totally unprepared to be facing a rapier-wielding slave. He saw no reason to kill crew members on the ship, so he did not immediately carry the attack to them. Instead, looking up at the forecastle he saw a wide brimmed hat bobbing above the rail about fifteen feet overhead. As his eyes adjusted to the light a man came into focus beneath the hat.

Captain Waverley was short and stocky, with broad shoulders and a small paunch from good living as a successful merchant sea captain. He was dressed in smart clothes typical of a wealthy man in the empire. Sturdy high boots were pulled over long trousers of grey hue. A red cotton shirt was tucked into a black leather belt and a topcoat of brown leather kept him warm and dry. Shoulder length blond hair fell from beneath the wide brimmed hat and a greying beard covered his thick chin. At his side was slung a seafarers cutlass, a typical weapon for any sailor.

Reynard decided that Waverley would be his point of focus. Behind him he heard the screams of the first mate trying to get the crew to react. He trusted Okoth and Kita to deal with him and looked for a way to get to the captain of the ship. The two crew members near him had recovered their wits by now and had drawn daggers.

Reynard crouched down then leapt upwards, timing his jump as the ship rose on a gentle swell. Stretching up and to his right as far as he was able, his fingers just grasped a stay supporting the foremast. He hauled himself hand over hand into the lower rigging, out of reach of the two crewmen. Finding a spare brail rope he grabbed it and wound it tight around his left wrist, drawing his rapier with his right hand. Springing into the air he swung on the brail rope, flying over the main deck. Pulling his legs in tight at the last moment he flew over the forecastle railing and planted both feet into the belly of the ship's captain.

Waverley went sprawling across the deck of the forecastle as Reynard smashed into him. Reynard released his grip on the brail and rolled. Tucked up into a ball he barrelled along and smashed into the ballista which was situated there. Momentarily dazed he shook his head and got to his feet. Captain Waverley had likewise recovered and was drawing his cutlass.

"Ah, so the little lordling has come out to play, has he?" sneered the portly captain, wiping a drop of sweat from his forehead with the back of his sword hand.

Reynard cocked his head sideways, "What do you mean?" he asked, assuming a fighting stance, rapier coming up to point at the chest of his opponent.

"Two weeks in my hold and you thought I didn't know who you were, didn't you? You have no idea what is going on. So cocky, so self-assured, even in the hold of a slave ship. You make me sick."

"If anyone here is cause for nausea I can assure you it is not me," countered Reynard. "I'm not the one running a slaving ship, forcing people to die so that I can turn a greater profit." He circled to his left, trying to put the sun behind him and into the captain's eyes. How did this slaver know who he was? He had been very careful to keep his identity secret when in the hold.

The captain circled right in response but his wide brimmed hat kept his eyes shaded. "You were worth a pretty penny to me in my hold, but somehow I think I will enjoy slicing you up more than I have enjoyed spending the gold I was paid to put you there."

Someone paid this slaver to capture me, thought Reynard. But who? And how could he get this captain to divulge the information? He edged forward, rapier ready, trying to get into range of a lunge. "Of course I know who sold me to you, idiot," he taunted, lying glibly. "I'm merely waiting for the opportunity to pay them back the compliment. And trust me: I have a long memory and am very patient. I will have my revenge in my own time."

The captain appeared annoyed, "Well, it will be of no mind that you know about your brother, for soon you'll be at the bottom of the sea, shark bait." Stepping forward Waverley launched the first strike, a high sweeping attack aimed at Reynard's neck.

Reynard was stunned. His brother? Maynard? He was so shocked he almost didn't parry the blow but his natural reactions brought his blade flashing up to block the neck strike without conscious thought. He blinked, trying to take in the news. Maynard had sold him for a slave? But why? What could he possibly gain from it? Reynard stepped back, trying to concentrate. There would be no use in dying here; he needed to find out the truth.

Waverley advanced, following Reynard as he retreated. The captain sensed confusion in his opponent after that last exchange. Had he just made a mistake? He was aware that he had just told Reynard Ferrand his brother had been the one who had paid for his capture, without Reynard mentioning the name first. Damn! Reynard had probably just tricked him into giving that information away. Oh well, there was no point in crying over spilt rum, he thought, he might as well make the most of the young whelp's shocked state of mind and finish him off. He would deal with the ramifications afterwards.

Waverley launched a new offensive, driving his opponent back into the ballista mountings. The captain was totally at ease on the ship's moving deck, probably better even in this setting than on land. His opponent was a landed gent and not used to the way a ship's deck moved beneath the feet. Clearly the young lord was an accomplished fighter but the terrain was his and he meant to take full advantage of it. Pressing the fight and continuing to rain blows on his cornered foe, Waverley began to gain the upper hand.

Reynard was trapped. His back was to the ballista mounting in the middle of the forecastle deck. He was still struggling to find his feet on board the gently rolling ship and his mind was reeling from the shock of the news that his brother had somehow arranged for him to be sold into slavery. The slaver captain was a seasoned warrior and was totally at home in this environment. Reynard had to find an advantage from somewhere.

He shook his head one last time, determined to put all thoughts of how he had ended up here out of his mind and concentrate on survival. Blocking strike after strike he was hard pushed to find an opening to riposte. However the sea captain was an older man and out of shape. The intensity of the onslaught was dropping off. Reynard took a risk, taking a slice across his left forearm as he launched a counter attack. The risk paid off at least enough to force his opponent to jump back and cease his attack.

Reynard immediately rolled to his right, coming back to his feet again in one action. He had moved away from the ballista mounting but now had his back to the port rail. Again the captain advanced and again Reynard was stuck with nowhere to go. He leapt nimbly up onto the rail and turned to face the advancing captain. Beneath him the sea rolled under the bow of the *Hammerhead* some forty feet below. It was a precarious perch. One false step or slip here could see him plummet into the depths.

The captain sensed an advantage and swung a low cut aimed at Reynard's feet. He jumped in the air with both legs tucked high and was landing back on the rail when the ship plunged over a large swell and dropped away from him. He landed badly on the rail, slipped and went over the edge.

*

Reynard slid down the port bulwark, grasping desperately at the strake which made up the hull, trying to get a purchase. One plank was slightly warped and his left hand grabbed a hold, his arm wrenching in the socket as he arrested his fall. His right hand still held tight to his family sword and he shook his head at the pig-headedness which had stopped him releasing his grip on his heirloom. Putting the sharp blade carefully between his teeth he took hold of the hull planks with both hands. The abrasion of the fall had ripped open his left hand, which was bleeding, and his forearm stung terribly from the cutlass cut inflicted on him by the slaver captain, but his sword hand and arm were both strong and fit.

He climbed quickly up the bulwark to the rail and peered over. The captain was standing on the forecastle deck, leaning over the main rail and looking down at the fight going on below him on the main deck. His cutlass was back in its scabbard. He had obviously assumed Reynard had been lost to the sea and had not bothered to confirm the demise of his opponent. Reynard vowed to make him pay for that mistake.

One crew member had climbed up to the forecastle deck and was checking to see what had happened to Reynard. Leaning over the rail next to where the escapee was clinging to the bulwark, the crew member spotted Reynard hanging onto the hull and was about to shout out. Reynard grabbed his collar and heaved. The sailor went flying over the rail and fell into the depths below. In the next second Reynard was over the rail and back inboard, rapier in hand.

He crossed quickly and quietly to the place where Captain Waverley stood and put his rapier up to the back of the captain's neck. "Surrender the ship, Captain," he ordered, speaking into the sailor's ear.

Waverley went rigid and pale, as he felt the blade dig into his neck. He had underestimated the young lord and not checked that he had fallen into the sea, as he had supposed. A stupid mistake to make, certainly, but there was no way he was going to surrender his ship to a slave, no matter what position he might find himself in. Whirling in place, faster than might be expected for a portly man, the captain moved smoothly to the side, his right hand flashing across to his left hip and in one fluid movement drawing his cutlass.

The speed of the captain's evasion surprised Reynard. He was not expecting such a move and the speed of the man's movement caught him flat footed. The captain had his cutlass out and was ready to defend himself. But even with this quick manoeuvre, Reynard still had the advantage. This time it was the captain who found the rail against his back – the one which separated the forecastle they were on from the main deck below. Reynard had the initiative and meant to keep it. And Reynard had the sun at his back.

The young noble began to attack with a measured but quick series of strokes, building up into a pattern. It was a regular combination, one well known to any trained swordsman. Waverley knew it and parried with the expected blocks and moves. Reynard continued to take him through the pattern, knowing it would soon climax with a powerful downward strike which Waverley would attempt to parry with an angled deflection. Waverley would need to judge his defence accurately but it was not difficult to a trained swordsman like the sea captain and the sailor continued to follow the pattern himself, clearly confident with his ability to defend the last strike.

There was no easy way for the defender to break out of the pattern as the nature of the routine left them very much having to put all their efforts into blocking and dodging each strike. But Waverley appeared content to let the series play out, knowing that the last strike of the combination left the attacker vulnerable to a counter strike - if the defender was capable enough of executing it, and Waverley knew he was.

Reynard built up the speed of the exchange, pushing the captain to his limits, trying to take him out of his comfort zone. The series continued, racing towards its finale, blades flashing silver in the afternoon sun. The pattern reached the section where the attacks would drop down, forcing the defender's guard to become lower and lower. Both combatants knew that any second now Reynard would lift his rapier high into the air and bring it slashing down at the captain's neck. The outcome of this exchange would be based on how well the captain could parry that attack.

The climax came and Reynard quickly flicked his rapier up into the air preparing for the final downward blow. But with the upward flick of the rapier he turned the blade sideways, intentionally catching the edge of the wide brimmed hat the sea captain was wearing, flipping it off his head and onto the deck. The rapier was now high in the air and Reynard brought it down with all his speed and skill, aiming for the captain's neck.

    Waverley looked up to block the expected strike, but looked straight into the blinding sun, the protection of his wide brimmed hat lost to him. His eyes reflexively closed, he lost track of the rapier as its blade flashed downwards and his block went awry. Reynard's blade sunk deep into the neck of his opponent and Captain Anton Waverley, captain of the *Hammerhead* fell to the deck, dead.

-Chapter Four-

Reynard took a huge breath of salty air, relief flooding him, thankful that his idea had worked. He had been certain Waverley had been a good enough swordsman to be capable of blocking the final attack of the sequence. He had been fairly sure Waverley was good enough to execute the advanced counter too. Reynard had been worried that he was setting himself up for a cutlass slash across the belly, but his hope that the sun's angle would blind the captain had paid off and his final blow had struck home.

He looked across the ship and saw that Kita and Okoth had Scraggs up against the quarterdeck wall, pinned down and weaponless. The fighting had stopped as the few crew members who had actually taken up their weapons against the slaves were either dead or defeated. It was time to take control of the ship.

"Crew of the *Hammerhead*, hear me!" Reynard bellowed. He had their full attention now. "You have long served under Captain Waverley, a hard and difficult master. As you can see, he has resigned his commission!" With that Reynard held the dead body aloft for all to see, and then dumped him down the stairs to come to rest in a crumpled mess at their feet. "I am Reynard. *Captain* Reynard, the new master of the *Hammerhead*. I offer you a choice: serve me and my command crew," he said, pointing to Kita and the slaves who had escaped with him, "and you will continue to be paid well. Refuse to work for us and we will put you ashore at the next port. We have no wish to extract revenge on you for your choice of captain. We will not be slavers; we will be releasing all the captives in the hold below. Those who wish to stay aboard the *Hammerhead*, move forwards. Those who wish to leave move aft."

"What about Scraggs?" asked one crewman. "What will you do with him?"

The first mate scowled and spat until Okoth backhanded him across the cheek, a blow which sent him reeling to the deck.

"What would you have me do with him?" asked Reynard, keen to gain the approval of the crew as quickly as possible. Scraggs was clearly every bit as bad as Tanithil had made him out to be and Reynard suspected every member of the crew had a reason to hate the surly man.

"The plank!" one member cried and soon the chant was taken up across the ship. "The plank! The plank!"

"Very well," agreed Reynard. "He will be given a traditional farewell as befits a sailor," he smiled.

The crew cheered and Reynard knew he had them.

*

"Do you seriously think we can just sail into any old port in the empire?" questioned Tanithil, incredulously. "This is the *Hammerhead*, a major Guild ship, and you're *not* Anton Waverley, its captain. The moment it is clear that something has happened to Waverley the Guild will be on us and our lives as slaves will seem pleasant in comparison."

"He has a point," agreed Kita.

"Then what do you suggest, Tani?" asked Reynard.

"I know a place on the south coast. It's a village port called Black Sail. We could take the ship there. They have a small shipyard and ask no questions. We could get the ship's name changed, documents and everything."

Reynard considered this. He could appreciate Tanithil's point. If Waverley was a captain high in the standings of the Guild then the *Hammerhead* would be well known. If they wanted to keep the ship they would need to change it enough that people would not recognise it as Waverley's. But they were currently anchored off the north coast of the Tail of Ursum. To get to the south coast would mean travelling half way around the whole country – a trip of a week or more.

And what would they do with the slaves in the mean time? He had no wish to keep them on board any longer than was necessary. They had been unlocked and were recovering on deck enjoying the spring sunshine. There was not enough food on board to get the ship, its crew and all the slaves all the way around to the south side of Ursum.

Reynard made a decision. He would find a secluded bay on the north coast near their current position and drop off all the slaves who wished to leave. The north coast of Ursum was fairly well populated and the slaves would find people to help them quickly enough.

None of the crew had decided to leave, so there were no concerns there. They were happy to work for the new captain as long as he paid them well and Reynard had promised to do so. They were still waiting for the old first mate, Scraggs, to walk the plank, and Reynard was not happy about it. It was not in his nature to order the cold blooded murder of someone, even someone as clearly evil as Scraggs. The crew wanted the man dead and Reynard needed to keep their loyalty, but he was not happy with what he might have to do to hold onto it. He was putting that decision off and had Scraggs held in the brig whilst he considered his options.

Reynard couldn't go home. He had no idea why Maynard had sold him to slavers. He had decided it was safer to remain at sea, where his brother thought he was a slave or dead, whilst he worked out what to do. He had no proof of his brother's treachery as only Captain Waverley had spoken of it and the captain was dead. Perhaps Scraggs knew – which was another good reason not to execute him. Turning up at home in Providentia without proof would only cause all sorts of issues. He knew his father loved him, but he was the second son and the big disappointment. If he turned up accusing Maynard of this vile deed and Maynard denied it, his father would have to choose whom to believe. Reynard felt he was bound to side with the elder brother. So for now he was content to take over the captaining of this ship and think on what to do about his brother. Of course none of his companions had any idea who he truly was, or that his brother had sold him into slavery.

Shortly after taking over the ship Reynard had entered the captain's chambers. There, along with sumptuous fixtures and fittings, he had found a ledger which detailed the cargos they were shipping. It appeared that Captain Waverley was, as Tanithil had suggested, a drug runner. They had a cargo hold full of spices, which were entirely legal of course, and various narcotics, which were not. Reynard knew the approximate resale value of the cargo, and it was enough to keep him and his crew well paid for months. However he was aware that Tanithil was right and that they would need to refit the *Hammerhead* and give it a new name. Doing so would cost money – a lot of money.

His companions appeared to accept Reynard as captain in the same way that they had automatically listened to his decisions and followed his ideas. He had named them his command crew. Okoth was first mate, Mosi ship's doctor, Kita was second mate and in charge of the security of the ship and Tani... Well, Tani didn't really have a role, but perhaps he was Reynard's advisor. He certainly seemed to know more stuff about more things than a dozen men put together did. He was a walking encyclopaedia. The group had not discussed how long they intended to remain together, but that was something they could sort out later.

"So, what do we do?" asked Okoth, bringing him back to the moment.

Reynard told them, "We find a secluded bay near here and drop off all those who wish to leave the ship. We will give each person disembarking a day's rations. Then those of us who remain will set a course for Black Sail. There we will sell the cargo and use the profits to get the *Hammerhead* renamed. With the ship ours we can decide what to do. I suspect the answer will be to sail into Selkie or some other major port and sell the vessel, split the money between us, and go our separate ways.

"Okay, that sounds like a plan," said Okoth, with a white grin.

"Agreed," said Tanithil.

Kita nodded her approval.

"By the Light, I believe we have an accord," finished Mosi.

*

The *Hammerhead* turned hove to, facing into the gentle winds coming off the north shore of Ursum. Reynard ordered the anchor dropped and the crew reefed the sails. The sun was still shining and the cliffs shone white in the afternoon glare. A dark smudge revealed a small cleft in the cliff line, beyond which a thin beach rose. The crew dropped the single rowing boat overboard and one nimble sailor climbed hand-over-hand down the painter rope into it. He then held the small boat steady whilst another sailor dropped a rope ladder down to him. The slaves made their way down into the ship's boat and two sailors rowed them through the gentle afternoon swell into shore. They pointed the boat at the crack in the cliffs and, as a line rolled through, they rode the swell into the gap, steering carefully.

Twenty minutes later the two crewmen were rowing the small boat back out to sea. As Reynard watched he caught sight of something which made him blink in surprise and do a double take. "Kita! Here! Now!" he called, not taking his eye from the shoreline. Kita was at his side in seconds.

"What is it?" she asked quickly, sensing his urgency.

"Look over there," he pointed, "and tell me what you see?"

Kita looked where Reynard was indicating, shielding her eyes against the glare of the sun reflecting off the cliffs. "Scraggs," she said simply.

"I'm not imagining it then. Damn." As the pair of them watched a furtive figure slipped away across the cliff tops after taking one last long look at the *Hammerhead* anchored out in the bay. "How did he get out?" he asked rhetorically, already turning to head down to the brig.

Kita and Reynard arrived down in the aft hold moments later. The brig door was open and a quick search showed no signs of forced exit or struggle. Someone had let Scraggs out – but who and why? Returning to the main deck they went to the side rail and looked down as the rowing boat was pulling alongside. Reynard wracked his brains to recall the sailors' names: Florus and Tito. Were they responsible? Or did someone else release Scraggs from the brig and help him to get on board the rowing boat? That was all assuming Scraggs had somehow stowed aboard the rowing boat at all, of course.

The two sailors tied lines to the fore and aft of the boat and then clambered up the ladder back onto the ship. The crew then hauled the now empty boat back on deck and carried it to its usual resting place in the centre of the main deck where they lashed it in place.

"Florus, Tito – with me please, "ordered Reynard, spinning on his heel and heading for his cabin. "Kita, you too", he added looking over his shoulder at the Niten student who had become his head of security. His mind was spinning with possibilities and thoughts. The main two were: Who and why? He reached his quarters, opened the door and went in.

The entire bow of the ship on the main deck under the forecastle was devoted to the captain's quarters. The main door in led to a short corridor with a door on each side and a door at the end. The two side doors opened into a private study on the left and a sitting room on the right. The door at the end led into sleeping quarters. Typically the captain would only permit the first and second mate in the study, but this is where he led the two sailors.

The study was square and tidy. A large, sturdy writing table rested against the side wall. Several bookcases, with leather straps across each shelf to hold the books in place in rough seas, were placed against the other wall. Captain Waverley had obviously been a well-read man as the shelves were full of histories, treatises on trade and geographical tomes. One shelf was dedicated to trashy fiction, full of stories about the end of the Rainbow Empire some five hundred years ago – Reynard supposed even a well-read man had to have entertainment.

Reynard moved to the desk and turned to face the two sailors who had followed him in. Kita entered last and shut the door behind her. Reynard decided to use the same tactic as had worked on the captain.

"We know you did it and we are not going to punish you for it. We just want to know: why?" he asked them, feigning a friendly but disappointed tone.

Florus and Tito looked at each other quizzically. "I dunno what you be meaning sir," replied Florus looking nervous.

"Me neither," echoed Tito, looking equally fearful.

"Which of you was it? Or did you work together?" Reynard probed again.

"Err, still don't know what yer on about, sir," came back the reply from Florus again. Tito nodded once more, agreeing with his colleague.

Reynard was a good judge of character and felt that these two were worried, but not so much about what they had to hide, but more because they felt they were about to be punished for something they had not even done. He suspected that was something which happened a lot under the old captain and his first mate. He decided to try a different tack and see what that revealed.

"Okay, you're fine – we were just checking," he said waving away the previous conversation dismissively. "Now, we brought you two up here as we want to know what you think we should do with Scraggs. You two are senior members of the crew, so what do you believe we should do with him?"

"Beggin' yer pardon sir but I don't care what 'appens to 'im, as long as he suffers", piped up Tito.

"Nah, it's got to be the plank," countered Florus. "It's traditional."

The two began arguing together and Reynard let it play out. It was clear that both hated Scraggs with a passion and, although they couldn't agree which punishment to inflict on him, it was obvious both wanted him to suffer greatly. By now Reynard was certain that either they were master liars, or had nothing at all to do with his escape. He sent them off back to work.

"What next then Kita?" he asked the woman from Honshu. He was coming to rely on her advice a lot. Or was it just that he wanted an excuse to keep her here in the study with him alone a moment longer? Since their escape she had been able to clean the grime and dirt from her body and Reynard found himself admiring the curve of her hips under the silk kimono. She truly was a beauty and he looked at her in open admiration.

"We can't tell the crew that Scraggs has escaped," she said. "There will be a mutiny." She stood as she often did with arms crossed across her chest; her feet planted comfortably shoulder width apart, in perfect balance as the ship rocked in place. Her *daisho*, never away from her, were tucked into the *obi* which kept her kimono shut tight around her.

"Agreed, but if they find out and we haven't told them it will be worse than if we just come out with it. How long can we keep this secret? As soon as someone goes down to feed him the word will be out. I think we need to tell them."

"Tell them he has escaped, without any explanation of how? You will lose the crew in that moment," she told him.

"I know," he said, "but I don't have any other ideas.

"Call Tanithil in here. He is a clever man and might have thoughts on what you can do."

"Okay, can you go and get him please?" asked Reynard.

She bowed curtly, turned on her heel and left.

*

"But how can you possibly know that?" asked Reynard bewildered and annoyed. It didn't make any sense.

"I just do," came back the terse reply from Tanithil, evasive as usual.

"I can't accuse Cyrus of letting Scraggs out of his prison without any proof, Tani," said Reynard exasperated. Reynard had asked Tanithil if he could help finding out how Scraggs escaped. Tanithil had told him he knew that Cyrus had released Scraggs and had helped him to get off the ship. "You tell me that you know Scraggs jumped ship when everyone was busy watching the slaves get into the boat and that he swam to shore, but you won't tell me how you know."

"I can tell you that Cyrus has a silver amulet in his possession that is Scraggs'. Scraggs gave him that amulet as payment for letting him out. Scraggs also promised to meet Cyrus in Selkie later where he would give him ten golden imperials for his help. The amulet is distinctive enough that the crew will know it was Scraggs'. He has the amulet pinned on the inside of his shirt over his right breast. "

"I still don't see how you can know that but, assuming you're right, I think I know the approach we can take here. But you have to be right Tanithil. Are you?"

"Have I ever told you a fact which was proved to be wrong?" asked Tanithil, fixing Reynard with his intent violet gaze.

Reynard found himself deciding to trust his new companion, against his better judgement. "Okay then, I know how we'll deal with this," decided Reynard. "Kita, please call the crew to assemble on deck now."

A short while later the crew of the *Hammerhead* were gathered on the main deck. No one was sure what the new captain wanted to speak to them about. Reynard came out of his quarters and made his way up the stairs to the foredeck so he could look down on the assembled crew.

"Gentlemen," he began. "I'm afraid I have some bad news." Murmurings of discontent rippled through the assembled crewmen. Reynard saw both Kita and Okoth place hands on their weapons, just in case things turned ugly. "Scraggs has escaped," he told them directly.

"What!?" shouted one seaman. "How did that happen?!" Many of the crew shouted out and Reynard had to hold his hands aloft to call for silence.

"I'm afraid we have a traitor in our midst, "he said. "Someone helped him to escape. One of you," his hand swept across the assembled host, "went down into the hold and released him as we were dropping off the slaves a short time ago. One of you, "he continued, "was paid off to let that foul brute of a man escape the justice we all desired he should face. One of you betrayed us all!"

"Who?" called out Florus from amidst the throng.

"You know who it was, don't you Cyrus?" said Reynard pointing his finger at the crewman.

Cyrus was swarthy and thin, unshaven and scruffy. His black troos were rolled up and he was barefoot. His white cotton shirt was a size too large for him and loose fitting. He began to look about him, casting for a way out as all eyes turned on him.

"I dunno know what you're talking about Cap'n," he stammered, looking scared as the crew began to close in on him.

"Grab him!" commanded Reynard and three crew members restrained him instantly. "Now, you all know the silver amulet which Scraggs possessed," said Reynard, fervently hoping that they did. "Well, I think if you search inside the right front of his shirt you'll find it pinned there. Scraggs gave it to him to help him escape, with the promise of gold at a later date."

Seconds later an angry crewman ripped a silver amulet in the shape of a mermaid from the inside of Cyrus' shirt. He held it aloft for all to see. "Proof!" cried the seaman, "He's guilty! He released Scraggs!"

Reynard breathed a huge sigh of relief – Tani had been right again. "Hold him still men and I will deal with him," he instructed forcefully. He did not want to see this sailor ripped apart by angry men. "Kita – take Cyrus into custody and throw him in the brig; and make sure it stays locked this time."

The warrior made her way through the crew, a passage opening up for her automatically as the sailors moved respectfully out of her way. She took hold of Cyrus and marched him off to the aft hold where she threw him into the brig.

"How did he know?" Cyrus asked Kita pitifully, as she locked the barred door. "Scraggs and I made the deal when I was down here feeding him. There was no one else down here – I checked thoroughly and pulled the trap door shut too. There was no way anyone could have seen or overheard us," he complained.

"Well, obviously someone did," replied Kita. But how did he manage it, she wondered?

-Chapter Five-

The weather turned stormy as they rounded the Tail of Ursum and headed into the Lucarcian Straits on a southerly setting. Gales blew up the Straits and right into the face of the *Hammerhead* as she struggled south. High winds and lashing rains pounded the ship. None of the ex-slaves had faced weather like this since they came on board. The ship listed and rocked and they began to understand that life on board ship can be harsh, even when not chained in the hold.

Okoth was violently sick, his stomach not coping with the sea sickness that came over him. He was the newest on board and still hadn't got used to the conditions. Mosi spent as much time as he could down in the crew quarters tending to the poor Nubian, but found that too much time below meant he too fell prone to sea sickness. Reynard found the days particularly unpleasant and Tanithil, who had been on board the longest of the group, occasionally had to heave over the side rail. Only Kita appeared unfazed by the whole experience, something which annoyed Reynard no end.

"How come you seem completely unperturbed by the rough seas?" Reynard asked her one day, turning his face into the rain which lashed down on the deck. The choice at the moment appeared to be stay inside and feel sick, or stay on deck and get drenched. He chose the latter. She was, as ever, standing with arms folded and feet comfortably planted; her body naturally in tune with the pitch and yaw of the ship beneath her.

Kita just shrugged, unwilling to take any credit for something which she had no control over. She just didn't feel ill at all. "We need to do something with Cyrus," she answered directing the topic of conversation back to what they had been discussing previously.

"I know. I'm not going to execute him for one mistake. He made a serious error in judgement but that's not enough for me to kill him. I will not be like the last master of this ship," Reynard replied, swallowing a lungful of fresh air and holding onto the rail as the ship plunged over a large swell.

"That is your choice, of course," Kita agreed, the rain making her long black hair stick to the side of her face, "but he needs to be punished somehow or the crew will be unhappy. Morale is a fickle thing and once lost it will take a lot of effort to bring back."

Reynard considered his options. He would not kill Cyrus. The man was weak and greedy but these were not reasons to put him to death. But Kita was right – he needed to use Cyrus to show the crew that he would brook no dissent. "Twenty lashes," he decided, "as soon as the storm passes."

"It will be so," she confirmed.

*

Two days later the storm had played itself out. The ships' crew gathered on the main deck and everyone not on duty was up on deck to watch the flogging. The sky was overcast and grey and a light drizzle was falling. Kita led Cyrus up from the brig, his hands lashed together with leather straps. She led him to the main mast which she then tied him to, facing inwards. Okoth took up the ship's lash. He had volunteered to perform the flogging, telling Reynard that he was skilled with the whip. At first Okoth's request dismayed Reynard because he believed the Nubian shared his hatred of inflicting unnecessary pain on another man. He was going to ask one of the crew to perform the flogging until the giant explained that he could control the damage done to Cyrus. It was better to have a skilled whip wielder than a brute with no touch. So Reynard had given Okoth the responsibility.

"Cyrus, you have been found guilty of releasing a prisoner of the ship, without the authority or consent of the captain or any of the senior crew. You are hereby sentenced to twenty lashes in accordance with the traditions of the Inner Sea," Reynard pronounced formally.

Okoth ripped the shirt from Cyrus' back, knowing that bare flesh would be better for the man in the long run – otherwise bits of cloth would get into the wounds and increase the chances of infection. The huge Nubian wielded the lash with dexterity and skill. Cyrus howled in pain as the whip tore the flesh from his back. The crew winced to a man as each blow fell. They began to feel that the captain had been harsh on the poor fellow.

When the flogging was over Cyrus could hardly stand. Kita untied him from the mast and supported him as she took him below deck to where

Reynard knew Mosi was waiting. The captain wanted to go below deck and see how the crewman faired, but he knew he could not. He returned to his quarters, a mask of cold indifference upon his face.

*

Down in the crew quarters Mosi examined Cyrus' wounds. His back looked a mess, but upon closer inspection it was clear the wounds were mostly just superficial and didn't run as deep as they appeared. Okoth had done a masterful job of making the flogging look horrendous, but in actual fact had spared the sailor from serious physical harm. Mosi took his golden sun disk from inside his robes and held it in one hand. The other he placed upon the back of the stricken sailor and began to chant in soft and gentle tones. As Kita watched she saw a subtle glow play across the poor man's back and the wounds began to close before her eyes.

There were priests in Honshu where Kita was born and raised. They generally fell into two camps in her experience: either wandering holy men who were more interested in their own poverty and piety than in actually helping people, or the warrior priests attached to the temples, who were more interested in killing people than in curing them. She had heard of the occasional healing supposedly performed by holy men, but had never seen it first-hand. She was amazed and more than a little humbled.

Mosi gave Cyrus a sleeping draught and told him to stay in bed for at least a day, sleeping on his stomach and letting the air get to the wounds. Mosi said he would check on Cyrus every hour to make sure the wounds didn't become infected, but said he felt they would be fine, given time. In fact Cyrus was ready for active duty again in two days, but Reynard refused to let him work.

"What does it look like to the crew if he returns to his post just two days after taking a flogging?" he asked Okoth and Kita who were gathered with him in his sitting room. The sitting room, part of the captain's quarters, was probably the most lavishly appointed room on the ship. Several burgundy chairs with gold trim surrounded a low mahogany table. Two lanterns hung on opposite walls, providing illumination to the room. An intricately carved liquor cabinet graced one corner, and a thick ornamental rug covered the rough floorboards. As in every room, bolts held the furniture to the floor, but here the carpenter had cleverly concealed the bolts so as not to ruin the room's ambiance. Tapestries decorated the walls. These depicted the catastrophe of the Writhing Death and the end of the Rainbow Empire.

"It would look like we don't take crimes against the ship seriously," replied Okoth.

"Exactly," replied Reynard, "and that is something I don't want to have happen." Reynard thought for a moment. "Hmmm, "he continued, "I have an idea. Bring him up to my study please, Kita."

"At once," she replied, bowing curtly and heading out of the sitting room. Reynard watched her go appreciatively.

"Be careful there," cautioned Okoth. "She is dangerous. Like the assassin vine - a plant which grows in my country. Enticingly beautiful, but get too close and it will ensnare an unwary victim."

Reynard looked up at his first mate, eyebrow raised, and Okoth laughed a deep throaty laugh at his own joke.

*

"So you agree then Cyrus?" Reynard asked.

"Yes sir, of course, and thank you very much indeed for this opportunity to repay my debts," the sailor replied, nodding vigorously. He was clearly relieved that his captain had forgiven him. In fact Reynard had given him an important task. Cyrus appeared deeply ashamed of his previous actions and determined to make amends.

"Then we will say no more about it. You will return to your quarters and stay there 'recovering' until we reach Black Sail when you will be put back to work. And when the time comes to find Scraggs again you will help us locate the nasty piece of work. You may go."

"Thank you sir," the sailor replied and hurried out of the study, heading back to his bunk.

"That went well I think," Reynard said to Okoth and Kita who were still in the room with him.

"Masterful," replied Okoth. "In one stroke I believe you turned him from a traitor into a loyal servant who will do whatever it takes to please you. I'm impressed."

"Masterful and dangerous," countered Kita, not as impressed as her colleague. "He is a weak man and his loyalty will be fickle at best. A treacherous personality will not easily change. You must watch him carefully and only trust him so far."

"I will," Reynard promised. "When the time comes to find Scraggs in Selkie we will watch Cyrus like a hawk and plan carefully," he finished, well aware that planning was anything but his strong point.

Overall Reynard was very pleased with how his approach had seemed to work out. Rather than punishing Cyrus further for releasing Scraggs from the brig, he had sympathized with the man and had almost apologized for the flogging, explaining that it was necessary for crew morale. He had then gone on to describe how he needed Cyrus' help in locating Scraggs. Everyone in the crew wanted Scraggs caught and punished. Reynard was going to give Cyrus a chance to play a vital part in finding and dealing with the renegade. He told Cyrus that this would change him from villain to hero in the eyes of the crew.

Cyrus appeared to lap it up.

Now Reynard's attention turned to Black Sail. According to the charts, and to Tanithil's description of where the small port lay on the south coast, they should reach there in about two days' time. The idea was to sail into port and find out who was in charge. Tanithil said that Black Sail was well known as a place where you could do deals on the black market and was somewhere they could sell the drugs they were carrying. They could also get their ship renamed and refitted.

After that Reynard wanted to go to Selkie. This was where Scraggs had gone. Reynard wanted to find him and get information out of him. He needed to know what Scraggs knew of his brother's betrayal. Once the ship's cargo had been sold and the refitting was complete, they could sell the ship, split the profits and go their separate ways. He would miss them, Kita especially he realized, but his number one priority was to find out what Maynard was up to.

Of course none of the rest of the group had any special reason to go to Selkie with him. The crew wanted revenge on Scraggs and Reynard had pointed out to his companions that Scraggs had been involved in most of their incarcerations and they too could gain revenge on him. It was a fickle reason and they were only buying into it tentatively. He would have to work on them.

*

The sun had gone down, two days later, when they reached Black Sail. From the open seas all that Reynard could see was the occasional twinkling of a light shining through a deep cleft in the otherwise dark and foreboding cliff face. They double checked the charts and confirmed that this was Black Sail's location.

Reynard ordered the sails reefed and they dropped anchor. Sailors lowered the ship's boat into the sea and the five command crew climbed down into it. Reynard gave Birgen, the boatswain, command of the ship in their absence and Florus and Tito were his seconds. There was a chance that the crew might make off with the *Hammerhead* whilst they were away in the port but Reynard was happy to take that risk. By showing trust in the crew he gained more of their respect and loyalty.

Reynard had told the crew that the command team would go and check out the port and make arrangements. Then Reynard would give the crew shore leave. The crew were not happy with the delay as they had not set foot on land in weeks, but Reynard gave them no choice in the matter.

Okoth manned the oars singlehandedly, his huge frame able to pull the boat through the evening tide as easily as two normal men did. Reynard took the tiller and guided the boat through the natural channel and into the deep water of the harbour itself. As they rounded the natural breakwater the whole place came into view.

The port was nestled in a circular cove with high cliffs surrounding and sheltering it. Two high fingers of rock extended out from the cliffs to form breakwaters and a natural channel between them provided protection from the seas and a great deal of shelter from prying eyes. It would be very easy to sail past and never notice this bay was here at all.

The granite cliffs formed a natural harbour and the settlers had built the port down in the bowl, out of sight of the plains which ran off landward from their tops. The buildings were all timber and mostly ramshackle. The place had the feel that it was built from driftwood and that it had been haphazardly erected, almost as if a strong tide had washed a bunch of planks into place randomly and then retreated, leaving Black Sail behind. Wooden walkways crisscrossed the whole town, going up, across and down all over the place; connecting different levels and sections of the settlement.

Three ships were anchored in the bay and Reynard found himself impressed. He was not sure if his crew had the skill to navigate the *Hammerhead* through the channel into the harbour proper.

Okoth rowed them into shore, pulling up by a jetty. The five climbed up a fixed ladder onto the wooden waterfront and Reynard tied the boat up to a bollard.

"Watch yourselves here," he warned them. "Keep an eye out for trouble, stay close to each other and be careful what you say. Remember we need to avoid mention of the *Hammerhead* until we know who we need to speak to. Best if we can avoid too much attention."

Reynard lead the way along the wooden decking, lantern lights casting shadows back and forth across the whole town. The waterfront itself was quiet, with not a soul to be seen, but Reynard could hear the noise of rowdy singing and drinking from at least one establishment ahead. He picked the first one, The Bawdy Mermaid, and pushed open the door.

A wall of smoke and noise hit him full on. Revellers packed the place, drinking, singing, smoking and carousing. This was his sort of place. He coughed, squinted to let his eyes adjust to the bright interior and stepped inside.

The place went quiet instantly.

Reynard looked around. He recognised the type of place perfectly. This was a regulars' tavern and everyone in here knew each other, if only by sight. There was no real threat here as long as one knew how to blend in, how to appear as one of the locals. He smiled at a nearby patron and nodded his head as if in recognition. The bar began to return to normal as people assumed others knew this handsome newcomer all dressed in black. Then through the door behind him came the seven foot tall Nubian, the white robed Hishan, the silver haired, violet eyed Lucarcian and the female Honshu warrior in scarlet kimono.

You could hear a pin drop.

It took Reynard ten silver sickles to buy enough drinks to get the group accepted and a further five to discover the name of the person in charge of the shipwrights.

*

Reynard was lead down a dark corridor at the rear of the Drunken Dolphin Inn by a short swarthy man, typical of these sorts of places. The rest of the group sat back in the common room, sipping at their drinks and trying, unsuccessfully, to blend in. The man stopped outside a wooden door and knocked twice, paused, then knocked three times, slightly faster.

"Come in," called a muffled voice through the door.

The swarthy man pushed open the door and indicated that Reynard should step through first. Reynard gave him a quick appraising look, judged it to be safe to do so and stepped through. The door clicked shut behind him.

Reynard found himself in a well-appointed office. A large cedar desk dominated the centre of the room. Book shelves lined most of the walls and multi-coloured tomes of different sizes and shapes filled them. A thick rug covered most of the floor, depicting a large ship on a storm-tossed sea. A single lantern lit the room but the light was comfortable and served to illuminate the attractive face of a young lady sitting in the large wooden chair behind the desk.

"You wanted to see me?" she asked smiling up at him, her eyes appraising his tall, strong frame.

Reynard took in deep blue eyes with a hint of ice and blonde hair pulled up in a ponytail and tied tightly, capturing all bar a couple of wayward strands which refused to be controlled. The strands dropped into the woman's face and she unconsciously flicked her head to get them out of her eyes.

"Yes, thank you," he replied, turning on his most charming smile and bowing from the waist in courtly fashion. "I am Captain Reynard of the *Javelin* out of Selkie. How do you do?" he asked.

"Well met Captain. I am Seneca. Now, what can I do for you?" she asked sitting back in her chair and lifting her pointed boots up on to the desktop, crossing them at the ankles, showing off shapely thighs. She put her hands behind her head and stared at him.

"I have a ship in need of some ... repairs. Some rather specific repairs. In fact the whole of the name plate is damaged and in need of replacement. I have been told that you control the ship yard here and are the person to talk to?"

"Repairs you say?" she queried. "Yes, we can accommodate all manner of work. Is it only the name plate which needs replacing?" she asked, her blue eyes staring into his intently.

"Yes, quite a freak accident really, it seems to have left the name plate all bar unreadable yet nothing else seems to have been damaged. Moreover the same strange event contrived to throw the ship's records overboard to be lost to the Inner Sea. It appears we will need a new record book as well, "he continued.

"I see," came back the response. "That sounds like a very complex administrative problem. It will take expert knowledge of the laws of the empire to solve. Fortunately you have come to the right place for I have that expertise. It does not come cheap however."

"I didn't imagine it would, somehow. How much?" asked Reynard, fearing the worst.

They began to haggle. Once Reynard and Seneca had agreed on the price, they went on to agree a value for the items in the hold. The villagers had told Reynard that she controlled the whole port and there was no one else to go to sell the illegal cargos here. Since they needed to sell the drugs and spices to pay for the new name for the *Hammerhead* they had no choice really but to sell to her. This left Reynard with coins in his pocket, but less than he was hoping for when he set out here.

*

"So what you're saying then is that us five get nothing?" asked Tanithil cutting to the point.

"Nothing *yet*," Reynard corrected him. "You agree that we need to pay the crew some money? We have not given them a single coin in weeks and if we lose them we lose the ship. We'll also lose any chance of picking up a new crew here in Black Sail and us five can't sail her alone. We lack the skills and knowledge. "

"Yes, yes," Tanithil retorted. "I get that we need to pay the bastards who kept us captive for weeks so that we don't annoy them," he finished sarcastically.

"So with them paid and the ship renaming performed there is basically just enough money left to take on provisions for the journey to Selkie," Reynard continued.

"I don't understand why we have the need to go there, specifically," commented Kita. Reynard had talked about going to Selkie ever since he had found out that this was where Scraggs had run off. She was curious to know why. She understood that he wanted revenge on the brute but she had a feeling it was something more than that.

"Because Selkie is the best place to sell the *Hammerhead*; sorry, the *Javelin*", Reynard explained. "There are some ports on the south coast near us – Providentia for example – but they have less passing trade and less ships visiting than Selkie. Its position on the north tip of the Tail puts it right slap bang in the middle of the empire and makes it a trade hub. Captains and ships are in and out of there all the time. There will be far more demand there and we'll be able to ask a higher price. Simple economics, my dear," he smiled up at Kita shrugging his shoulders.

"I'm sold," said Okoth, grinning.

"I have heard that Selkie is a place of debauchery and low morals where the ruling lord deals in the dark arts and necromancy," proclaimed Mosi. "It is a place I would like to avoid, but just the sort of place where the Light can do much good. I will come."

"Anywhere I can get a good cut suits me," stated Tanithil.

"Then Selkie it is," declared Kita wondering if she might find out Reynard's true motives for wanting to go there.

*

Less than a week later, the local pilot coaxed the newly named *Javelin* out of Black Sail harbour. Once clear of the entrance channel, Florus rowed the pilot back to shore. Upon his return they set sail off to the east once more, retracing their steps along the south coast of the Spine then around the cape and north into the Lucarcian Straits heading for Selkie on the Tail.

Reynard sat in his study, going over the books. He realised that if he was to become a success he would need to pay more attention to detail. He had got a fair deal for the spices in the hold but having checked the ledger and Captain Waverley's notes he realised he could have got considerably more for the narcotics. No wonder the Guild were happy for merchants to ship these illegal goods – the margins were huge.

The *Javelin* was on its way to Selkie where the plan was to sell the ship and split the profits. Reynard had still not told the crew – there was no point in giving them any warning at this stage. Morale was high – the crew had spent a whole week in the port, had blown all their wages and were hungry to be earning again. Unfortunately Reynard had no money to buy any cargo in Black Sail so they were basically travelling empty. As such, they would make no profit when they reached Selkie, but he figured they would pay the crew when they sold the ship.

Reynard's mind went back to his brother. Maynard was two years older – he would be turning thirty this year – and had always been the cleverer of the two. Not as tall or strong as his little brother since the age of about ten, but always the more crafty. Maynard had proclaimed himself a pacifist on his twenty-first birthday, and this proclamation had prompted their father, Lord Caer, to delay naming him as heir. Maynard was oldest and typically would inherit the title when their father died. Tradition held that the father would name his heir on the eldest boy's twenty first birthday. Now, some nine years later, the Earl had still not named his official heir. Should Lord Caer die before naming one of his sons then the title and estate would pass to Maynard by default.

Was this what his betrayal was all about – a way to ensure his father didn't name him? Reynard knew his father would never name him heir. He was always the disappointment. His father had tried and tried to make Reynard see the importance of the estate and the responsibilities of his position but had failed. Funnily enough two weeks in a slave hold, and the knowledge that his brother had put him there, had caused Reynard to re-examine his life and now the idea of being heir to the Earl of Providentia was quite appealing.

The Empire of Lucarcia was at a turning point. The emperor was old and had no living heir. His line, which could trace itself back five hundred years to the original Emperor Lucar, was at an end. There were doubts as to what would happen when the emperor died and there was no one to take control of the ruling Azure House. With Azure House leaderless, and maybe gone forever, a huge power vacuum was looming. Some said the death of the emperor would mean the end of the Lucarcian Empire itself. Most agreed civil war was coming.

There were five major houses in the empire. The Azure house was the imperial house, ruled by the emperor. This house had been the ruling house for five hundred years. It was based in the Spine of Ursum centred on Lucar, the capital. Then there were the Ruby and Ebon houses, also based on Ursum, in the Head and Tail of that island respectively. The Ice King, who ruled the entire island of Manabas in the north, headed House Snow. Finally the mysterious and reclusive Verdant Queen, Lily Jade, headed the Jade House. She ruled the jungle island of Ibini in the east of the empire. Rumours said that each of the latter four major houses was preparing for civil war – but it was unclear exactly what each house was doing to prepare.

If Reynard's father died and Maynard became Lord Ferrand, Earl of Providentia, the Iron House and its lands would fall into his control and be under his protection. House Ferrand was a direct vassal of the ruling Azure House. When the emperor died, if the Azure House crumbled, any protection the Iron House had enjoyed over the years would end instantly. So if civil war broke out and word got out that Maynard was a pacifist then the Iron House would become a target. One of the other major houses on Ursum would sweep down and attack Providentia. If Maynard refused to defend the city then House Ferrand would quickly cease to exist.

If a strong Earl ruled Providentia and remained resolute against anyone threatening it, then House Ferrand's future was much more secure. One of the major houses would still probably aim to take Providentia under its control but would likely do it politically, by seeking to get the Earl to swear fealty to them. This would mean the Iron House and its lands would continue to belong to the Earl and his family. All that would be different would be that they would now owe fealty to House Ebon or Ruby, instead of House Azure.

Lord Caer knew this, Reynard was sure, so perhaps he had spent the last nine years trying to convince Maynard of the necessity to be prepared for war so that he could name him heir. There was just no way that Reynard could know the truth without digging deeper into this mess. And Scraggs was his first lead. It was time to get to Selkie and find out what the old first mate knew.

Reynard would drag it out of him by force if he had to. He was no pacifist.

-Chapter Six-

A week later the *Javelin* rounded the headland which marked the end of the Lucarcian Straits. A league or so ahead they could see the sprawling city of Selkie. Selkie was draped across the low lying hills either side of where the Iceflow River emptied into the Inner Sea. The largest settlement in the Tail of Ursum, Selkie was a major trade hub with strong links to Manabas and Ibini, the other major islands of Lucarcia. The Old Coast Road linked Selkie with the fishing villages of Kelp in the west and Derketo in the east. Guild merchants used the Iceflow River to transport their wares up to faraway Frostgard.

The ship weighed anchor outside the port and a pilot rowed out to the ship and came aboard. He asked them some perfunctory questions about where they were from and what their purpose was in the city and then he skilfully navigated the ship into port and brought it to a stop alongside a wooden jetty. The crew threw ropes out and stevedores tied them to the bollards on the wharf, securing the ship. Seabirds wheeled and screeched above and the gentle afternoon sun warmed the air. They thanked the pilot and put the gang plank out for him to leave the ship.

The crew looked out on the port of Selkie, most happy to be home. Reynard had organized their time off already and the first rota disembarked with the pilot. Many chose to stay aboard, having already spent their pay in Black Sail. Only those who had won at cards in the dens of Black Sail still had money to burn. Cyrus went with them, his mission to locate Scraggs and report back.

Reynard stood on the port rail and looked out at the city. He had never been here before. The harbour was large and fed by the river which flowed gently out to sea. There were currently about a dozen large ships and scores of small boats moored up. Sailors scurried about the place fixing things, carrying stuff or running errands. There was a lot of noise and bustle.

On either side of the river, buildings led up the low hillside in neat, grey rows. The builders predominantly used rock quarried in the nearby Frosthold Mountains. Looming over the whole city high above was a dark and foreboding castle, home of Lord Barrius Ebon. Lord Barrius ruled the noble Ebon House which controlled the whole of the Tail of Ursum. A huge standard hung from the castle flag pole, shifting lazily in the gentle afternoon breeze. Reynard knew that fully unfurled the flag would show a giant raven on the wing, the coat of arms of the Ebon House.

Looking across the wharf Reynard's eye was drawn to a group of men making their way down the water front. There were half a dozen of them, all dressed in black leather with red flashes. They wore helms which looked like oversized human skulls and had long curved swords at their sides. These were the Dread Guard, personal soldiers in the employ of the Ebon Lord. As they moved down the wharf everyone scrambled out of their way, giving them wide berth.

Looking more closely Reynard noted that things were not quite as they seemed at first glance in Selkie. Where the harbour front had a certain bustle and energy about it, as he studied the people there more closely he noticed there was something missing. There was no laughter. Nowhere could any music or singing be heard – something quite common on most waterfronts. As he watched the patrol of Dread Guard pass down the wharf he noticed something which *was* there: fear. It was subtle but present. The people of Selkie were afraid.

Looking back up at the foreboding castle on the hill, Lord Barrius Ebon's reputation sprang to mind. The common folk said that the Ebon Lord was a necromancer who spoke with the dead. There was no doubt he had a preoccupation with the deceased – you only had to look at the helms of his Dread Guard to know that. Reynard had never met the man, but was sure these rumours were no more than that – just folklore and superstition. Still, it was clear that the populace believed it and were more than a little afraid of their ruler.

*

Three hours later the sun had set and Reynard had Kita and Okoth in his office. "Kita, Cyrus and I will go," he told them. "Cyrus has located Scraggs holed up in a waterfront hostel called the Inn of the Dying Minotaur. He will lead us to him. The plan is to capture him and bring him back here to the *Javelin* so we can let the crew feel that they have had their revenge for all the terrors he imposed on them under Captain Waverley."

"You're going to kill him?" asked Okoth, surprised.

"No, it won't go that far. A flogging perhaps – out to sea of course where no one will ask any questions. But I won't let them make him walk the plank," Reynard answered.

"I'm not sure what we stand to gain from this venture," commented Kita. "It seems a lot of risk for no real purpose," she continued. What was Reynard up to here? Why was he so insistent on bringing Scraggs back to the ship?

"We need to keep the crew happy," replied Reynard. You said it yourself – morale is fickle and easily broken. We have not paid the crew in two weeks and we have no money to pay them now. We need some way to keep them ours."

"Your logic is flawed," pointed out Kita. "You have no money to pay the crew. You have no money to take on new cargo, so we have no way to make more money. Yet you expect the crew to be happy to set sail once more? What are you going to tell them? That our sole purpose for this journey is simply to flog Scraggs?"

Reynard knew she was right. The plan had always been to sell the *Javelin* here, pay the crew their dues and split the remainder of the money between them. But he needed to talk to Scraggs, needed to find out what the man knew about his brother.

"Okay," conceded Reynard, "you're right. That won't work." He decided to be honest with them – to a point. "I'll come clean," he confessed. "I need to get some information out of Scraggs. It's personal and I have no wish to share it with you all just yet. I need to get him alone for a while. Just a while. Will you help me to do that?" he asked.

Kita considered for a moment. "Yes," she replied after a short pause. "I will help you. You should just have told us this at the start. It would have been easier." So, that was what it was all about. Reynard wanted some information. She could understand that. She was curious to know what that information related to but it was none of her business so she was content to leave it be - for now.

"Fine by me," said Okoth, obliging as usual. He wasn't worried about all these complex issues. He was simply happy to follow where Reynard led. Okoth was reasonably content. He knew he would never be able to return home as there was a price on his head. He intended to ask Reynard if he wanted a travelling companion once they had sold the ship. If not Reynard, then maybe one of the others would want his company. He didn't really have anything else to do.

"So, Kita, Cyrus and I will go," repeated Reynard. We will head down to the inn where Cyrus says he is staying, and have a word with him. Once we have done that, we will find a shipwright and look into selling the *Javelin*. Agreed?" he asked.

All were.

*

Reynard gave it another couple of hours. Cyrus had said that Scraggs was drinking in a hostel by the waterfront and giving him more time to drink could only help Reynard's position. It was getting late when Cyrus led Kita and him to the side of the ship ready to disembark. As he was about to follow them onto the gang plank Reynard felt a hand on his arm. He stopped and looked to find the silver haired Tanithil stood there.

"Don't trust Cyrus," the violet eyed man warned him.

"It will be fine, I'm sure, Tani," Reynard assured him.

Tanithil looked deep into his eyes, then merely shrugged and walked away.

Reynard shuddered as he felt someone walk over his grave. He shook his head to clear the moment's feeling of foreboding and then followed Kita and Cyrus off the ship.

The three reached the main wharf and turned right to head down to the Dying Minotaur where Cyrus said they would find Scraggs. As they did, a dark hooded figure detached itself from the shadows of some cargo crates on the waterside. Unnoticed, it trailed them down the wharf.

*

Standing in an alley, Reynard pressed his face up to the grubby glass of the inn window and peered into the common room. The Dying Minotaur Inn was dark. Mahogany made up the majority of the floorboards and the walls were panelled in the same deep red timber. The furniture was heavy wood and uncomfortable looking. The place was full of sailors and the discordant sounds of an out of tune singer filtered through to the alleyway through the window.

Sat in one corner, darker than the rest, was Scraggs. He was deep into his cups, Reynard could see, and he was alone, just as Cyrus had told them. Scraggs was wearing the same clothes as when Reynard had last seen him, disappearing off into the distance of a cliff top a few leagues west of here. He looked thin and hungry. It seemed life was not treating him well. Reynard was glad.

"Okay, it's your turn now then Cyrus. Are you ready?" asked Reynard.

"Yes sir," came back the reply from the sailor, who looked a bit nervous.

"Go through what you're to do again."

"I go in there and talk to him. Put him at ease. Then get him to come out here into the alleyway where you will, err, have words with him. Obviously I don't mention that you're here," replied Cyrus.

"Yes, that's about the size of it. Good man. Now get going."

Reynard and Kita watched through the window as Cyrus entered the bar. He looked around and then approached Scragg's table. Cyrus and Scraggs exchanged a few words and then Cyrus pulled up a chair and sat. The two continued to talk for what seemed like a long time. It was impossible to tell exactly what they were saying to each other.

As the conversation continued Reynard thought he saw Scraggs glance at the window through which they were peering. Tanithil's warning repeated in his head as he watched the conversation play out. Was Cyrus selling them out? Was he still working with the old ex-first mate of the *Hammerhead*? Reynard prided himself on being good at reading people, but at this distance, through a grubby window, it was hard to tell.

"Be on your guard, Kita. I'm not sure I like the look of this," he instructed her.

"I always am," she replied shortly, loosening her swords in their scabbards.

At that time Scraggs and Cyrus pushed their chairs back and stood. Cyrus led Scraggs towards the back door of the inn and they disappeared from sight. Shortly they would arrive in the alleyway and Reynard would be able to find out what Scraggs knew of his brother's treachery. He felt his palms were clammy as the moment approached. He was not sure he really wanted to know.

Minutes passed. Too many minutes, Reynard realised with a start. His hand dropped to the basket hilt of his rapier as two men entered the alleyway from the direction of the back door of the inn. It only took a moment to realise they were not Scraggs and Cyrus. These were typical sea front thugs and there was only one thing they were here for: violence. Looking back over his shoulder Reynard saw that two more thugs had entered the alley at the water front end. The thugs had surrounded them and cut them off.

As he drew his sword he felt Kita draw her twin blades behind him. The two warriors instinctively moved back to back. The thugs advanced and as they did Reynard saw Scraggs move into the alleyway behind the two at his end, cutlass in hand. Risking a quick glance behind him he saw that Cyrus had moved into the alley at that end. Tanithil had been right: Cyrus had sold them out.

Reynard felt his anger rise and focussed on the two men directly in front of him. The alley was thin and they would struggle to flank him. Reynard decided to press the fight and moved quickly in their direction. He lunged at the first goon and the sheer speed of his blade caught the ruffian off guard. The blade pierced his chest and blood fountained out of his mouth. He dropped to the floor as the second swung a clumsy slash with his long knife. Reynard ducked easily and punched him in the face with the hilt of his blade, stunning him. He grabbed the thug's tunic and pushed him into Scraggs. Scraggs caught the ruffian and shoved him back – right onto the end of Reynard's blade. The thug slid off the rapier and onto the floor, dead.

The initial anger subsided and Reynard dropped into his more typical fighting stance. He was a natural counter attacker and favoured a defensive stance. Raising his rapier to point at the chest of his opponent he steadied his breathing and waited.

Scraggs looked at him and sneered. "What brings you after me, rich boy?" he asked as he slashed his cutlass across the space between them, warming up his sword arm.

"I have a few questions I'd like answering," replied Reynard.

"I'm sure you do," Scraggs taunted, launching a wicked curving strike with his cutlass. Reynard parried the blow easily, deflecting it downwards and away from him.

Behind him Reynard heard Kita let out a great shout. It was more a sharp exhalation of breath articulated into a very loud scream than any particular word. He turned Scraggs to the side with a wide thrust which allowed him to flick a glance behind himself. Kita had just cloven Cyrus in two with her *katana*. The other two thugs already lay dead at her feet.

"It seems your companions are taking a break from the fighting," Reynard teased, smiling his easy smile. This seemed to enrage the ex-first mate who dipped his shoulder and barrelled into Reynard's midriff. Reynard fell heavily and dropped his rapier.

Instinct kicked in and he smashed a fist into Scragg's nose as the sailor landed on top of him. Rolling sideways Reynard tried to get out from under the dangerous opponent but Scraggs was too good a brawler and, even with blood dripping from his broken nose, he battered Reynard with a quick serious of punches to the face. Reynard was beginning to see stars.

Scraggs stopped punching abruptly. Raising his hands above his head he moved off Reynard and stood to the side. Kita was pointing her *katana* directly at his throat.

"Thank you," Reynard said to Kita, getting to his feet and bowing politely. He received a curt nod in return. Reynard leaned down to pick up his rapier and turned to Scraggs. "So, we have some issues to discuss, sir," he said pointedly. With a lightning fast move Reynard struck Scraggs in the temple with the hilt of his sword and the sailor slumped to the ground unconscious. "But I think the brig of the *Javelin* is the place for such a discussion," he finished.

"Not before we have a little chat ourselves," said a hooded figure as it detached itself from the shadows deeper in the alleyway.

*

"What the...?" exclaimed Reynard, spinning to face the newcomer. "Who are you and what do you want?"

"Let's start with a simple drink, shall we? Back inside the Dying Minotaur," he answered, pulling his hood back from his face to reveal a full head of auburn hair and a pointed beard, neatly trimmed. A heavy dark cloak hid the rest of him. No weapons were visible on the stranger. "You can leave Scraggs here in the alley for a few minutes. He won't be coming around any time soon."

"Why should we listen to you?" asked Reynard, pointing his sword at the man's chest.

The stranger stepped forward, pushing the blade aside with a black gloved hand. He looked deeply into Reynard's steel blue eyes, "If you don't want me to call out to the Dread Guard patrol that are passing the alley about now, and have to explain to them all these dead bodies, then I suggest you take me up on my offer and allow me to buy you a drink," he stated.

Ten minutes later the three of them were in the common room of the Dying Minotaur Inn, a glass of frothy local ale in front of each of them. Scraggs was piled unceremoniously in a crate in the alleyway outside, still unconscious.

"So, what is it you want?" asked Reynard coming straight to the point.

The stranger picked up his ale with his gloved hand and took a sip. "Not the best Lucarcian ale in the city," he noted, "but there are worse. I am Varus," he introduced himself, "and I'm here to deliver you a summons. You are wanted in Cansae. The Trade Lords would like to meet you - all five of you."

Reynard and Kita exchanged glances. The Trade Lords? This could not end well. "What is it that the leaders of the Guild want with us?" Reynard inquired.

"They know about the *Hammerhead*," Varus answered simply.

"I'm not sure what you mean," said Reynard evasively. If the Trade Lords knew they had killed a Guild captain and taken his ship their lives would not be worth living. The Guild was extremely protective of its own.

"Then let me explain," began Varus, lowering his voice. "The five of you who are now the command crew of the *Javelin* – that is: you two, the Nubian, the Hishanite and the silver haired Lucarcian - were, until about a month ago, working as 'oarsmen' in the *Hammerhead* out of Selkie. About that time you rose up, killed the captain – Anton Waverley – and took over his ship. You threw the first mate – Mr Scraggs, our friend in the alley – into the brig and sailed off to Black Sail. There you had the ship renamed and reregistered as the *Javelin*. Does any of this sound familiar?" asked Varus, taking another sip of his ale.

"Why talk to us about this? If this is true and the Trade Lords know all this then why have they asked you to find us? Why not send assassins to kill us?"

"I'm merely the messenger, sir," answered Varus with a shrug. "All I know is that it is my job to get you to arrive in Cansae and appear before the Trade Lords by the end of this month. That gives us about two weeks. I'm sure there is no need for me to warn you not to disobey the Trade Lords."

Reynard took a long pull of his ale. "We have no money to pay the crew. There is no way we will be able to get them to take the long journey to the other end of Ursum." Cansae was right up at the Head of Ursum, a long distance away and Reynard could not see any way in which they could get that far without a crew mutiny.

"I have enough money to pay your crew for the journey to Cansae and then some bonus on top of that. However, the five of you will get nothing," came back the reply.

Reynard thought hard. Varus seemed to have all the angles covered. "What is to stop us from weighing anchor and sailing off into the distance?" he asked after a pause.

"I will be coming with you," answered Varus, draining the last of his ale. "And anyway, if you're not in Cansae by the end of the month, nowhere in the empire will be safe for you, ever again. You're right – the Trade Lords would have killed you if they wanted you dead. So you have nothing to lose. Go to Cansae and see what it is they want with you."

Reynard considered his options but quickly realized there were none. They had no choice. The power and influence of the mysterious Trade Lords was such that there was nowhere they could run, nowhere they could hide.

He looked at Kita for an opinion. A simple nod of her head was all he got, but it was enough. "Okay. It seems we have no choice. We'll escort you to Cansae and go and visit the Trade Lords. But before we go, I need to speak to Scraggs."

"Scraggs is unimportant," said Varus. "Leave him."

"He is important to me," came back Reynard, leaning forward to make his point.

Varus considered for a moment, "Very well," he replied. "You have five minutes."

Reynard rose from his seat. "Kita will escort you to the *Javelin*. I'll be along presently."

"Five minutes," repeated Varus, also rising.

Reynard gulped down the last of his ale and turned to head out the backdoor to the alleyway. As he did, Kita rose and led Varus to the front door, her ale left completely untouched on the mahogany table.

*

"It's very simple," said Reynard, "You tell me what I want to know and I let you go. You refuse and I gut you here in this alleyway, right now." Reynard had Scraggs by the throat with his left hand and his right was pressing a long knife into the sailor's stomach.

Scraggs turned his head and spat at the floor next to Reynard. "Okay," he answered, "I get the point. What is it you want to know?"

Reynard could smell the fetid stench of stale ale on the man's breath and clothes. It was pretty unpleasant and he didn't want to be in this position any longer than necessary. Relaxing his grip on the sailor's throat he grabbed him by the shirt and kept him at arm's length but still close enough to plunge his knife into his chest if required.

"Let's start at the beginning. You know who I really am, and you know how I ended up on the *Hammerhead*. I want to know everything you know about that," Reynard explained.

"Fine," said Scraggs, crunching his neck from side to side and feeling his throat where Reynard's hand had been gripping it a moment before. "It's like this. Your brother paid Cap'n Waverley to take you into slavery. The Cap'n did tell me that apparently someone had ordered your brother to 'get rid' of you. He didn't know who had the influence to order that of your brother but us sailors never did understand the workings of you nobles. The Cap'n ordered me to find you, and it wasn't difficult. I slipped some narcotics into your drinks on the water front in Providentia and before too long you was sleeping like a baby and it was easy to get you aboard the *Hammerhead*. That's it," finished the ugly sailor. "That's all I know."

Reynard's mind went into over drive. So someone had ordered Maynard to get rid of him. Who had the influence or the power to do that? His father certainly, but there was simply no logic behind that idea. So, who else? Who stood to gain from Reynard's death? With Reynard gone only Maynard stood to control House Ferrand in the event of their father's death; and Maynard was weak.

Two obvious factions stood to gain from a weak Iron House: The Ruby and Ebon houses. With Maynard in control the Iron House would be frail: perfect pickings for the Ebon or Ruby houses to swallow up.

An offer of protection from one of the major houses in the case of the death of the emperor would no doubt appeal to Maynard. And with Reynard out of the way the Iron House could easily be controlled by one of the major houses when their father finally died. It all made sense. But which major house was responsible, Ebon or Ruby?

"So, I have told you all I know. I can go now, yes?" asked Scraggs.

Reynard plunged the knife deep into the sailor's heart, watching as surprise washed over his face and then the life slowly drained from his body. "No, not really," came the reply as he dropped the lifeless body to the floor of the alley and turned and headed back to his ship.

-Chapter Seven-

Reynard looked up at the dark castle above him. The sun had just risen in the east and blood red light bathed the fortress. From the castle flagpole, the raven standard was fully unfurled as a sharp breeze drove in from the Inner Sea to the north, bringing cold winds and the occasional rain shower. The Ebon Fortress, home of Lord Barrius Ebon, known to some as the Dark Lord, loomed over the city of Selkie like a watching sentinel.

Reynard looked and wondered. Was Lord Barrius responsible for his current plight? Had he ordered Maynard to kill his own brother? Reynard was pretty sure it was either the Ebon Lord, or his main rival on Ursum, Lord Ignatius Ruby, also known as the Dragon. One of these two nobles had caused Maynard to sell him into slavery and end up on a ship, about to set sail to Cansae and the home of the mysterious Trade Lords. How had life construed to bring him to this sorry state?

Tearing his eyes from the Ebon Fortress, Reynard returned to his quarters in the fore of the *Javelin*. He was going to have to explain to his command crew that rather than selling the ship, dividing up the profits and going their separate ways, both free and with good coin in their pockets, they were going to be embarking on a journey to the other side of the empire and an interview with the Trade Lords. It would not be an easy pitch to make.

Presently the others arrived in the sumptuous living quarters of the captain's cabin. Varus also joined them. Reynard made sure they were all seated and then offered them some refreshments. Once they were settled he began.

"You're probably expecting this conversation to be about selling the *Javelin* and going our separate ways," Reynard said. Looking around he could see that Okoth and Mosi were nodding their heads at this opening. Kita, who already knew their position, was sitting with an unreadable expression on her face. Tanithil was staring at Varus with an intense look, his concentration so focused that Reynard doubted the silver haired Lucarcian was even listening to what he was saying. "Well, it would appear that this plan will have to be put on hold for the foreseeable future," he continued.

That grabbed their attention; or at least Okoth's and Mosi's. Kita remained unreadable and Tanithil continued to stare at Varus.

"Why is that?" asked Okoth, voicing the obvious question.

"It seems that the Trade Lords have taken an interest in us and want to speak with us, personally, face to face, in the Guild Hall in Cansae," Reynard explained. "They said something about being unhappy with us for killing their Guild captain and stealing one of their ships."

"I do not know much about these Trade Lords," stated Mosi, brushing out an imaginary crease in his white robe, "but from what I have heard I would have expected them to have ordered our deaths, rather than summon us for an interview."

"That's correct," said Reynard, "which means we are at least not likely to be summoned there and then killed. It would be a waste of time and energy." Or at least he hoped so.

"And who is this fellow?" asked Okoth, nodding towards Varus.

"I am Varus," he replied, bowing low, "and I'm here on behalf of the Trade Lords to help ensure you reach Cansae as swiftly and safely as possible."

"In other words, he is here to baby sit us," came in Tanithil, finally dragging his eyes from Varus.

"So do we have a choice?" asked Okoth, of Reynard.

"Not really," came back the reply. "And worse, still, although the Guild has paid the crew so we won't get a mutiny on the way, they will not give us a penny. This means we'll be sailing to Cansae with an empty hold and will have no way to make any money either. Varus here has given us enough funds to equip us with basics – so we have provisions for a two week journey but that is it. Any questions?"

"Would it matter if we did?" asked Tanithil, of Varus.

"No, not particularly," he replied.

*

Later that morning as they waited for the tides to rise ready to set sail, Reynard was in his office. He was studying the maps and charts and was making some calculations. He determined that it would take about twelve or thirteen days to reach Cansae if they took the southern route, following the southern edge of Ursum past Providentia. If they took the northern route then it would take only eleven days. This was clearly the most favourable route but involved a two or three day crossing of the Inner Sea away from the coast. Which route should they choose?

He went out onto the main deck where the crew was hard at work preparing the ship. There was a positive buzz about the place and Okoth was there moving among them and encouraging them in their work. Standing at the starboard rail looking out across the harbour was Tanithil. Reynard approached him. Tanithil turned as he got near.

"Good morning Tani. Ready for our new adventure?" he asked.

Tanithil looked deep into his eyes. "You want to speak to me about our route," he declared.

"Err, yes. Yes, I do," replied Reynard, a bit surprised that he was so readable to his companion. "Will you come up to my office please?" he asked.

Minutes later the two were stood overlooking the charts on Reynard's desk. Before Reynard had a chance to explain the options Tanithil said, "The crew won't be happy if you decide to cross the Inner Sea. The route from here to Lucar – the obvious point to aim for on the northern coast of Ursum – would take you pretty much right over the site of Antissa," Tanithil pointed on the maps. "That area of the Inner Sea is considered cursed and you would struggle to get the crew to go there, unless it was absolutely necessary," he continued. "Your best bet is the southern route, even though that will take a day or two longer and may expose us to the southern storms. We have fourteen days to reach Cansae and perhaps a day or two of slack to play with. It will be close but it is the best choice," he concluded.

Reynard looked at Tanithil closely. He always seemed to know what Reynard was about to ask him. It was uncanny. He also always seemed to have useful information to impart. He must remember to ask his advice more often. "Okay," Reynard conceded, "We'll go south."

*

Pulling out of the harbour of Selkie the *Javelin* turned east and headed towards the Lucarcian Straits once more. The sky was blue overhead and small white clouds scudded swiftly across the sky on a strong northerly wind. Reynard took his place up on the quarterdeck and watched as the crew did their thing. Okoth had become quite accomplished on the wheel and stood there tall and strong looking across the ship and on towards their heading. The wind whipped Reynard's shoulder length blond hair back from his face and caused his black waistcoat to slap at his side.

In the rigging above him skilful sailors climbed and scurried, working hard to get the ship moving as quickly as possible. Down on deck more crewmen worked the sheets and lines, keeping the sails trimmed. The *Javelin* fairly flew across the wind-swell moving east across the seas.

Reynard felt a surge of pride. These were not originally his men. A man who had thrown him into slavery picked this crew. A man he had killed. Yet they now worked for him, working as a well drilled and well organized team. Of course he could claim no credit for their skills, but he did claim responsibility for the morale of the crew. He knew a motivated team when he saw it, and this was one. Of course, the bonus pay that Reynard had been able to lavish on them helped.

The *Javelin* moved east, and by the time the sun was setting they had turned south into the Straits proper. They navigated deeper out to sea, to avoid any chance of running aground in the night, and pressed on. Reynard watched as the crew rotated for the next shift and then retired to his cabin to think. He felt like he had no control over his life at the moment. Only a few weeks ago he had been a happy-go-lucky fop with plenty of money in his pocket and no responsibility. Then suddenly he was a slave in an oar deck. Now he was free from slavery but still subject to the whims of the Trade Lords. They were telling him what to do and he didn't like it. All this was Maynard's fault. No, actually, all this was the fault of the person who had told Maynard to get rid of him. And that was either Lord Barrius Ebon or Lord Ignatius Ruby. Either way, Reynard had some serious enemies – and he wasn't even sure who they all were.

*

A couple of days later the *Javelin* rounded the southern tip of the Tail and turned west to follow the southern edge of the Spine of Ursum in the direction of the Head. They still had over seven hundred miles to go till they reached Cansae, the Red City, but they were making excellent progress. The winds had stayed in the north and had driven them through the Straits at breakneck speeds. But now, as they moved into the Southern Ocean, they were at the mercy of the spring storms which wracked the coast at this time of year.

Reynard had grown up on this coast. He was born and raised in Providentia and had never really been that far from home. The occasional visit to outlying villages which his father's men protected was the majority of his travelling experience. He had once taken the overland journey to the capital Lucar and been to court with his father. That had been many years ago. Growing up here he was well used to the weather in this part of the world and had much experience of the violent storms which were prone to strike this region in the spring.

Within hours of rounding the Tail the lookout up in the crow's nest shouted down. All eyes went to where he pointed and in the distance out to sea ahead of them they could see a dark mass of clouds, roiling across the sea. Flashes of lightning lit up the clouds, making for an impressive display of purples, oranges and yellows in the dark cloudscape. It would have made enjoyable watching were it not for the fact that the *Javelin* was heading almost straight towards it.

Reynard tried to judge the movement of the squall. If it was moving south, away from land, then it would miss them totally. A few minutes of watching it gave him the impression it was coming towards them, but that it might miss them on the port side. If they tucked in tight to the coast it might pass by out to sea and give them nothing more than a bit of a bumpy ride for a few hours. But if it turned more inland or he had misjudged it, it could be catastrophic. It looked like a particularly violent storm.

Reynard turned to seek out the boatswain on the main deck, "Birgen! Get up here now!" he shouted.

A little man, slim and wiry, with black hair, greying at the temples and pulled back into a pony tail, came rushing up the steps to the quarterdeck. "Yes, sir?" he reported.

"We need to get the ship into shore. That storm might pass us by but we can't risk it. Get the ship prepared for a stop in a sheltered bay. Do you know any around here?" Reynard asked.

Birgen put his hand to his chin as he thought. "Yes, I think I do, sir. We are not too far from Black Sail but that would mean turning around and heading back where we have just come from. Or if you would prefer then there is a deep water cove a little way along from here. We could shelter there," he told Reynard.

"The cove sounds perfect, thank you. Speak with Okoth. I need the two of you to get us to safety."

Suddenly Varus was at his side, appearing almost out of nowhere. "What's all this about, Captain?" he enquired.

"The storm is coming up fast on us, so we are heading to safety," replied Reynard.

"A word in your ear, please Captain," came the reply from Varus as he turned and walked to a corner of the quarterdeck away from Birgen and Okoth.

Reynard cursed inwardly and followed him. "Yes?" he asked.

"We need to push on, Reynard. We have an appointment in the Red City and you do not make the Trade Lords wait." Varus rocked up onto the balls of his feet and back down as he spoke.

"That will mean taking us right into the storm," countered Reynard, looking down on the shorter man.

"I know full well what it means, Captain. But we push on."

Reynard cursed, aloud this time, "So be it Varus, but any damage to this ship is on your head. I cannot afford to pay for any repairs – so you had best agree to foot the bill now, or we are going nowhere."

"Agreed. Now get this ship moving, Captain," Varus ordered.

Reynard considered the situation. They had gained a day or so in their rush south through the Straits but they still had a long way to go. Perhaps if the storm looked like it was going to actually hit them, they could find a place to dive into cover for a short while. He returned to the wheel and gave the command to Okoth to steer the ship a little nearer to shore but on a generally westerly heading still, taking them nearer the raging mass of clouds and lightning.

"Carry on into the storm, sir?" asked Birgen, still on the quarterdeck alongside the wheel.

"Yes, that's what I said."

"Sir, the ship won't survive a headlong collision with a storm of that power. At the very least it will rip parts off the ship and toss them into the ocean. At worst it will capsize and sink us. We need to avoid it, sir," advised the boatswain.

"I know your job is to look after the ship," Reynard conceded, "but mine is to get us where we need to go, and on time at that," he said, with a sideways glance at Varus who was stood nearby. "We press on. Do what you need to do to get the ship ready to face the storm," he finished.

Birgen paused as if about to say something, then merely nodded and rushed off to the main deck shouting commands to the crew as he went.

*

Up on the foredeck as the sun began to set, Reynard knew they were in trouble.

The *Javelin* had made fair time pressing west along the coastline. The storm had moved steadily closer. Reynard had been constantly balancing the options of making a run for cover on the coast or staying out and pushing on further, nearer to the storm. He had watched the storm move closer and yet had elected to push on and on, hoping that the storm would pass by on their port side. Varus had been by his side each moment, making sure they did not deviate from their course. Now Reynard realized he had misjudged it and the storm would crash headlong into them.

The swell rose as the seas grew in intensity. Ahead lightning lit the black and grey storm clouds in multicolour and now the crew heard the sounds of booming and rolling thunder, getting louder as the storm approached. Reynard rushed across the ship back up to the quarterdeck and found Okoth at the wheel. "Can you get us into shelter?" he asked the giant Nubian.

"I will try, but it looks like that storm will be here before we can find somewhere safe," Okoth replied.

"Yes, I think I might have misjudged the speed and direction it was heading," admitted Reynard.

"Well, there is nothing to do now but deal with it, little man," said Okoth with a big smile.

Reynard turned to the boatswain, "Birgen! Get up here now!" he shouted.

The little man came rushing up the steps to the quarterdeck, tying his hair, which had come loose, back into its accustomed ponytail as he ran. "Yes, sir?" he reported.

"I know we should have stopped when you suggested it, Birgen. Now it's too late and the storm is going to hit us. Can you get the ship ready before it does?" Reynard asked.

Birgen looked over his shoulder at the roiling mass of black and grey clouds and gulped. "I'll do me best sir!" he said and spun on his heel, commands bellowing from his mouth as he set about sorting the ship.

*

The *Javelin* was like a small toy on the seas as the storm hit. Carracks like the *Javelin* were the biggest and hardiest ships in the empire but their construction tended to make them wallow in rough waters. In a storm like this one they were prone to being tossed about violently. Birgen had everything which could be tied down secured. Only those sailors who Birgen had ordered into the rigging were up there – the rest had lashed themselves to the deck. No one was below decks. This was an event that everyone wanted to experience first-hand – so if they survived it they could tell their grandchildren about it.

Darkness had engulfed the ship as the storm enveloped it. Occasional flashes of lightning lit the scene with a surreal brightness which was there and then gone. Okoth was steering the ship, tied to the wheel to stop the crashing waves from sweeping him away. Wind and rain pummelled him as he tried to get the *Javelin* into shore as much as possible, to remove it from the worst of the thrashing that the storm was giving out, but even still the effects on the *Javelin* were terrible.

The ship fought its way against the wind, climbing slowly to the top of a swell. There it stuttered as if nervous of what it might find on the other side. The height and angle of the wave made it seem that it would never reach the top. Finally it crested the wave, pitched over the far side and dropped like a stone into the deep valley beyond. The fore of the ship plunged deep into the sea and a powerful wave swept over the prow and crashed onto the deck. It washed two sailors screaming right over the starboard rail and into the abyss of the pounding surf.

Suddenly a blinding flash split the darkness and the mizzenmast exploded in a ball of fire, the mizzen sail smouldering in the dark, despite being soaked through with the rains. The mast split and the top half crashed down onto the quarterdeck, splintering much of the railings there and crushing one sailor's skull. Birgen had men there in an instant, dealing with the fire and getting the remains of the mast secured safely.

"We need to stop fighting the storm, sir!" Birgen told Reynard. "There is no way the ship will survive this. Reef the sails, drop anchor and try and ride it out," he advised.

Reynard was reticent to do so – they needed to push on and get to Cansae – but the loss of the mizzenmast was enough to convince him. "Okay. Do it," he commanded.

Birgen gave out the orders and the sailors brought the ship to a state where it would no longer fight against the storm. The crew dropped, wrapped and stowed the sails as fast as was possible. They threw the anchor over the side in an effort to reduce the distance that the ship might drift and got out of the rigging, preparing to wait out the storm.

At times it felt like the ship would roll over. Okoth stayed at the wheel, fighting with all his strength to keep the prow facing into the storm, to stop the waves turning the *Javelin* sideways on. The ship continued to rise and fall over the great swell, battling to stay afloat and upright. It was the hardest fight Okoth had ever known. And he was a seasoned warrior.

Okoth was born and raised in the far-off land of Nubia, across the other side of the known world, thousands of miles from Lucarcia. The Nubians were hunters and farmers. A simple race, far less advanced than their neighbours the Rodinians were. Hence they were easy pickings when the Rodinians decided to invade them and subjugate them many years ago. Since that time Nubia had been a colony of Rodinia and a regular source of slaves for the Rodinian Empire.

Okoth had been a hunter. The Rodinians allowed the Nubians to continue their traditional cultural practices and hunting was one of them. Standing the best part of seven feet tall Okoth stood out in a crowd so it was inevitable that someone would notice him one day. When the Rodinians were looking for Nubian slaves to take part in their gladiatorial games, of course someone spotted Okoth and realized his potential. The Rodinians dragged the huge warrior off to the gladiator school where they had trained him to fight. He was already a capable warrior and of course was incredibly strong, but when the Rodinian arms masters got hold of him and gave him formal training, he became deadly.

His masters sent Okoth into the ring to fight against other Nubian slaves, the occasional foreigner and all manner of wild animals. He was lethal. He fought in the ring for three years and was undefeated; the Gladiatorial Champion of Nubia. Then the call came. The emperor was holding a huge tournament at the capital of Rodin and the emperor's aides told Okoth's masters that Okoth was to attend. The road from Nubia to Rodin was long and Okoth had found an opportunity to escape. Okoth was never actually sure if he wanted to be a gladiator or not, and had never really thought about what he would do if the chance to escape arrived. When it did, he had taken it on a whim. It was then, when he experienced true freedom, that he had come to understand that he never wanted to be a slave again.

Okoth had headed east across the Rodinian Empire until he reached Nagastan. Here the legionaries of the Rodinian army had no sway. The Nagastani were nomads, in many ways similar to the ancient Nubian culture, and Okoth had felt that he would be happy there. But when the bounty hunters came searching for him, he came to see that nowhere in the regions around the Rodinian Empire would be safe. The Gladiatorial Champion of Nubia was worth enough money to tempt mercenaries into Nagastan on his trail, trying to bring him back to Rodinia.

Okoth got on a ship and headed further east to the Empire of Lucarcia and freedom from the yoke of the Rodinians. He had nearly completed the treacherous crossing and was in sight of the island of Ursum when the *Hammerhead* hove into view. The *Hammerhead* came alongside and before the captain of Okoth's ship had appreciated what was happening the slavers were swarming all over them. The slavers had killed many on Okoth's ship but had taken a few captive. Okoth had killed three slavers single handed before Scraggs and four of his men had overwhelmed him. Just when in sight of the land he thought would mean his freedom, he found himself in the hold of a ship, a slave once more.

There he had met Reynard, the 'little man' as he called him. Reynard had organized their escape and now led the group of ex-slaves who were trying to win their freedom once and for all. Reynard, a natural leader by birth and breeding, had simply taken control of the group and everyone seemed happy with that – Okoth especially.

Now Okoth found himself strapped to the wheel of a ship, in the biggest storm he had ever experienced, trying desperately to keep the ship afloat. Birgen had explained to him that the safest position for the ship was heading directly into the waves. His job was to try and keep the *Javelin* on that heading as the winds and waves tried to turn the ship and capsize it.

Okoth braced his feet wide and put his entire body into keeping the wheel straight. The ship was trying to turn to starboard, moving to face towards the shore as the prevailing winds turned that way. He has fighting and straining to stop the wheel turning, muscles bulging and tightening. He had been battling the wheel for nearly an hour now and the strain was beginning to take its toll. He was not sure how much longer he could keep up the fight.

Suddenly a huge wave smashed over the side of the ship. Okoth's feet slipped from under him and he crashed into the deck. Only the rope which tied him to the wheel kept the wave from washing him overboard to be lost to the seas. Stunned for a moment he lay there, trying to recover. The ship began to turn, pushed sideways by the howling winds. If it turned too far the next wave could capsize it.

Okoth shook his head to clear it and pulled himself to his feet using the rope around his waist. Straining against the powerful winds he got himself upright. He grabbed the wheel once more and began to fight the ship, trying to pull it back into the winds. But it was a fight too far and the ship continued to turn sideways. Even with Okoth's prodigious strength and power, he simply couldn't get the *Javelin* back under his control.

Then Reynard was at his side. The noble had untied himself and risked a dash across the quarterdeck to the wheel. Now he grabbed hold of the structure and was quickly tying himself to the wheel in case of another powerful wave. Once secured to the wheel he leant his strength and leverage to the fight.

Ahead they could see a huge wave bearing down on them. With their current facing, the wave would smash into the side of the ship and capsize it. They had to get the wheel turned. They both grasped the wheel and put their entire focus into turning it. For long moments the wheel refused to move and the giant wave got ever closer, building in size as it loomed towards them out of the darkness.

Then, finally, the wheel turned.

Okoth and Reynard managed to bring the ship back into the face of the storm. Only just in time, as the huge wave smashed down on the forecastle, splintering wood and destroying one of the ballistae mounted there. The wave flooded across the ship's deck ripping anything which was loose free, and dragging it off into the depths. One sailor had his shoulder dislocated just trying to hold onto the ship and stop the surf from washing him overboard.

But the wave passed on and the *Javelin* stayed afloat.

The giant wave heralded the end of the worst of the storm. It was almost as if the storm had tried to break them but they had survived and it had agreed to let them live. Over the next hour or so the waves and winds slowly abated as the storm finally passed beyond them and turned inland, battering the coast and heading in to flatten trees and damage houses. The seas slowly returned to some kind of normality and the ship settled down in the calm after the storm. The crew got to their posts and made the ship ready to sail again as Birgen began an inspection of the damage caused.

The *Javelin* had survived, but it was badly broken. The storm had claimed three men and injured half a dozen, and now there was no way they could reach Cansae on time without stopping for repairs.

They were going to be late for their appointment with the Trade Lords.

-Chapter Eight-

"I can't sail the *Javelin* into Providentia," Reynard told them. The five command crew were in his lounge discussing what to do next. Varus was due there any moment and Reynard had to make a decision. The *Javelin* would not make it to Cansae on time with no mizzenmast. It would limp along at a slow pace and get there but they would be late. They could turn around and go back to Black Sail where they would be able to get repairs made, but turning around would delay them too much. The only option was to drop into nearby Providentia and get the *Javelin* repaired there as quickly as possible, and hope to make up lost time on their way west. But dropping into Providentia would risk getting spotted by someone who knew him – and there were a lot of people who would know him on the waterfront. The ship needed to go to Providentia, but he could not be seen.

Could he trust the ex-slaves with his true identity? Could he tell them the reason he didn't want anyone to see him? It was a big risk. He was certain he did not want to let Varus know, but the others he felt he could trust. They had been through so much together.

"Why not?" asked Mosi the priest. "Why can we not take the ship there?"

There was no time to ponder so Reynard made the decision to risk it. "It's not that the *Javelin* can't go there, it is more that I cannot be seen there," he told them. "You see, I'm supposed to be dead."

Reynard laid out the situation briefly, explaining that he was the second son of the Earl of Providentia. He told them how he had found out that his brother had sold him into slavery. He didn't tell them of his suspicions that it was one of the two noble houses who had ordered him imprisoned.

Okoth let out a low whistle. "You're full of surprises, little man," he said cracking a big white smile.

Reynard grinned back. "That I am. Now, quickly, we need to work out what to do. I do not want Varus to know who I am and why I can't take the ship into Providentia."

"How good is your acting?" asked Tanithil from his position by the door.

*

Four days later the *Javelin* pulled out of Providentia harbour and back into the Southern Ocean. Okoth, currently acting captain of the ship, ordered the crew to their stations and they bore right to plot a westerly course once more, heading along the coast of Ursum. They were two days behind schedule and had a lot of ground to cover. The command crew knew what was at stake – Varus had been quite clear about how unforgiving the Trade Lords would be if they were late. A steady easterly breeze followed them as they turned into deep water and the sails filled. It was a good omen.

The dockyard had patched up the mizzenmast. There was no way they could complete a full repair in the time the crew had given them. They just hoped it would hold for the remainder of the journey to Cansae.

That afternoon Reynard miraculously recovered from his 'debilitating illness' that had kept him confined to his quarters all the time they had been in Providentia and returned to his station on deck. Varus approached him. "Feeling better?" the red head asked.

"Yes," replied Reynard tersely.

"Do I assume from your tone that you're not best pleased with me?" asked Varus, stroking his beard between fingers and thumb.

"Not best pleased!?" raged Reynard, struggling to control his anger. "Come with me to my quarters! Now!" Reynard marched off towards the prow of the ship without a backwards glance. Varus followed. Reynard went into the lounge and poured himself a large glass of Pembrose Red, and did not offer one to Varus. He drained half of it and put it down on a mahogany table by one of the comfortable sofas. He resisted the urge to grab a hold of Varus and punch him in the face.

"What's the problem?" enquired Varus calmly.

"Because of you, three of my crew will never see their families again!" Reynard roared. "Because of your stupid idea to sail on when we should have holed up and taken shelter three men are dead and another six are only working because my doctor is an excellent surgeon!" Mosi had cured all the injured men, calling upon the powers of his god to heal their wounds, some of which were serious. He had got all six men back at work within the four days they had spent in Providentia. He truly was working wonders. "Because of you we are now two or three days behind schedule, when we would have only been a day behind if we had taken refuge from the storm as I suggested. Because of you, we will probably end up late to Cansae and the gods only know what will become of us then!"

"Are you quite finished?" asked Varus, crossing his arms across his broad chest.

"For now," said Reynard, trying to calm himself.

"You're right," agreed Varus, "we should have taken shelter. I misjudged the storm and its ferocity. I'm not used to the Southern Ocean and the tempests it can generate. I apologise. But now we have to put that behind us if we are to reach the Red City in time. By my calculations we have five days to reach Cansae and it's about a week long trip to get there under usual circumstances. What do you suggest?"

Reynard took a long, deep breath and counted to five slowly in his head. In many ways Varus was right: though he was extremely angry at the Guildsman, Reynard had nothing to gain by sulking. He had to try and make up two days in just five days of sailing; otherwise the Trade Lords would make their experiences with the storm seem pleasant. "There is only one answer I can think of: get lucky. The winds seem to be in the east right now. Our local weather expert tells me that the chances are it will stay that way for the next few days, maybe as long as the five days we need, if we are fortunate. If we get favourable winds all week, and push on at night, making sure we don't slow down for anything, we might just manage it. Maybe."

"Then let's hope the Windbringer is on our side," said Varus, invoking the local god of the weather.

*

The winds stayed in the east all week. As the last day of the month dawned the *Javelin* rounded the headland and entered the Aper Sound. It was thirty miles to Cansae's harbour mouth – less than half a day's sailing. They had made it. They merely had to get to the Guild Hall in the city before the sun set, to make their appointment.

The winds had stayed in the east, filling the sails and pushing the Javelin along at great pace. They had dodged another large storm which had followed in behind them but missed them by some distance and which had actually helped buffet them along – making for an uncomfortable few hours but allowing them to make up some time.

The *Javelin* skipped along. The sun was high in the sky and a light breeze pushed her along to her destination. Reynard stood at the prow overlooking the wide Aper Sound and breathing a deep sigh of relief. They had got to Cansae on time. Now all they had to do was deal with the Trade Lords.

*

Cansae straddled the Nabor River where it flowed into the Aper Sound. The Nabor was a thin, fast moving river which spilt out into the Sound a mere two score or so miles from its source in the foothills of the Aratas Mountains. Three bridges crossed the Nabor in the city and each was constructed able to be raised up to allow high masted ships to pass below – although in those days the only ships making this journey were the ships tasked with carrying building stone to the city from the quarries in the Aratas hills.

The majority of the buildings of Cansae were built from the stunning ruby-red bricks quarried in the Aratas hills near the source of the Nabor. These rocks were cut out of the hillside, loaded onto barges and shipped down river overnight to the city where they were used in the construction of most of the city's buildings.

Cansae was one of the oldest cities in the empire. Founded back in the days of the beginning of the Rainbow Empire, the discovery of the unusual red bricks here caused the head of the local ruling house to name his house the Ruby House, and to build his palace out of this amazing rock. Incredibly the supplies of 'ruby-rock', as it was known locally, had lasted even though an entire city had been built from it. The work had nearly expended the quarries of the Aratas hills.

The districts of Cansae had developed over many years and the city appeared to have no real plan or layout. Perhaps it did at one stage but it was so old that any original plan had been lost and engineers and architects tended to just build wherever they could find spare land. Fortunately the Cansae Plains on either side of the Aper Sound were vast and there were no real restrictions on the size the city could grow.

Cansae was the capital of the Head of Ursum and was still the centre of power for House Ruby. The Dragon, Ignatius Ruby, current overlord of the house, made his home in the Ruby Palace. The palace sat surrounded by warehouses, inns, residential houses and shops, in a haphazard collection of styles and structures. It overlooked the harbour and the approach to the city by sea along the Aper Sound. The red dragon standard of the Ruby House flew from the flag poles atop the palace and on all significant buildings in the city. All significant buildings bar one.

The city had one new and notable addition. The Guild of Master Merchants and Sea Farers had set up their base here. The mysterious Trade Lords went against every standard in the city and built a huge Guild Hall out of white marble, transported at great cost from the mountains of Manabas. This stark white monolith stood out like a single tooth in a full red mouth. It was testament to the power the Trade Lords wielded that the Dragon did nothing to stop them building it, in complete contrast to the rest of the city. The Guild standard of a fox atop a set of merchant scales hung from the flag pole on the building.

Cansae's location on the southern side of the Head made it difficult to get to and yet it maintained its position as a major trade hub, probably in no small part due to the influence of the Trade Lords. People would often see Guild ships sailing up and down the Aper Sound on their way into or out of port. The people of Cansae were interested in the latest fashions from Lucar, the jewellery from Selkie and other more exotic goods from the further parts of the empire and beyond. In exchange, Cansae was rich in simple foodstuffs that grew in abundance on the plains outside the city. Typically, Guild ships were loaded up with grains, rice and fruits when they left the city for their next port of call.

The Javelin docked in the sprawling harbour and Reynard watched as the first crew rotation disembarked. They had made sure that the crew was unaware of the importance of this stop. None of them knew of the command crew's urgent appointment with the powerful Trade Lords nor did they realise that the future of the ship they served on was about to be decided. The men ran down the gang plank and rushed off into the gambling dens, taverns and brothels on offer. Reynard wished them well.

A few minutes later the command crew had all assembled on the main deck, Varus with them. Reynard passed command of the ship over to Birgen and told him they would be back in a couple of hours. He hoped that would be true. The six of them moved down the gangplank and into the city. Reynard could see the Red Palace from the harbour and, on the opposite side of the Nabor River, he could make out the white monolith of the Guild Hall, a few hundred yards up the hill. They moved off in that direction.

*

  Tanithil wandered along in the middle of the group, not really looking where he was going. He let his mind float free and let his senses push out to explore the area around him. It was hard to achieve whilst moving but he was able to explore some of the city this way as they walked. The city felt much as any other, there was a lot of energy here – a natural build-up resulting from so many people in such close proximity. He heard the murmuring thoughts of passers-by as they came and went, but didn't let his mind focus on any of them, keeping his thoughts loose and free-floating.

  As the group climbed towards the bright white Guild Hall, a wave of heat energy assaulted Tanithil's mind. He staggered and had to grab hold of Okoth to keep from falling. Pretending to have stumbled on a steep step he thanked the giant for his help and then gathered his thoughts. Pushing gently back in the direction he had felt the heat coming from he quickly located its source: a large building not far from where they were now. Stopping and turning to face back down towards the harbour as if taking in the view, Tanithil pushed his thoughts carefully into the building and was amazed at what he saw.

  The room inside was a big hall, dimly lit. Groups of men and women in red robes stood inside. Some were holding hands, others worked alone. But all of them were engaged in one activity: creating fire. The robed figures were alight with arcane power to Tanithil's searching mind's eye. One figure stood out from the rest. A tall dark haired man also in a red robe moved from group to group giving advice here and sharing an insight there. He was teaching these students how to channel arcane energies from the Void and to turn those energies into raw fire. He was teaching them the ancient skills of the Pyromancer.

  Emperor Lucar had banned the practice of studying arcane lore when he first formed the Lucarcian Empire out of the remains of the Rainbow Empire five hundred years ago. Blaming the Writhing Death on the study of these arcane mysteries, the emperor had decreed that their study would from that time forward be punishable by banishment from the empire. The knowledge and lore had slowly been lost until all believed that no one in the empire knew how to harness these energies any more.

Clearly someone here in Cansae did know, and he was teaching others.

Bringing his mind quickly back to his body, Tanithil took a deep breath and turned to continue the climb up the hill, hurrying to catch up with the others. He tried to decide what to do with this new found knowledge. Should he tell Reynard and the others? Doing so would raise the obvious question of how he knew and he was not sure he was ready to share his talent with the group yet. Then again Reynard had told them all about his heritage on this trip, and no one had betrayed that knowledge. Perhaps he really could trust them. But perhaps it would wait until they had spoken with the Trade Lords.

*

The Guild Hall of the Guild of Master Merchants and Sea Farers stood at the top of a rise, overlooking the harbour and the Aper Sound. Made entirely of white marble quarried in far-off Manabas, and shipped here at great expense, it made for an exceptional visage. Three stories high and glinting in the late afternoon sun the group had to shield their eyes from the glare. Two guards in polished chainmail with long spears stood to attention either side of the entrance doors but they did nothing to stop the group as Varus led them in. Whether they knew him or just let anyone past was unclear.

Varus led them into a huge entrance hall which took up all three floors with a sweeping staircase of the same white marble ascending one side. A massive drapery hung from the wall opposite the staircase, hanging the entire height of the hall. It depicted a cunning looking fox sat atop a set of scales – the symbol of the Guild. They mounted the spiral staircase and came out onto a balcony overlooking the main hall. Below them they could see giant golden letters etched into the floor, spelling out 'The Guild of Master Merchants and Sea Farers' in a large circle. It was an impressive sight. Large numbers of people scurried about the floor on various errands and missions. The place was a hive of activity.

Varus led them onward, clearly knowing his way around the place. He took them to a double door of polished ash, and pushed it open. It swung open silently on well-oiled hinges to reveal a long hallway with a thick soft carpet down the centre. Stylish wall hangings along the walls showed scenes of ships at sea, of village markets, of busy city shops and of carts rolling across open farm lands. It was clear the decorators had meant to show that the Guild was everywhere.

At the end of the hallway was a comfortable looking room appointed with couches of soft leather and various tables. Refreshments were already waiting for them and Varus invited them in and told them to sit and help themselves. He made sure they were all settled and he then knocked gently on a door located on the other side of the room. Seconds later he pushed it open and disappeared through it.

Reynard stood and addressed the group. "Whatever happens here, we stick together," he said. "I suggest you let me do most of the talking. As a noble's son I'm used to dealing with powerful men and know how these people think. I think I'm best suited to speak with them."

"Fine with me, little man," replied Okoth with his usual smile.

"I am also happy with that arrangement," said Mosi, twiddling his white rope belt nervously.

Tanithil nodded and Kita was her usual impassive self, though Reynard noted she did loosen her swords in their scabbards. She would not go down without a fight, he knew. He decided that if they had to die, he would rather die fighting and would be happy to do so at her side. He moved next to her and made sure his rapier was also loose in its scabbard.

No one made any move to tuck into the refreshments provided. They were all too preoccupied with the situation ahead of them. No one was even sure if they would be alive an hour from now.

The door opened and Varus popped his head through. "The Trade Lords await your presence," he told them.

*

The Trade Lords held court in a large circular room. A long cedar table had been placed so as to make a wall across the room and behind it were twelve large cedar seats, almost more thrones than chairs. The Fox and Scales standard hung behind the table, covering the rear wall section. Five simple wooden chairs were arranged in a line facing the table. The light in the room was dim, almost dark, with only two flickering torches illuminating the whole of the large chamber. Trade Lords occupied ten of the twelve thrones.

Each of the Trade Lords was dressed identically. Wearing grey, deep hooded robes with the hoods pulled up over their heads, none of their faces was visible in the dim light. The long arms of their robes hid their hands, removing any possible way to identify the people under the hoods. It was not possible to tell what sex, race or creed each was. The Trade Lords maintained their anonymity and their reputation for mystery and power in this way.

Varus moved to stand next to the five chairs and motioned for the others to sit.

"I'd rather stand, thank you," said Reynard, aware that reacting to trouble would be much easier if standing rather than if sat.

"Sit down Captain," ordered the middle of the Trade Lords, his voice deep and commanding. "You have nothing to fear here."

Reynard knew that it was indeed unlikely that they would have summoned them all this way just to execute them here and now, but was still on edge. The silence grew as the others looked to him for a decision. The Trade Lords did not move, allowing the weight of their command to grow as time passed. Reynard sat.

"Thank you," came back the deep voice again. The others in the group followed suit and took a chair each. "Now," the central Trade Lord continued, "to business. You took something which belongs to us. We have brought you here to bring you to account for your crimes."

"Hang on one minute, sir," interrupted Reynard loudly, half rising from his seat, "A captain in your employ had us in his hold as slaves! If we are talking about crimes, it is you who are at fault."

"Never," said the deep voice menacingly, "interrupt me again." Reynard felt a chill go through his spine and sat back down heavily, looking down at the floor. "As I was saying," the hooded Trade Lord continued, "You killed a Guild Captain and took control of his ship. You then proceeded to sail it to Black Sail and get it refitted and renamed in order to cover your tracks. Furthermore we have proof that you sold illegal contraband including a large stash of narcotics. Clearly you do not want us to take this information to the authorities. Would you agree?" he asked.

"Agreed," replied Reynard, looking up and trying to see into the shadowy hood for a glimpse of the man beneath it. It was impossible. The dark light in the room meant his face was totally in shadow.

"Now, we commend you for your resourcefulness. Taking control of a ship from its command crew and having the knowledge and skills to sell its illegal cargo and get it renamed and reregistered so quickly was a sign of great ability and initiative; and we like to reward people when they show initiative. And as it happens Captain Waverley was not entirely loyal to the Guild," continued the deep voice.

"What do you mean?" asked Reynard intrigued in spite of himself.

"Captain Waverley had allowed himself to fall under the influence of a major noble house, rather than keeping his loyalty focussed on the Guild. As such, you have done us a small favour in getting rid of him. This is the only reason you are not all dead now."

Reynard considered this information. If Waverley was working for a major noble house then it was clear that would have been the same house which asked Maynard to get rid of him – hence Reynard was placed on Waverley's ship as a slave. So if he could find out which house Waverley was working for that would tell him which noble house wanted him dead.

"Which noble house was he working with?" he asked, hoping to find out who had ordered his death.

"That is no concern of yours, Captain," the voice answered dismissively. "The important fact is that Waverley is dead – at your hands – and you're now in control of his ship. But in actual fact with all that we know about you and your actions - murder, piracy, trade in narcotics and so on – it is clear that we are in control of your futures. So you work for us now."

Reynard sighed. So, he had escaped from slavery in the hold of a ship to take control of it and win his freedom. Then to find that, in fact, his freedom was still not his own and that he was now in the thrall of the most powerful organization in the empire – one with a sinister reputation against those that cross it. Out of the fire and into the pan, he thought.

"What do you want from us?" he asked, resigned to his fate.

"A simple task to pay us back and win your freedom," came back a new voice, this one from the left of the table. This new voice was light and high, maybe a female voice, but it was hard to be certain. "A few days ago one of our Guild ships was attacked by corsairs. They sunk the ship but one of its crew survived long enough to tell a tale. The ship was carrying a suit of golden armour which the corsairs stole, along with a sizable collection of Guild treasures. We want you to recover that armour and return it to us here. Do that and you're free," the new voice finished.

"What information do you have on the corsairs?" asked Tanithil, from Reynard's right.

"The sailor who survived told that the corsair ship was flying a flag he had not seen before, that of a red eel on a blue background. The name of the ship was the *Moray*. He told of a tall rapier-wielding captain of the *Moray* and that the first mate was a bull of a man, bigger even than you, Nubian," the soft voice said, a long sleeve gesturing towards Okoth, "if the dying sailor's story is to be fully believed."

"Furthermore, a ship matching this description sailed into Lucar harbour a few days ago," added a third voice, this time from the far right of the table. "Our reports tell that the captain strolled into the capital wearing the suit of golden armour. Someone like that should not be difficult to track down."

"Find him and recover that armour," continued the first Trade Lord in his deep voice, "then you go free."

"It seems we will be heading for Lucar as soon as our ship is properly repaired," said Reynard.

"I'm glad we understand each other, Captain," finished the deep voice. "You may go."

*

Back on the *Javelin* the group gathered in Reynard's lounge. Varus had not returned to the ship with them – the Trade Lords were leaving them to their own devices to find the *Moray* and the golden armour. The Trade Lords had given them an advance – enough money to run the ship for a good few weeks, even months. They could report on their progress at any Guild Hall in the empire and could also request more funds to run the ship when they ran out. Furthermore the Guild shipwrights would begin work on the ship first thing in the morning, replacing the broken mizzenmast and making all the repairs which Birgen said needed doing after the storm.

"So, we have our freedom – to a point," said Reynard. "Okay we have a mission to undertake for the Trade Lords but we are free to proceed however we think best. We have enough money to keep the ship running till the summer comes. And we have a promise: find the golden armour and return it to the Trade Lords and we have our freedom, permanently. Are we agreed that we stick with what we have been asked to do?" he queried.

"What we have been ordered to do, more accurately," said Kita, hands crossed over her chest as usual.

"Yes, I guess so," Reynard agreed, "but will we do it?"

"We have no choice," said Tanithil. The Trade Lords will find and kill us if we don't. I want my freedom back and this is our chance. Let's take it."

"Agreed," said Okoth.

"The sun appears to be peeking out from behind the clouds again," said Mosi, scratching his goatee. "Let us be thankful for this opportunity and embrace it."

Kita nodded.

"Okay, then we must head to Lucar next," said Reynard. We'll set sail on the first available tide once the ship is fixed. And now I bid you all good night. I for one am going to sleep soundly this evening. I can taste freedom on the wind."

"May I have a quick word, please?" asked Tanithil as the others prepared to leave the quarters.

"Certainly, Tani," Reynard replied. He got up and shut the door after the others had all left the room. "What is it?"

"You want to know which house Waverley was working for," stated Tanithil. "Well, I know the answer."

"Which house?" Reynard asked, feeling a surge of excitement at the prospect of finding out who had ordered his death.

"The Ebon House," stated Tanithil simply.

"How do you know?" enquired Reynard.

"Because I was put aboard the *Hammerhead* as a slave in punishment for getting caught cheating in a Selkie gambling house," he replied.

Reynard knew that the Ebon House was rumoured to control all the gambling dens in Selkie – the base of the House's power. So if the Ebon House had given Tanithil over to Waverley for cheating in a gaming den, then that did indeed strongly imply that Waverley and the Ebon House were linked. It all made sense.

So, Reynard had a name for the person who was responsible for putting him in this position: Lord Barrius Ebon. Now all he had to do was find the *Moray*, recover the golden armour and then he would be free to take his revenge on the leader of the Ebon House.

He couldn't wait to begin.

-- PART TWO --

-Chapter Nine-

A week later the repairs on the *Javelin* were complete. They had a brand new mizzenmast and the shipyard had replaced all the broken, frayed or generally worn parts which Birgen had listed. The Guild shipwrights didn't bother to actually fix anything – if it was damaged they simply replaced it. Birgen reported himself extremely happy with the results, saying that the *Javelin* was in better condition now than it had been in years.

Spring was in full flow by then and the temperatures were slowly rising. It was a warm morning and the sun was bright in the sky when the *Javelin* pulled out of Cansae harbour into the Aper Sound and headed out into the Southern Ocean once more. The seas there were mercifully calm and it was Reynard's intention to round the Head of Ursum as quickly as possible and reach the relative quiet and safety of the Inner Sea.

Reynard stood on the quarterdeck alongside his first mate, Okoth, watching as sea birds wheeled above the deck. Many fishing vessels plied the Aper Sound and as a result gulls looking for an easy meal visited nearly all the ships out here. They were clearly unaware that the *Javelin* didn't have any fish aboard.

They whipped along the coast, close to shore, with a view to turning north around the Head as soon as they left the Sound. They passed a few merchant ships on their way into Cansae and followed in the wake of a small fishing boat out netting the day's catch.

Reynard turned his head to the sky, closed his eyes and let the spring sunshine warm his clean-shaven face. It was good to be out at sea again. Not a sailor by nature or profession he was growing to enjoy the freedom that came with owning a ship. Okay, so this ship was only theirs because the Trade Lords had allowed them to keep it after they had effectively pirated it, but that was as close to owning a ship as he had ever been. And they were free to come and go as they pleased now, as long as they were making progress towards recovering the golden armour.

Reynard wondered what sort of man would steal a suit of golden armour from a Guild ship and then proceed to wear it into the capital city of the empire. Golden armour was hardly something subtle, and surely he would have realised that wearing it would only make him stand out in a crowd and be easy to find. He must be either very confident or very stupid. Reynard hoped it was the latter. A stupid man would be easy to find. If it was confidence, then it appeared the man was confident in his abilities to deal with whomever the Guild sent to recover their armour. That was a worrying thought. As Reynard mused on the mission ahead of him he heard laughter coming from down on the main deck. Opening his eyes he took a second to work out what his eyes were seeing.

Kita was down on the deck in her red silk kimono and barefoot. She had placed her swords carefully on deck nearby and was proceeding to move about the deck in a series of slow, measured steps. With each step she performed a pre-planned strike, kick or block, fighting off one imaginary opponent after another. The moves were very precise, performed slowly and with great control. At times she balanced on one leg, spinning slowly and kicking out with her other, demonstrating superb poise and execution. At others she was in a deep stance, showing great strength and flexibility.

A few of the crew had stopped to watch her performance. Some were pointing and muttering comments to each other under their breaths. There were a few sniggers. Reynard also watched, entranced. The movement was spellbinding. He had seen warriors performing drills before but there was something magical in the flow and control Kita was showing. He found himself annoyed at those who were laughing. He thought about reprimanding them for it but decided that as Kita was stoically ignoring them he would not add to their importance by recognising them. He kept quiet and continued to watch her.

Once she had finished going through her set of moves slowly, she returned to the starting point and performed a neat bow. She took a deep breath and let it out slowly. Then she exploded into action. She repeated the same series of moves she had just gone through but this time at incredible speed. The movement remained tight and controlled. Each kick or strike powered out and snapped to a dead halt as she used her muscles to focus each attack or block. She reached the last strike in the form, a double handed blow to face and chest, and let out an enormous shout, as she had done when she struck down Cyrus in the alleyway in Selkie. The shout startled the few birds who had settled on the mast and they flew off squawking. None of the crew was laughing now. It was all too easy to imagine being hit by one of those punches, strikes or kicks.

Kita bowed once more, took another deep breath and then moved to her *daisho* and picked the swords back up. She looked up at Reynard where he was watching down from the quarterdeck and smiled at him. He felt his heart race a little as she did and realized this was the first time he had seen her really smile. And her smile was mesmerising.

*

It took a week to sail around the Head of Ursum, into the Inner Sea and down the coast to Lucar. The weather stayed fair and they avoided any further storms in the Southern Ocean. Once into the relative calm of the Inner Sea they made good time and the journey was nothing short of pleasant.

Kita continued to practice her unarmed forms each morning and now commanded a regular audience - so much so that Reynard had to tell the crew they could only stop to watch if they were off duty. She carried on with her training unfazed by the growing interest in her demonstrations. Her skill and technique had achieved one thing: no one laughed at her anymore. In fact at times Reynard noted a few crew members trying to copy her moves. She ignored them and just continued to do her thing.

Six days into the journey, as the *Javelin* passed by the waters around the town of Tunis, about a day out of Lucar, a carrack of a similar size to them appeared before them around a headland. Its sails were full and it was moving at a good speed. From his position high on the quarterdeck, Reynard noticed that as soon as the other carrack spotted them it changed its sail configuration and slowed considerably.

The two ships neared each other and as they did etiquette forced Okoth to steer closer to the shore, as it was usual in the waters of the empire to pass port-to-port. The approaching ship appeared to alter its course a little too, but rather than steering away from the *Javelin* to give it more space, they seemed to turn in to shore as well, thus giving Okoth virtually no sea in which to manoeuvre.

A call went up from the crow's nest above as the look-out spotted rocks ahead. To the starboard side of the ship the white cliffs of this part of the Inner Sea rose, and jutting out from them was a line of mostly submerged reef. The *Javelin* was heading straight for it.

"To port!" ordered Reynard shouting at Okoth and running to the starboard rail to see how much space they had.

"I can't," replied Okoth, "We'll head right into the path of the oncoming ship!"

Reynard cursed. What was the captain of the other ship playing at? They needed to stop the *Javelin* and quickly. "To oars!" he bellowed to the crew, "Birgen, get the sails reefed, now! We need to stop the ship. Florus! Get down onto the oar deck and get them backing water!"

The crew sprung to action. The rowers rushed down into the lower deck and grabbed the oars. Florus ran down there and took up the drums, beating a measured cadence out. Birgen shouted instructions and the crew took all the air out of the sails, slowing the *Javelin's* forward momentum. The rowers dipped the oars into the water and strained to paddle against the direction the ship was already heading. There were still plenty of yards till the rocks but it was hard to stop a ship the size of a three masted carrack when in full flow.

Reynard moved to the port side to get closer to the other ship as it passed. He wanted to shout out and give the other captain a serious piece of his mind. As he reached the other side he saw that the other carrack was really close now, and was closing further. Rather than steering away, the other ship was getting even nearer. From this distance Reynard could read the name of the ship: the *Hag*. As he looked he noticed that there were lots of men on the deck of the *Hag*, and rather than trying frantically to avoid a collision, they appeared arrayed along the port rail, looking out at the *Javelin*. The sun glinted off a bared steel blade held by one of the sailors on the *Hag* and it suddenly dawned on Reynard they were ready to fight.

"Prepare to be boarded!" he screamed, drawing his rapier. "We are under attack! Ship the oars!" There was a great cracking noise as the *Hag* pulled alongside the *Javelin* and smashed into the oars which the men were still pulling on. Reynard heard the screams of men below deck and knew that the oars had just crushed the rowers on the port side as the *Hag* ploughed into them.

Men from the other ship threw grappling lines and the two ships were entangled together, stopping any chance of the *Javelin* escaping – not that it had anywhere to go with the prow of the ship pointing into the reef and the *Hag* blocking any chance of turning. They were stuck and only a fight would save them. Above Reynard, men from the *Hag* were swinging on ropes, some were landing on the main deck, others were flying into the rigging overhead. Crew from the *Javelin* were responding now and melee broke out all across the ship.

As he turned away from the *Hag* he noticed the flag they were flying: a red eel on a blue background. This triggered a memory in his mind: this was the same flag that the Trade Lords had told them the *Moray* had flown when it had attacked the Guild ship and stolen the golden armour. Why was the *Hag* flying the same flag? Were these corsairs operating under some sort of truce with the *Moray*?

Reynard easily parried a thrust from one raider and ran him through, ducking under the swing of another as he pulled his blade free. Deflecting a follow up attack he stabbed this man through the neck and gained some breathing space.

All across the main deck the fight surged. Reynard saw Kita in the middle, feet planted easily, perfectly balanced dealing with a large number of raiders and drawing the defenders to herself like a beacon of calm and solidity. Up on the quarterdeck near Reynard, Okoth had lashed the wheel tight to stop the *Javelin* turning, had taken up his spear and was heading towards the steps down to the main deck. The fight was looking like it might be close but Kita and Okoth would certainly turn it in their favour. Still, it was important to stop it as fast as possible – the longer it went on the more men he would lose from his crew.

Across the far side of the ship on the forecastle Reynard spotted the *Hag's* captain. Short and stocky, dressed in black trousers and a puffy red shirt, the man had a cutlass in one hand and with the other was still holding onto the rope he had used to swing across to the *Javelin*. He spotted Reynard about the same time as Reynard spotted him, and raised a salute with his cutlass. Reynard decided that if he could take out the captain then the fight would quickly end.

He took the stairs down to the main deck two at a time, shouldered into a raider he met at the bottom and leapt over him. It was fully seventy feet across the main deck to the stairs up to the forecastle and it was crammed full of struggling sailors. He had to find a quick route. The only option available to him was the port rail. Grabbing hold of the shroud he pulled himself nimbly up onto the rail and set off along it.

The *Javelin* was pretty stationary by now and wasn't pitching too much so he made quick progress. About half way along, his passage was interrupted when a raider swung a large cutlass at his legs, but Reynard simply skipped up and over it, landing deftly on the rail and not even pausing to look behind to see what the raider was doing. Quickly he was at the far side of the ship and moving up the stairs to the forecastle where the other captain waited.

"Impressive manoeuvre," complimented his foe, bowing a mock courtly bow and dropping into a fencing stance. His heavy cutlass was not well suited to the role of fencing blade but he seemed adapt with its use from his balance and weight distribution.

Reynard decided there was no time to lose and lunged. The speed and accuracy of the attack caught his opponent by surprise and it was all he could do to deflect the blow from his heart into his left shoulder. Howling in agony the red shirted man dropped his sword and clutched at his arm. "You've killed me," he complained.

"Hardly," said Reynard, "but I will, unless you call off the attack," he continued, holding his rapier to the man's throat.

*

The fight was over. Eight of the *Javelin's* crew were dead and many more were injured. Reynard had captured their captain and the remainder of the *Hag's* crew had surrendered. Reynard now had to decide what to do with them. He stood on the main deck with Kita and Okoth next to him, watching as Mosi moved among the men.

The priest of the Light was directing the crew to gather the injured - from both ships Reynard noted – and place them in a row in the middle of the main deck. Slowly he was forming a collection of bleeding and maimed sailors, some of whom, it appeared, would soon die from their injuries. When the crew had assembled all the injured Mosi knelt down in the midst of them, held his hands aloft in supplication and began to chant a soft, slow prayer.

As his chant continued it grew in speed and intensity. As it did so the few clouds in the sky above seemed to part and the sun burst through. Beams splashed down on the main deck and lit up the scene. Mosi's chant got louder and louder, and the warmth of the sun seemed to intensify. The moans of the men around him ceased and all stood dumfounded as wounds healed before their eyes. Mosi continued to chant, his arms held aloft, for a few minutes, swaying from side to side as he did. Wounds seemed to mend and Mosi brought men on the brink of death back from the edge and into a stable condition.

Mosi collapsed down to the deck, exhausted. As he did a cloud passed back over the sun and the intense light faded. Okoth moved forward and picked the priest up. Slinging him effortlessly over his broad shoulder he took him off to his quarters to recover.

*

Reynard had the captain of the *Hag* on the quarterdeck. The young noble was standing and his prisoner was sitting on the floor, back to the rail. "Who are you and why are you flying the red eel flag?" Reynard asked, looking down.

"I'm saying nothing," replied the captain, looking up at Reynard defiantly.

"There's no need to be like that," said Reynard in reply, smiling his easy smile, trying to put the captain off guard. "I'm a very forgiving man, captain, and am not holding any grudge against you for attacking my ship. All I want to know is who you are?"

"I'm Captain Cimber of the *Hag* out of Lucar," the red shirted man replied, "And you'll not get anything else out of me." He winced as he spoke and his right arm moved to hold the wound in his left shoulder.

"Captain Cimber, you're in pain and not thinking straight. As you have seen the priest who is among my crew can heal the wounded. I can have him come up here and fix your arm up – if you'll only tell me what I want to know. I'm purely interested in how you come to be flying the red eel from your mast, that's all. Surely you can tell me that, and I'll see your pain removed."

"I don't want your help or healing. I'm fine," replied the injured man, gritting his teeth against the pain.

Reynard sighed, unhappy with what he was about to do but determined to get the information he needed. He knelt down and gripped

Cimber's injured shoulder, giving it a squeeze. Cimber cried out in pain. "Come now, this shoulder wound really is nasty. A few words from you and it will all be over. You can be resting in a soft, comfortable bed with no pain, if you just tell me what I want to know."

"Go to the depths," spat Cimber.

Reynard rose back to his feet and as he did so, he noticed that Tanithil and Kita had joined him on the quarterdeck. The silver haired Lucarcian was looking intently at Cimber.

"He's really not going to tell you what he knows, Reynard," Tanithil said, shaking his head. "Trust me on this - I know when people will break and when they won't. This man won't." Tanithil had listened to the interrogation and had tried to sense what the man was hiding but he couldn't. All he felt was a huge loyalty to the person this captain was trying to protect - an almost unnaturally strong loyalty at that. Tanithil wondered if this was the time to tell Reynard about his talent but there were simply too many people around.

"Okay, Tani, I have learnt to trust your judgement on these matters," Reynard replied. Turning back to the sitting Captain Cimber he continued, "It appears you win, captain. You will not need to tell me anything. But I might have lied a bit about not holding a grudge. Kita, take him and put him in the brig. He can walk the plank when we get back out to sea."

*

On the *Hag*, Reynard went through the documents in the captain's study. The study was small and poorly appointed; nothing in comparison with his one back aboard the *Javelin*. A rickety old pine table, on wobbly legs and crudely lashed to the floor, dominated the room. Faded and torn tapestries lined the walls, depicting great sea monsters of myth and legend. On the large pine desk was the cargo manifest. The *Hag* was carrying some valuable cargo which the crew were even now moving across to the *Javelin*. The booty would pay for the repairs the ship needed and allow them to hire on more crew to replace those killed by the raiders.

Also on the desk, next to the manifest, was a map of the seas around Tunis. The map was very detailed and had shipping routes marked on it which Reynard realised were common trade routes that Guild ships and privateers would take when shipping cargo from port to port, into and out of the town. It was like a map to the corsairs' targets.

The large pine desk had a single locked drawer, but Reynard had the key. Kita had appropriated it from Captain Cimber when she had searched him, before throwing him in the brig. Unlocking the drawer Reynard discovered a letter.

My Dear Captain Cimber,

As agreed, I would like for you and the Hag *to work the waters around the town of Tunis. Strike at any ship which seems a suitable target. Guild ships will obviously form the majority of our prey. The group need finances to fund our mission, and we can find them by doing what we do best: piracy.*

Bring any booty you recover to our new base when you feel you have acquired enough to make the trip worthwhile.
Yours,
Captain Nikolai Kester.

Reynard read the letter three times. So it appeared that the corsairs were uniting under a new leader, Captain Nikolai Kester, a name Reynard had never heard before. They had a base somewhere, although there was no indication where it might be. Finally, it seemed that Kester had united the corsairs with a particular goal in mind, but again there was no hint as to what that purpose might be.

All that information was unimportant to Reynard at that time. What he really needed was a lead on where to find the *Moray*, but there was no clue in the letter. Presumably the *Moray* was part of this group as it was flying the same flag, the red eel on a blue background. Was it possible that this Kester was the captain of the *Moray* and the leader of the corsairs? He supposed it was. For now though it was time to head on to the city of Lucar, and see if they could find the *Moray* and the man in the golden armour.

*

Reynard stood on the back of the quarterdeck as the *Javelin* sailed north east away from shore. He watched behind him as the last planks of the *Hag* burnt to the waterline. A trail of black smoke rose high into the afternoon sky and was carried away on the breeze. Reynard's men had removed all the valuables and put the last of the *Hag's* crew ashore with no food or weapons, then fired the ship. The enemy crew could fend for themselves as best they were able. Captain Cimber was still in the brig. Reynard wasn't happy about executing the man, but he was a corsair and had tried to kill him and his crew. Reynard's crew wanted revenge. He supposed it was the way of the Inner Sea.

The *Javelin* picked up speed on a following southerly wind. Although Lucar lay directly east along the shore from there, they were heading out into deep sea. The waters near shore were too heavily travelled and Reynard wanted privacy for what was about to happen. Cimber was to walk the plank.

As they moved further from the shore the lookout called down. He had spotted five sails on the eastern horizon, rounding a headland. Five ships were vaguely visible in the far distance, seemingly moving in a group along the shore. It was unusual for that many ships to sail in convoy in these waters, but Reynard had no time to consider the implications. He ordered the *Javelin* to push on at full speed, putting as much distance as he could between them and the other ships.

The other ships moved on westward, following the shoreline, passing way behind the *Javelin*, and not seeming to pay the fleeing ship any mind. Reynard was pleased as he didn't want any more complications in his life right now. The *Javelin* pushed on into open sea where Cimber was to meet his doom.

If he had been closer to the five ships, he would have seen that each flew a flag with a red eel on a blue background. And at the wheel of the lead ship was a man dressed all in golden armour.

-Chapter Ten-

As the sun reached its zenith the next day, it glinted off a structure above the cliffs in the distance. As they moved further east the glints resolved themselves into the towering Imperial Palace which dominated the skyline of the city as one approached from sea.

Lucar was the capital city of the Lucarcian Empire and was named after the first emperor who founded both the city and the empire itself. It was founded five hundred years ago at the time of the destruction of Antissa and the end of the Rainbow Empire. The emperor moved his court to the promontory which overlooked the new Inner Sea and the site of the destruction which broke the Rainbow Empire apart.

The city was built entirely on one huge headland which stuck out into the Inner Sea for a few miles. The promontory was rounded, with the neck of the headland only a few hundred yards across. A large granite wall circled the headland, making it a very defensible place, but in the five hundred years it had stood it had never been attacked so its defences remained untested.

The city boasted two harbours, one on either side of the headland, in the coves formed by the neck. Harbour walls had been built out on each side to produce two very sheltered bays. The eastern bay was the deeper of the two harbours and the harbourmaster directed deep hulled ocean-going ships to dock there. The western bay was shallower and tended to be full of smaller ships and boats. Both harbours had multiple granite staircases leading up to huge gates which lead into the city through the city walls. Each harbour had also given birth to its own waterfront district, complete with all the usual trappings these places acquire: taverns, gambling dens and brothels.

The *Javelin* sailed east and passed by the city to the north, heading for the deep-water harbour on the eastern side. They sailed beneath the white cliffs which rose from the sea straight up for one hundred feet. Directly atop the cliffs the Imperial Palace continued to rise, seeming almost to be part of the rock face.

The ship turned and sailed into the east harbour, coming to rest by a jetty and tying up to the bollards there. A representative of the harbourmaster came aboard to speak to Reynard about their purpose in visiting the capital and to take an inventory of any cargo they were selling. When he was gone Reynard summoned his command crew to the lounge.

"Kita, Tani and I will head into the city and find out what we can about the *Moray* and its captain. Okoth you're in charge here," instructed Reynard.

"What is the plan?" asked Tanithil. "What are we trying to find out?"

"We need to know exactly when the *Moray* was here and what they were doing here. If possible it would be good to find out the name of the captain and find out where he may have visited in the city. I suggest we start with the harbourmaster's office," Reynard answered.

*

"All I want to know is when the *Moray* was here. I'm trying to track down its captain, a good friend of mine," said Reynard, spinning a gold coin suggestively between the knuckles of his right hand.

"I'm sure that sort of information would be okay to pass over to someone as obviously honourable as yourself," said the harbourmaster, eyeing the coin greedily. Reynard flicked it in the air and the harbourmaster's hand shot out and grabbed it before the chance was gone. He moved to a large ledger and flicked back through it. "Two weeks or so ago, you say?" he queried, turning pages with his thumb. "Yes, yes, here we are."

Reynard moved to the book and looked. The *Moray* had docked here just over two weeks ago and had stayed in port for three days. The ship was registered as belonging to a Captain Nikolai Kester. So that confirmed it: Kester was the leader of the corsairs. "Yes, that's it, perfect. Old Nikolai was here then, good. Now do you know if he visited the city?" he asked, pulling another gold imperial from his money purse and setting it spinning across his knuckles again. "You would remember him, my friend has a tendency to wear a ridiculous suit of golden armour," he continued.

The harbourmaster looked at the coin again and Reynard made it disappear into his palm. The harbourmaster's eyes narrowed until Reynard reached across, brushed some imaginary lint off the harbourmaster's jacket and in doing so produced the coin again, with a simple act of legerdemain. He dropped it into the official's pocket.

"Yes, the man in the suit of gold armour. Caused quite the stir on the water front, it did. He went into the city for the three days the ship was here, I think. Don't recall him returning each night. The ship was watched over by the first mate in his absence – now there was a giant of man. He was the size of a bull, that fellow."

"Yes, of course," said Reynard. "Thank you for your aid – you have been most helpful. Just as befits a man with the responsibility of looking after the harbour of the Imperial capital," Reynard smiled. The harbourmaster looked at Reynard carefully, unsure if he was mocking him or not. Reynard turned on his heel and marched outside where Kita and Tanithil were waiting. "We go into the city," Reynard told them.

"I suggest we head up the southern staircase and enter the city from Poor Town," said Tanithil. "We will be less obvious to the Azure Watch that way – they don't tend to watch the South Gate at all."

"Ah, of course, this is your home town Tani, I forgot. We will take your advice then, certainly."

The three climbed the granite staircase which led up from the east harbour to the mainland. After a long hard climb they reached the top and came out into the slums on the southern side of the city. There the neck of the headland stretched out into the mainland. The city overflowed out from the city walls at that point. Many of the city's poorer inhabitants lived in this place, outside the protection of the walls, and the Azure Watch who patrolled the city streets inside the wall, rarely went there. Gangs of thieves and thugs roamed the streets in Poor Town, as it was known, and violence was a way of life. No one accosted the three of them though, sensing that a group armed with swords were more bother than they were worth. The group passed through the South Gate which led into the city proper. As Tanithil had suggested there were two guards on the gate who steadfastly ignored all traffic coming in and out of the city there.

Inside the walls life was safer, but the city was still rough and ready. The Market District lay just inside the South Gate and the thieves of Poor Town populated this area too, picking on merchants and their customers alike. Beyond the Market District were rows of shops and residential areas, clustered tightly together. Many alleyways and short cuts crisscrossed the area and litter and rundown buildings were common. A lot of these buildings were five hundred years old, built when the city was originally constructed. Some looked like they had not been renovated at all during their lifetimes.

Lucar was known as the Azure City, which conjured all sorts of images of a bright, clean and sparkling city of blues and whites. In fact the capital was anything but. It was a dull and grimy place which many said represented the state of the empire today: old, dirty and past its prime.

As they moved north from the Market District they passed into the Temple District where large temples to the city's main gods could be found. These were fairly well looked after, testimony to the religious nature of the populace. The Azure Watch patrolled this part of the city regularly, keeping unsavoury types away. Hanging onto the edge of the Temple District, almost as if it was trying to infer it was a temple to a new god, lay the Guild Hall, home of the Guild of Master Merchants and Sea Farers. This place was constructed of white marble, much like the main Guild Hall in Cansae, but was a smaller structure than the Guild base in the Red City. It was in pristine condition and very clearly showed the wealth and power wielded by the influential Guild.

"The East Gate, which comes into the city from the harbour, leads into the park," said Tanithil. "He will be hard to track from there as he could have gone anywhere."

"Is there an expensive inn around there?" asked Reynard, "A man who wears a suit of golden armour into a city is not going to stay in a cheap tavern in Poor Town. He'll be heading for somewhere rich. He has a cargo hold full of Guild treasure to enable him to afford good lodgings too."

"The Palace Gate Inn then," said Tanithil. "It lies right next to the Imperial Palace gate, as its name suggests. Plush and well to do."

"Perfect. Lead us there," commanded Reynard.

"It is just the other side of the park," said Tanithil heading on deeper into the city.

Beyond the Temple District was a large park with tree-lined avenues and decorative ponds. This was once the jewel in the crown of the city but now was like a tiny vision of the state of the empire. The paths were cracked and had weeds growing through in places. Low walls which separated the ponds had bricks missing and algae and reeds were beginning to choke some ponds. The few fish which still swam in the pools looked brown rather than golden and in places the odd tree on the avenues stood dead and leafless even in summer. The park, like the empire it was at the heart of, lay decayed and broken, in its last days of life.

Past the park, right on the northernmost edge of the island stood the Azure Palace. Built by command of the Emperor Lucar and the very first building to be raised in the city, the palace still looked an impressive sight. The emperor had kept it regenerated, perhaps at the expense of the rest of the city. The palace was made of white marble, flecked with blue in places. Azure decorations broke up the stark white façade and complimented the colour scheme. Pendants showing the great blue whale, which was the sign of the Azure House, fluttered from every available cornice.

Emperor Jovius Azure II lived in the palace. He was old and rumour had it was in his last days of life. He was the last living descendent of Emperor Lucar Azure, who formed the Lucarcian Empire five hundred years ago. When he died the line of Lucar would end. House Azure had no heir and would likely crumble too, leaving no royal house in place.

The Palace Gate Inn was an impressive building of the same white marble as the palace. It was three stories high with rows of windows overlooking the park to the south and the deep water harbour to the east. If the city had properly maintained the harbour and park, the views would have been stunning. A doorman outside nodded to the three as they walked in, opening the door for them.

They entered into a huge open entrance hall and crossed the carpeted floor to the desk where a young lady smiled up at them.

"Good day, milady," greeted Reynard, turning on his easy smile. "I'm trying to track down an old friend of mine, Captain Kester, owner of the *Moray*. You can't miss him, tends to wear his ridiculous golden armour all over the place. Can you tell me if he's stayed here recently?"

"I'm sorry, sir, I can't give out the names or details of guests. It's the policy in the Palace Gate."

"Of course it is," Reynard smiled, "and you're very professional to refuse. However this is a good friend of mine and I'm trying to find him for I have sad news. His mother's dying and I have to make sure he gets home to visit her before it's too late," Reynard said, leaning slightly on the table and looking intently at the woman.

The young woman looked a little flustered, "I'm very sorry about your friend, sir, but I still can't help you. Perhaps you should talk to the manager?"

"Yes, of course," said Reynard, realising he was getting nowhere fast. "Please can you call him for me?"

*

An hour later the three of them were back aboard the *Javelin*. The manager had proved even more reticent than the receptionist had, and nothing Reynard had said would get him to change his mind. He had proven completely immune to bribery and had in fact thrown the group out when Reynard had tried to hand him a gold coin. Perhaps he should have tried platinum.

"So we are stuck. We have no idea what Captain Nikolai Kester was doing here, nor where the *Moray* went after it left here about two weeks ago," said Reynard to the group who were assembled in the captain's lounge. "Does anyone have any ideas?"

There was a long pause as everyone looked around at each other. No one seemed to. Reynard sipped at his glass of wine and racked his brain.

"I know Kester was there," said Tanithil breaking the silence. Pulling his silver hair up into a ponytail behind his head he let it all fall back to his shoulders again. "He stayed in one of the suites on the top floor. And he met two men in a back room in the Palace Gate, two weeks ago. "

Everyone turned to look at Tanithil. Reynard asked the question they were all thinking, "How do you know this Tani?"

Tanithil took a deep breath. He had been debating whether or not to divulge his secret past to his new companions for weeks now. When he sensed the Pyromancers being trained in Cansae he had almost told Reynard, but that would have meant revealing his talent. Now it seemed the group were stuck but he knew things which would help. It was time to open up and trust that this group of people would not judge him too harshly for his past.

"I have a talent," He began. "When I was young I realised I could sense things which others could not. If I have some time and peace I can let my mind flow out and feel places and things. I find it easy to read people's emotions and feelings. With people who are feeling very strongly about things I can even sometimes pick out words and ideas from their minds. "

"You're a telepath?" asked Reynard, amazed.

"That is an overly simple word for it," replied Tanithil. "I can very rarely just read words in someone's mind and some people are more guarded than others."

"You should make good use of your ability," said Kita, "it is a rare gift."

"I did," replied Tanithil, turning to the woman from Honshu. "I joined the Thought Guard," he said. The Thought Guard were the emperor's personal bodyguard. They protected the Imperial Palace inside and out. Dressed in polished breastplates with spears in hand and swords by their sides, they wore long flowing cloaks of azure and plumed helms with bright blue feathers. Their surcoats were white with the blue whale of the house emblazoned on the front. The Thought Guard were so called as they were said to be trained telepaths, able to tell what a man was thinking and so protect the emperor from assault and treachery by being able to tell what people were planning before they acted.

"What happened?" asked Reynard, sensing there was more to this story.

"I was removed from my position and dishonourably discharged," confided Tanithil, his violet eyes staring at the floor in shame.

"Why? What for?" asked Okoth, putting a huge arm around the silver haired Lucarcian's shoulder in a friendly manner.

"Gambling," he said, looking up, "No, worse than gambling - cheating at gambling. I became addicted and couldn't help myself. There are gambling dens a plenty in Lucar if you know where to look. I was in there every night, spending my wages. When I started to run out of wages I began to turn my thoughts to those of the people around me and I found I could often tell how good their hands were, sometimes I could even see their cards. I always knew when people were bluffing. I started to win and win big. Then someone recognised me as belonging to the Thought Guard. That was the end of my position in the emperor's personal guard. I was discharged."

Reynard looked at Tanithil with sympathy. He knew how easy it was to fall into unscrupulous habits and knew the lure of the gaming tables. He had spent far too much of his inheritance in the dens of Providentia and knew what it was like. He had always avoided getting addicted though, but not by much. He knew he could easily have fallen into that trap. "That's how you knew about Cyrus and Scraggs, isn't it?" he asked.

"Yes, I was able to sense what had happened down in the brig, when Cyrus released him," nodded Tanithil.

"And how you were able to stop the slaver dead in his tracks in the hold of the ship, back when we escaped? I thought he was going to gut you."

"Yes, I can sometimes influence weak minded people's actions if I really focus."

"That's amazing. Well, if the Thought Guard can't make use of your fantastic talent, we certainly can," affirmed Reynard.

*

Reynard moved silently through the park, flitting from shadow to shadow in the moonlight. On his tail came Tanithil, moving as stealthily as he could, but Reynard could hear him stepping on the odd twig or rustling leaves under foot. The sound was loud to the noble's ear but there seemed to be no one around to hear. Behind Tanithil, Reynard knew, followed Kita. He couldn't hear a single sound from the Niten student, but he was sure she was there.

Soon they reached the edge of the deserted park and looked out across the road at the Palace Gate inn on the other side. The inn was dark for the most part with a lantern burning over the main door and a few candles flickering in the windows of the bedrooms upstairs. It was the middle of the night and all was quiet.

Reynard waited as his two companions caught up with him. He pointed to a side alley which led down the right side of the inn. The others nodded in understanding and he prepared to move off. Just as he was about to step out of the shadows and cross the road a patrol of the Azure Watch came into sight around the corner. Reynard ducked quickly back behind a bush and froze. It wasn't illegal to be creeping around the park at night armed with swords, but it was likely to get him and his group questioned if seen and this was something he was keen to avoid.

The patrol moved off and Reynard took a moment, checked the street was clear again, then whipped swiftly across the road and ducked into the alley. Seconds later Tanithil and Kita joined him. They moved deeper into the dark alley and found a side door which led into the inn. It looked like a kitchen door and there were piles of rubbish outside.

Reynard pulled a small tool out of his pocket and inserted it into the door's lock. He pried and poked the inner workings of the lock carefully until he located the latch and shifted it up gently. There was a faintly audible click and the lock was open. Kita raised an eyebrow at him as he pocketed the tool and he grinned at her. "Misspent youth," he shrugged.

Pushing the door open quietly Reynard slipped inside and the others followed. They were in a kitchen as he had guessed. He looked to Tanithil and the silver haired Lucarcian took the lead. He led them quietly into a corridor and turned right, heading towards the back of the inn.

As they moved down the dark corridors of the inn, all was quiet. Then from up ahead Reynard saw a flickering light: a candle. Someone was coming. He looked around quickly for a place to hide, but there was none. Only an alcove which contained a large potted plant suggested itself. Reynard moved in, trying to hide behind the thin leafy tree in the pot. Tanithil and Kita joined him.

Moments later, around the corner came a servant, carrying a candle on a plate. He was hurrying forward on some important mission for his boss, but there was no way he wouldn't notice three armed people hiding behind a potted plant. Reynard began to draw his rapier, thinking to knock the servant unconscious, but Kita stayed his arm, nodding at Tanithil. Reynard looked and saw the now familiar intense look on the violet eyed man's face. The servant moved up to their hiding place, yawned deeply, then moved past never giving them a moment's notice.

"I pushed the feelings of extreme tiredness and a longing for his comfy bed into his head," Tanithil explained after he had gone around the corner. "He wasn't exactly at his most observant."

Reynard shook his head and smiled, "Great to have you in the team, Tani," he said.

Presently they arrived in a plush part of the ground floor, one that contained numerous rooms, which could be booked out and hired for business meetings, private rendezvous and the like. Tanithil closed his eyes for a moment, and then walked to one of the doors. He pushed it open and quietly entered. The others joined him and Reynard shut the door behind them.

"This is where Captain Kester had his meeting," Tanithil told them. He closed his eyes and moved slowly and carefully around the room, stepping around furniture he couldn't see, using his sense to feel the objects in the room and what had happened here. A few minutes later he opened his eyes and blinked a few times.

"What did you see?" asked Reynard quietly.

"Two men met Kester here. From their dress all three were ship captains. A discussion took place and I got the impression that Kester was the lead role in the conversation. Some sort of agreement was forged in this room and I think Kester was pleased with the results. And there is one more thing: I got a strong feeling about a grate in the floor in part of the park. I'm not sure of its significance but it was important in Kester's mind at the time."

"Well done, Tani, excellent," congratulated Reynard. "Could you find that grate now, in the dark?"

"I think I could, yes."

"Then let's go."

*

A clump of bushes near a once beautiful fountain bubbling from a statue of a man in ceremonial armour hid the grate. Now the warrior's right arm had fallen off and a large crack had appeared in the side of his stained and dirty face. Reynard grasped the grate handle and pulled up. The rusty iron grate opened on stiff hinges and a waft of sewage drifted over him.

"Wonderful," he commented, wrinkling his nose. "Who's going first?"

Wordlessly, Kita dropped into the hole, climbing down a ladder set into the wall of the shaft. Reynard looked at Tanithil and indicated he should go next. He then followed, pulling the grate shut over his head. They were plunged into total darkness.

Seconds later a spark flared to light below him. Reynard looked down to see the floor of the sewer some forty feet beneath. Kita was lighting a torch using a flint and steel. By the time he reached the floor she had it going and had passed it to Tanithil to hold.

The sewer tunnel led off in only one direction from here – to the east – which Reynard realised took it towards the harbour where they were docked. A deep channel of sludge and water filled the centre of the tunnel and a thin walkway ran along each side. Reynard headed off at the front, stepping carefully, but quickly realised that his lovely black boots were going to be covered in muck no matter how cautiously he moved.

The tunnel was straight and well defined. It headed directly out under the city, dropping steadily but not sharply downwards. They followed it along and after a few minutes they could see soft moonlight ahead and felt a fresh clean breeze touch their faces. The fresh air was a welcome relief. Presently they came to the end of the tunnel where the sewer flowed out into the sea. Peeking out Reynard determined they were just north of the harbour wall. Why had Kester been thinking of this tunnel, he wondered. Had he come down here, and if so, why?

As he was contemplating these things Kita started knocking at the wall next to where she was standing. Reynard cocked his head and watched her, wondering what she was up to. She began to move up the tunnel again, away from the sea and back where they had come from, knocking all the time. Tanithil looked quizzically at Reynard who shrugged and the two followed her up the tunnel.

Soon she stopped and knocked intently at one section of wall over and over again. "Here," she declared. "There must be a catch to open this."

"Open what?" asked Reynard.

"A secret door," she answered. "Back in Honshu they are everywhere," she explained. "Most castles have secret passages built into them to allow swift and secret movement from one area of the castle to another. Doors which lead into those passages are obviously concealed. You can find them by tapping and listening – when you get a hollow sound you've usually found a door."

"Great work," said Reynard, impressed. "Can you find the catch?"

"Give me a moment," she replied, running her fingers along the brickwork around the area she had identified. Moments later she stopped; her fingers gripped a small brick which jutted out a tiny bit from the otherwise flush wall. She pulled on it and they heard a soft click. "Yes, I believe I can," she said, pushing the door open.

Beyond the secret door a natural passage led. Where engineers had cut the sewer tunnel into the rock and had walled it with dressed stone, the passage beyond was rough and looked like a natural twisting fissure in the rock face. The floor was sandy and showed the passage of many feet. Curiously it was lit, a low burning torch flickering in a wall sconce a few yards down the passageway. Torches like that burnt for about an hour which meant this torch had been lit some forty or fifty minutes ago. Someone had been here recently.

*

Reynard took the lead, stepping into the natural tunnel and drawing his rapier. The passage led slightly downhill, winding a little, such that it was impossible to see more than a dozen feet ahead at any given time. As they proceeded down it they began to hear the sounds of waves, and the smell of salty air replaced the rank smell of the sewers behind them.

Soon the passage opened out into a dark, natural cave. Across the far side of the cave was a small, dark beach with waves lapping in. The opening to sea was very low indeed, so low in fact that the sea would completely submerge it at most tides and it would only be open when the tide was furthest out. The tide was currently out far enough to mean the entrance to the sea was only inches high. Pulled up on the beach inside the cave mouth was a small row boat.

In front of the beach in the middle of the cave were a table, some crates and a few chairs. The cave was lit – some natural moonlight was coming in from the cave mouth and the rest was provided by a lantern sat on the table which threw the place into shadows.

A man stood behind the table. He had both arms on the table top and was studying something upon it. He was tall and gaunt looking, with dark trousers and shirt, the colour of which were hard to determine in the shadowy light. He had medium length blond hair which marked him as Lucarcian. Reynard noted the cutlass at his side.

Moving into the cave, Reynard headed towards the man who looked up, furrowed his brow and moved around the table, drawing his cutlass.

"What are you doing in here?" demanded the man, accenting each word with a poke of his sword.

"I was just about to ask you the same question, sir," smiled Reynard, moving forward and dropping into a fencer's crouch.

"Who are you?" came back the reply.

"Captain Ferrand of the *Javelin*. And you?" said Reynard, still smiling.

"I'm Milo and you're not welcome here," came back the response.

"I'm here to find out about Captain Kester," said Reynard. "What can you tell me?"

"That you're outnumbered and surrounded, mate," said the swordsman, returning the smile.

Reynard looked quickly over his shoulder and saw three previously unseen men had just moved from the shadows in the corner of the cave. These men had an assortment of knives and cudgels in hand and were moving into position behind him. "Ah, but you don't have a Niten warrior on your side," Reynard countered, as Kita stepped out of the tunnel and into the light, her *daisho* in hand. Behind her Tanithil dropped back into the darkness of the tunnel.

"Kill her," ordered the leader, "I'll deal with this one."

"How very generous of you," said Reynard moving closer, confident that Kita could deal with three thugs single handed. He launched one of his favoured lunges as an opening but the swordsman stepped lightly out of range, easily deflecting the attack downwards harmlessly.

Reynard brought his sword back up to guard and then countered an attack from his opponent. The attack was fast and powerful but the fighter remained in control and did not over balance. He clearly knew how to handle a cutlass.

Reynard moved across the sand, blocking, parrying and countering. His footwork had always been one of his strong points in fencing and he used it to his advantage now. He pushed his opponent back slowly towards a row of crates. Soon he had him pinned back. "Nowhere to go?" he taunted as his enemy backed into one of the crates.

Milo blocked a high strike and grabbed Reynard's sword arm with his left. Reynard did the same and it became an arm wrestle. The two came face to face and Reynard could smell the last meal on the man's breath. The warrior was strong and pushed Reynard back away from him, giving him a second of space. Spinning, Milo leapt upwards to land on the crate which Reynard had previously backed him up against. He swung his cutlass down at Reynard as the noble moved back in. Reynard parried just in time.

Milo jumped from the crate to the top of the table nearby, flying over Reynard's shoulder as he went. Reynard slashed low and the man nimbly skipped over the blade. Turning to face him Reynard could see from the corner of his eye that Kita had dispatched two of the thugs and was facing down the last.

Reynard ducked under a head height slash and as he came up he put his shoulder into the table, knocking it backwards and spilling Milo to the sandy floor with a grunt. The lantern fell off and smashed on the ground, a small pool of burning lamp oil sinking into the sand. Various papers also slid off the table and one landed in the pool, igniting instantly. In seconds one of the crates had caught and a small fire had started.

Reynard moved around the table quickly, putting himself the other side of the fire from Milo, who was getting to his feet. Reynard had the swordsman trapped. Behind Milo were the upturned table and a growing fire. At that moment Kita appeared at Reynard's side, the three goons all dead.

"Time to surrender," said Reynard, levelling his blade at the leader's throat. The warrior looked at the bodies of his three men and dropped his sword.

*

"I think a summary is in order," said Reynard cutting in on the discussion. They were back on the *Javelin* the next morning and Reynard had the group in his study. They were still docked in Lucar and were discussing what to do next. "This is how I see it," he continued. "We know Captain Kester owns the *Moray* and we are pretty certain he is the leader of a band of corsairs. These appear to be growing in number – there are at least five ships in his fleet from what we can tell.

"We recovered two maps from the hidden cave under this city. One was of the town of Tunis, and the other was of my home town of Providentia. Both had scrawled notes on them which looked to us like battle plans. It seems they plan to strike at Tunis and Providentia. We have no idea what they are trying to achieve, nor do we know the order they plan to strike the two towns.

"From the notes on the maps, we think that five ships, headed by the *Moray*, will be used in the attack on Tunis. Coincidentally we spotted five ships heading in the direction of Tunis yesterday morning on our way here, after being attacked by the *Hag*. It's quite likely therefore that they are, even as we speak, attacking Tunis – and that Providentia has either already been hit or will be next."

"On top of that," added Tanithil, "both the men we captured, we tried to interrogate. We encountered exceptionally high levels of resistance to telling us anything, probably unnaturally high resistance. I tried to read them both. Each had huge feelings of loyalty for someone – we assume Captain Kester – and would do anything not to let him down. Again I was faced with unnaturally strong feelings in both the men," he finished. "I suspect some sort of supernatural effect on both men but I have no idea where it might be coming from."

"Thanks Tani," said Reynard, continuing, "Tunis is a day away and we won't be able to get there to stop them, and I'm not sure I would even be inclined to do so if we could – the *Javelin* is not going to be able to take on five ships and win.

"Their battle plans seemed to indicate that only the *Moray* will strike at Providentia – which seems very strange. We don't know if they have struck at my home town or not yet. We do know that the *Moray*, and the man we are after, is probably this very second in Tunis, a day's sail from here.

"I think that's about the size of it," finished Reynard.

"That pretty much sums it up, little man," said Okoth.

"So what do you plan to do?" asked Kita, arms crossed over her chest.

Reynard shrugged, "Follow them to Tunis and see what they are doing there – I don't see that we can do anything else."

-Chapter Eleven-

The *Javelin* pulled out of Lucar's deep-water harbour and turned west, setting sail for Tunis, some eighty miles along the coast of the Inner Sea. It would take them a day to reach the port town. Reynard left the ship in Okoth's steady hands and retired to his quarters to plan and think.

As soon as they broke into open water Kita arrived on deck in her customary red kimono. She was barefoot. Removing her *daisho* she placed them carefully on the floor near the main mast. Four crew men gathered around her. They were also all barefoot. She spent a few moments talking to them and then got them to line up in a row, facing her. She put her feet together, hands by her sides. They all copied. She then bent her knees, sinking into a squatting position, her back still perfectly upright. The four crewmen copied her again, one wobbling and having to stop himself falling by putting a hand on the deck. From there Kita placed her left knee slowly on the deck, then her right. She was now kneeling. At all times her body had remained perfectly upright. Her four students copied her movements. Then she bowed to them, placing each hand on the floor in front of her. Again they mirrored her actions. Reversing the bow she slowly stood, again at all times maintaining poise, balance and control. The students all followed as best they could.

Next Kita took them through a series of exercises all designed to get the muscles warm and ready for action. By now there was a large crowd gathered on deck watching. They gave the lesson space and no one laughed or sniggered, not even when the students tried and failed to copy their teacher. Once the warm ups were over Kita began by teaching the four men to make fists. She emphasised the importance of a solid contact point when striking. Then she began to show them a simple punch.

Two hours later the lesson was over. The men had learnt a simple punch, one kick and two blocks. They were exhausted. The students went off to their hammocks to rest and others came over to Kita, asking if they could join the next lesson. She agreed and before she was done she had ten more students signed up for lessons the next day.

*

As the sun began to set in the west the *Javelin* rounded the headland just east of Tunis. The town came into view and as it did it was clear that parts of it were aflame. Heading out of the harbour and towards the *Javelin* were four ships under full sails, moving rapidly. One of them had a small fire on the forecastle, which the crew were tackling. Another's aft staysail was burnt and hanging limp. All four were showing charred and singed timbers.

Okoth took the *Javelin* slightly further out to sea to let the four pass on the port side, as was the correct etiquette. The ships got closer and it was quickly obvious that they were all flying a red eel on a blue background. Corsairs.

The lead ship drew closer still and as it did it was possible to read the name carved into the hull: the *Moray*. Stood on the quarterdeck holding the wheel was an absolute giant. Standing well over seven feet tall the huge man was bare chested, wearing only a large loin cloth around his waist. Strangely the man also wore a massive helmet crafted out of the head of a bull. Huge horns completed the look of the head gear and made for a ferocious visage. A giant axe was strapped across the man's back.

Stood next to the bull of a man was a more reasonable sized figure. This one had shoulder length blond hair and a rapier hung at his side. He was well built and tall – but still dwarfed by the helmsman – and looked born to the role of sailor, feet planted easily shoulder width apart, perfectly balanced as he looked out at the *Javelin*. The man was clothed head to foot in golden armour.

"What do you want to do?" asked Okoth of Reynard who was stood next to him on the quarterdeck.

"There isn't much we can do," replied Reynard, "I'm not about to attack four ships, even if they are all looking like they have been set alight by someone. It would be suicide." Reynard stared at the man across the divide. They were a hundred feet from the goal of their mission for the Trade Lords, one hundred feet from freedom. But it was out of reach.

"Shall I swing the *Javelin* around to follow them?" asked Okoth.

Reynard considered this. They could try and follow the four ships now but there was no way they could do it without being seen. What would stop Kester simply turning around and attacking them if they did? At present Kester had no idea that Reynard and his friends were after him.

Making an obvious move like swinging around to follow would tip him off. But if they didn't follow they might lose him. Unless he still had to strike at Providentia. They could maybe get there first and take on the *Moray* when it arrived – after all the notes on the maps seemed to indicate that only the *Moray* herself would be going into Providentia. It was a big risk but he felt it was their only option.

"No, let's pass by and head into Tunis harbour as if we didn't know them," he told Okoth. "Whilst we're here we might as well find out what happened. It might help us piece together what the corsairs are up to, which can only help us."

*

Alone on the forecastle Kita stared out across the water at the *Moray*. Unlike the others she was not looking at the quarterdeck where the golden armoured Kester and his bull-like helmsman were stood. Instead her eyes were on the opposite forecastle where a lone man leant on the port rail. The man had black shoulder length hair, greying a bit in places. He was dressed in a red kimono and had a pair of finely crafted swords at his side, one long and one short.

"Father," she whispered.

A year ago, when Kita was approaching her tests to graduate from the Niten dojo at which her father was a teacher, he had disappeared suddenly. He had left without the permission of his *sensei,* causing his *sensei* to declare him *ronin*. Shortly thereafter the school had also banished Kita for duelling and she had set off to try and find her father and discover the truth in why he'd left, and hopefully clear both their names. Once in Manabas she had met the Ibini, Bayo, who had coerced her into taking passage about the *Hammerhead.* There she had been imprisoned as a slave. Now she was in debt to the Trade Lords. All she had to do was recover some golden armour and she would be free to find out what had happened to Heremod.

And just when she had found the man in the golden armour, she had found her father too, working for him.

*

135

The *Javelin* rounded the sea wall and sailed into Tunis harbour. Behind them the four ships in Kester's fleet sailed on eastward into the distance. There was no Imperial Navy in Lucarcia and no one was about to chase four well-armed ships off into the Inner Sea so there was no pursuit. Pulling into the harbour, the sight of a huge conflagration greeted them. A ship was fully aflame, a raging inferno. At the top of the main mast, Reynard could just make out its flag through the heat haze: a red eel on a blue background.

Reynard watched as the flag was engulfed. Parts of the ship were falling off into the harbour to be doused in the sea water. A large number of people were gathered on the docks, watching the ship burn and no one was doing anything to save it. The ship itself seemed devoid of life – presumably all the corsairs had been killed or had managed to get to the other ships before they fled.

The *Javelin* gave the flaming hull a wide berth and docked alongside a caravel called the *Poacher*. From this vantage point Reynard could see a few other fires in the town. Three or four buildings were ablaze although fire fighters were slowly bringing them under control. There had clearly been a serious confrontation here and Reynard wanted to know what it was about.

As soon as the *Javelin* was docked Reynard took Tanithil and Mosi off the ship with him into the town. Okoth stayed aboard as he usually did as first mate and Kita had expressed a desire to stay behind – something was clearly bothering her but Reynard didn't have time to find out what it was at that time.

The three men moved down the water front and up into the streets. Tunis was built on a slight rise with three main streets leading up away from the waterfront. The buildings were of local sandstone and were a pleasing uniform sandy brown colour. Most had simple clay tiled roofs, typically of a reddish hue. The streets here were cobbled. A few merchants had carts and stalls arrayed along the street the three climbed. Reynard approached a fruit seller.

"Well met sir," he greeted the man, who was grey and thin.

"And to you sir," replied the merchant with a theatrical bow. "Can I interest you in some fresh fruit? The plums are from northern Manabas and the apples from the vineyards of the Tail. Or if you prefer something more local I have some oranges from just up the road?"

"Ummm, a fresh orange sounds lovely," replied Reynard, "Thank you. It seems like there has been some excitement here recently," said Reynard, gesturing at a nearby building which had been put out, but which was still smouldering.

"Yes, quite the tale if you have time to hear it?" asked the merchant, taking the silver sickle offered by Reynard and fishing in his pockets for change.

"I'm all ears," encouraged Reynard.

"Well now," he began, "a group of five ships sailed into the harbour an hour or so ago. A large force of men disembarked from the ships and made their way up this very street. They were all sporting knives, cudgels and even cutlasses. Many bore lit torches – which I thought was strange given it was only late afternoon. At their head was a man dressed like out of a legend of old, wearing golden armour and carrying a noble's sword. At his side strode a giant of a man, maybe ten feet tall and built like an ox, wearing a bull's head helmet with a huge axe in his hands.

"The raiders passed straight up the street past my stall, but not one laid a hand on me or any of the others in the market. Nothing was stolen either. They simply passed by and disappeared up the road, one giant gang, intent on some unknown purpose. Very strange behaviour for raiders," the fruit seller noted.

"Minutes passed and nothing happened, then suddenly there was a loud whoosh and a ball of fire rent the air over the tops of the houses. Seconds later large numbers of the raiders came rushing back. The local town watch pursued them. The raiders regrouped around the man in gold and his bull-like friend and took a stand, right here in front of me. Well, I was hiding in that alley over there by this time of course," he continued, pointing to a small dark alleyway nearby. "A huge melee began right on the street here. The raiders were giving as good as they got, but then around the corner came half a dozen men in red robes. I've never seen their like before.

"These robed men began to chant strange words. Some held hands together. I felt the hairs on the back of my neck rising. Then, incredibly, fire lanced from the hands of the robed men, shooting out and engulfing some of the raiders. The giant bull-helmeted man broke off the melee and charged up the hill into the robed men, goring two on the horns of his helmet and disembowelling another with his axe. The remaining men in red robes fled back into the town away from the fight.

"The raiders retreated back to their ships. I followed at a distance, along with many of the merchants, keen to see what came next. More robed men appeared at the harbour and conjured flames across the water. One ship was completely engulfed – it's still burning now, down in the harbour I think – and the others were all damaged, but four ships got away. The robed men disappeared off back into town to who knows where."

"That's quite the tale indeed," complimented Reynard.

"I know you probably don't believe me," replied the merchant, "but ask any as has been here all day and you'll hear the same."

"I believe you," said Tanithil from Reynard's side, "every word."

*

Reynard, Mosi and Tanithil had followed the road that the merchant said the raiders had taken. By asking a few other people on the streets they had come to a large building which was now a smoking ruin. According to the people they had questioned in this area of the town, the raiders had singled out this building, surrounded it and torched it. They then waited for any who tried to escape the building and slaughtered them as they came out. Only the arrival of the town watch caused the raiders to run back in the direction of the harbour.

"What is this all about?" queried Reynard, "and can we really believe all this talk of flame-throwing robed wizards?" he smiled, amused at the ability of simple folk to give fantastical explanations to what were obviously perfectly normal occurrences.

"Pyromancers," answered Tanithil, shaking his head sadly, "It's about Pyromancers."

"What in the Inner Sea is one of them?" asked Reynard confused.

"Pyromancers are people who have learnt the arcane lore to control fire. The study of this or any form of Elementalism was banned at the collapse of the Rainbow Empire and their kind has not been seen in these lands for five hundred years. Now they have returned and the corsairs know it and are trying to kill them."

"What? What are you talking about, Tani?"

"This building is…" Tanithil pointed at the smoking ruins, "…was a training hall for Pyromancers. There was one back in Cansae too. Inside a master was teaching novices the banned arcane arts and they were learning how to summon, control and throw fire. Tunis lies just inside the lands controlled by the Dragon of House Ruby. The Ruby House are training Pyromancers. There can be only one explanation for this: they are preparing for war. Civil war."

"What do you mean, there is one in Cansae too?" asked Reynard, struggling to take all this in.

"I sensed it when we were in the city there," explained Tanithil. "I almost told you about it at the time, but had no logical way to explain to you how I knew. Now you know about my talent I can tell you about it. They are training Pyromancers in Cansae and in Tunis. And these are the only two settlements in the Head of Ursum we have been to recently. I suggest they may be training them in secret all across the region."

"Okay, let us suppose that is true," conceded Reynard. "Why would the corsairs be attacking these robed fire mages – whatever you call them?"

"Pyromancers," repeated the violet eyed Lucarcian, "and I have no idea why."

*

"And that is Tani's theory," concluded Reynard. They were back in the lounge of the *Javelin* with Okoth and Kita. Reynard had just explained Tanithil's idea that the Ruby House were training Pyromancers in preparation for war, breaking a ban which the emperor had imposed five hundred years ago at the formation of the Lucarcian Empire.

"Quite the story," noted Okoth with a large white grin.

"Why would Kester want to strike against the Pyromancers?" asked Kita, arms folded.

"This is the big question," answered Reynard. "According to the merchants we talked to, the corsairs didn't steal a single thing from the town, nor kill anyone save these robed fellows and the town watch who tried to stop them. It was definitely a planned strike with one purpose only: kill Pyromancers."

"So what do we do next?" asked Kita. "We still have one goal: recover the golden armour. That wins us our freedom. I suggest that, interesting as all this politics maybe, we focus on that."

"Indeed," said Reynard. "This means our next move has to be Providentia. The maps we found seem to imply that the *Moray* would be going there and going there alone. We have no idea why but that is our best hope to find Kester and get our lives back. Any questions?"

"I have an observation," came back Tanithil.

"Yes?"

"I know why Kester seems to inspire such confidence in the men under him."

"Why?"

"It's the golden armour. I recognised it when I saw him on the ship's deck earlier but it has taken until now for me to figure out where I knew it from."

"Go on," prompted Reynard.

"When we were back in Lucar there was a statue in the park, near where the grate led into the sewers. It was of a man in ceremonial armour and in a real state of disrepair."

"I recall it," said Kita, "What of it?"

"That statue was of the Emperor Lucar. And the golden armour is his. It's identical."

"You're saying that Kester wears the golden armour of Emperor Lucar?" asked Reynard.

"I am. That armour has many stories told about it. Some say it was enchanted with powerful incantations which imbued the wearer with supernatural charisma and the power to dominate weak minds and bend people to his will. Certainly all the stories tell that Lucar himself was an inspirational leader. Many non-historical documents attribute that to his armour being magical. Kester is wearing it and we have seen first-hand that his subordinates demonstrate almost supernatural loyalty to him."

"The Armour of Lucar," said Reynard. "No wonder the Trade Lords want it back."

-Chapter Twelve-

Spring was thinking about giving way to early summer as the *Javelin* scooted along the Inner Sea heading once again for the Lucarcian Straits. The sun was high in the clouds and the brisk wind out of the south was warmer than it had been in previous weeks. White caps dotted the sea to the port side and the low beaches of northern Ursum lay off the starboard, breakers rolling in to crumple lazily against the shore.

Aboard the main deck rows of crew were arrayed. Kita stood in front of them, arms folded across her chest. She was calling out numbers in her native tongue, counting from one to ten. With each number called out, the class of sailors would move forward in unison, performing a combination of kicks, punches, blocks and strikes as she directed them. Sometimes she would move between the crew, adjusting a technique here, correcting a stance there. Each crew member she spoke to would give a curt bow of acknowledgement and she would move on, continuing her count, watching the students with a critical eye.

Occasionally she would call the sailors to her and they would sit down around her. Then she would demonstrate the point she was trying to get across. She would call up a student – often Florus who was proving to be one of the most advanced of the students - and get him to throw a punch or a kick at her. She would move like lightning, blocking, grabbing, and then striking, kicking or throwing Florus with great speed, yet perfect control. He would always be unhurt, yet she always hit him hard enough for him to know he'd been struck.

Reynard watched the training as often as he could. He resisted the temptation to join in – he would have liked to learn but felt that as Captain he would make it harder for the crew to enjoy their lessons if he was one of the students.

Daily the crew's respect for Kita and her unarmed skills grew. And daily the crews' skills grew with it.

*

Ten days after leaving Tunis the *Javelin* moved into waters familiar to Reynard. He recognised each headland and craggy shore. He knew the names of the villages and fishing ports dotted along the coast here and even knew some of the better inns to visit for a pint of good ale.

Providentia itself was a small town which straddled the Old Gore River as it flowed down out of the Vacheron hills. The town lay at the back of a large, wide bay and was nicely sheltered from most of the bad weather that the Southern Ocean had a tendency to throw at this coast. The bay was a little craggy in places, like most of this coastline, but also boasted some stunning sandy stretches which made for wonderful places to spend lazy summer days.

The town flowed up the small hillside on which it had grown, developing over hundreds of years since the first settlers to this region had decided this would make a good place to live. Providentia had grown organically, never really planned, and had expanded as needed with no real direction. But in recent times the Earl had modified and organised the settlement. Lord Caer Ferrand, Reynard's father, had added fortifications to the town since he had become Earl of Providentia some thirty years previously.

The fortifications were only simple wooden walls which now surrounded the town. They were wide enough to support a thin battlement on which watchmen could patrol. Every few hundred yards the Earl had added a small wooden tower, where more guards could be stationed and weapons and provisions stored in times of need. He had also built dividing walls through parts of the town, again only wooden and this time just large fences really, but they had the effect of channelling traffic from one part of town into another through the wooden gates which had been placed strategically in various locations. This was a source of minor inconvenience to the population but the Earl saw the benefits should Providentia ever come under attack. And the Earl feared that if the emperor were to die, that time might come sooner than anyone here would like.

At the top of the hill overlooking the town was the Iron Fortress, home of the Ferrand family, the Iron House. Made of grey local granite the fortress was an imposing building. It was not built for show but for defence and was a dour and dreary looking structure, but an impressive one none the less. A high stone wall surrounded a courtyard which contained many wooden buildings and the keep. The keep, three stories high, was dominated on one side by a huge stained-glass window depicting a smith at work on a great forge – the symbol of the Iron House. The window was a masterpiece and one of the most beautiful pieces of art anywhere in the empire. The builder of the Iron Fortress, the founder of the Iron House, Lord Hiberus Ferrand, the first Earl of Providentia, had commissioned it. That was over three hundred years ago.

The *Javelin* rounded the manmade breakwater and cruised into the harbour gently, moving into the deep water bay and settling alongside the wharf. Crewmen rushed to secure the ship to the bollards on the water front, the anchor was dropped and Birgen had the sails reefed and readied the ship for its time in dock. Not fifty yards away the *Moray* was already at anchor.

They had found her.

*

"Yes, he went up to the keep I believe, sir," said the merchant on the water front. "Obviously some sort of a noble wearing armour like that, sir. Looked like quite the hero he did. I expect he's gone to visit the Earl and his son," he continued.

"Doesn't the Earl have two sons?" Reynard asked, aware that the merchant obviously didn't know who he was.

"Not anymore sir, no. Very sad thing it was. Seems the youngest son fell into the harbour and drowned dead he did, sir. A few months back."

"Did he now?" asked Reynard. "That's very interesting – thank you for your time." Turning to Kita he nodded up the street, "This way then."

Reynard set off along the waterfront for a few yards, and then stopped abruptly. He turned and stared at the building in front of him, the Drowned Hippogriff. This was the inn he had been drinking in. This was the place that Scraggs had found him, drugged him and taken him off to be a slave. This was where this whole sorry affair had all started.

"Something wrong?" asked Kita appearing at his side.

"No, sorry. Just thinking. Let's go." Reynard led her up a winding street which soon came to a wooden gate between one of the palisades which divided the town. Reynard put his hand up to his face as if to scratch an itch as they passed through and the guards, clearly not expecting to see a ghost walk through the gate, did not recognise him. They passed two more similar gates before they reached the keep.

The guards at the keep were not about to let just anyone in. "Halt! Who are you and what is your business in the Iron Fortress?" said the guard, stepping across in front of Reynard and Kita as they made to enter. The second guard on the other side of the large gates put his hand on his sword as if to emphasise the question.

Reynard drew himself up to his full height and looked down on the guard who had addressed him. "Really Maursus, I've only been gone a few weeks and you've already forgotten who I am?"

The guard blinked in surprise and did a double take, "Reynard? I... that is to say they..."

"They said I'd drowned?" Reynard asked, cutting in, "A misunderstanding as you can see. We are going to visit my father. Good day to you," he finished as he moved past the stammering guard and into the courtyard, Kita a step behind.

The courtyard of the Iron Fortress was busy. Market stalls were arrayed across the open space. Many were set up abutting the keep walls, their bright colourful canopies lightening the atmosphere and providing a gorgeous counterpoint to the dreary keep walls. High above, the smith depicted in the huge stained glass window looked down on proceedings in the courtyard as if the hustle and bustle of a market was beneath him.

Reynard shouldered his way through the crowds, eager to get into the keep. He reached the keep doors which were guarded and was pleased to see recognition on the face of the guard there. "My lord," he said, snapping to attention, "Welcome home, sir."

"Thank you, Thaddeus," he replied. "It is good to be back. Tell me, has a man in golden armour come through here?"

"Yes, sir," the guard replied quickly. "He is in the Great Hall visiting with your brother I believe. Would you like me to take you there?"

"I think I know the way, thank you," Reynard said moving forward.

"Yes, of course," replied Thaddeus, stepping out of the way.

Reynard led Kita into the entrance hall where a huge granite staircase led up. He took the stairs two at a time, passing astonished servants along the way. Kita was always just a step behind him as ever. Presently they came to huge double doors which were shut.

"Something's wrong," Reynard told Kita. These doors are never left unguarded. There should be a guard here, always." Reynard pushed at the doors but they wouldn't open. From beyond the doors he heard a shout and the clash of metal on metal. He shouldered into the door with all his strength but it would not budge. "Where is Okoth when you need him? Kita, we need to get this door open, quickly!" he said.

She looked around and saw a bench nearby. Gesturing to it she moved into place and Reynard joined her. They picked it up and ran at the door with it. The door smashed open and the two almost fell into the Great Hall.

The Great Hall was, as its name suggested, great. It was almost as long as the *Javelin* from end to end and wider by far. Dominated by the massive stained glass window at the far end, a long table lay across in front of the window. This was the head table at which the Earl would dine or hold court – whenever the need arose. Down each side long rows of tables also ran, with benches alongside them. These were where the assembled guests would congregate and sit to eat or feast. Three great fireplaces warmed the room and various tapestries decorated the walls.

There was no Earl present and no guests were feasting. Instead a battle was raging.

*

Kita drew her swords and moved forward quickly. Ahead there were two distinct fights going on and one of them attracted her attention instantly.

At the far end of the Great Hall in the shadow of the giant stained glass window a man in golden armour was fighting three guards. Behind the guards stood a thin, scared looking version of Reynard, who Kita assumed must be his older brother, Maynard. The guards were trying to stop the golden warrior from reaching their lord. From the looks of the other dead guards around Captain Kester, they were not likely to succeed. However, this was not the battle which took her attention.

Instead she focussed on the other fight. Here, a lone swordsman took on five of the Earl's best – and was winning. The lone swordsman was wearing the distinct red kimono with emblazoned dragon on the back which was the garb of the Niten dojo. The man had a long and short sword in hand and was a blur of motion. It was her father.

Even as she rushed to close the distance from the door to the fight, Heremod killed two guards, leaving three still standing. She knew they would not last long against him. "Father," she called out, hoping to distract him. Instead one of the guards looked up to see who had entered the room and died on the end of a thrust of Heremod's *wakizashi*. Two left.

Kita reached the fight as Heremod blocked a counter from one guard and spun in place his *katana* whipping around lightning quick to decapitate the next guard. One left. The remaining guard dropped his sword and was about to run when the *wakizashi* sliced into his guts. All dead.

Heremod continued the spin and came to face his daughter, swords ready. He blinked twice and stepped back, struggling to hide the look of shock on his face. "Kita," he said finally. "What are you doing here?"

"I've travelled all the way from Sapporo to find you father."

"Then we'd best talk," he said, putting away his blades in one smooth motion.

*

Reynard spotted Captain Kester instantly. Right over the far side of the Great Hall, behind the head table and under the stained glass window, Kester was fighting three guards who were bravely protecting his brother, Maynard. It rapidly became apparent that three onto one was not good odds for the guards. Kester moved as a man wearing silks even though he was clad from head to toe in heavy armour. His stance was deep and solid, yet his footwork took him across the floor at great speed, darting in and out of range of the guards faster than they could react.

Reynard saw Kita rush across the other side of the Great Hall to another fight and left her to it. She was more than capable of handling herself he knew. He had to get to Kester and stop him. He rushed forward towards the fight. As he ran a deep lunge from Kester's rapier gutted one of the guards. Sprinting across the floor Reynard leapt onto the head table and flew into the air. He struck Kester in the back at full tilt and knocked the man sprawling to the floor.

Kester rolled and was on his feet in an instant. "Ah, I see you have caught up with us at last, Captain Ferrand," he said smiling a surprisingly genuine smile. The golden armoured warrior blocked a thrust from a guard and moved back into a more defensive stance.

"How do you know me?" asked Reynard.

"I do my research," replied the corsair. "The Guild wants my nice new acquisition back," he said gesturing to his armour," and they hired you to get it for them." The warrior blocked an attack from the second guard easily and sliced his rapier across the man's throat. The guard dropped to the floor gurgling and was dead in seconds.

"And now you will hand the armour over to me," demanded Reynard, "or I will take it off your still-warm, dead body." As he spoke the last, he lunged forward hoping to catch Kester off guard with the speed of his attack, but the corsair was fast and blocked easily.

"You'll need to do better than that, Reynard," he chided.

"I think you had best put down your blade," suggested Reynard, "You're outnumbered. Extremely outnumbered." Nodding in the direction of the doors into the Great Hall, Reynard indicated the dozen guards who were moving into the room, spears in hand.

"Hmm, it seems you have thwarted me this time, Captain Ferrand. It will be the last time, I assure you." Spinning on his heel, Kester rushed to the back of the room directly away from the incoming guards. He had nowhere to go. Nowhere, until Reynard realised what he was planning to do.

"No! Not that!" shouted the noble, as the golden armoured man dived headlong into the three hundred year old stained glass window, smashing it to pieces and falling right through it into mid-air.

Rushing to the shattered window Reynard looked out and down. Kester had plummeted to the ground and crashed through the canopy of a rug merchant's stall. The canopy had slowed his fall and the piles of rugs had made for a relatively soft landing. Reynard watched as Kester rolled to his feet and rushed off through the market and out of the main gates into the city before the surprised guards thought to stop him. It was almost as if the corsair had planned his escape route perfectly.

*

"I'm so sorry, brother," blurted Maynard, close to tears. "I was just so scared."

The two brothers sat in one of the drawing rooms of the keep, near a roaring fire. Their father, the Earl of Providentia, sat nearby, wrapped in a blanket, listening intently. The Earl's body may have been old and tired but his mind was still keen. He had listened to Reynard's tale with interest. The boy had always been good at spinning a yarn but this was the most extreme he had ever heard. He was close to disbelieving it totally, until Maynard, the sensible one, had admitted his guilt.

So, one of his sons had sold the other into slavery in an effort to get rid of him, all because he was being pressured into becoming the lackey of the Ebon House. He knew Maynard was weak but he never expected this of him. To sell his brother to slavers? Ridiculous.

Reynard had shown remarkable initiative, ingenuity, guile and courage to get this far. And it seemed he had shown the leadership to take a ship of cutthroats and vagabonds and turn them into a motivated crew who would sail around the empire just because he asked them to. Lord Caer was impressed. This was not the behaviour he normally associated with his second son. Drinking, carousing and wenching were more his style.

"What I don't understand," said Reynard "is why Kester was trying to kill you. What have you done to upset him?" he asked his brother.

"I have no idea, none at all, I swear to you both," replied Maynard, looking from one to the other.

"It is clear to me what he would have achieved had he succeeded," said the Earl. "He would have weakened the Ebon House's position in this part of the empire. With Maynard dead the Ebon House would no longer have a man in our house. I would have had to pick a new heir, one of your cousins I suppose, and the Ebon House would no longer have their puppet."

"Puppet?" said Maynard, raising his voice. "I would be no one's puppet!"

"Quiet son," ordered the Earl. "You have already shown your worth. Do not speak until you're spoken to."

"But..."

"Silence!" demanded Lord Caer sternly. "This whole affair saddens me and at the same time I find myself relieved. I have long wondered about who might be suitable to be named heir to the Iron Fortress. As you're both aware I have put off naming an heir. Until now." The old man looked from son to son.

"Maynard, you are the oldest. I have long trained you and taught you all the skills required to run this household and to manage our affairs. You have shown yourself skilled, intelligent and capable. Yet today I find that you're also a liar and have no honour whatsoever.

"Reynard, you are a wastrel and have always been a huge disappointment to me. You have never applied yourself to the lessons of leadership nor been interested in this family, its traditions or its history. Yet today I find that you're also clever, resourceful and brave. And most of all you're a man with honour who understands the truth and respects it."

The Earl of Providentia stood up, moving his blankets aside and walked slowly to Reynard's chair. He placed his hands on his son's head and said, "Reynard my son, I name you heir of the Iron Fortress and Earl Apparent to the lands and title of Providentia."

*

Kita and Heremod strolled along the Providentia waterfront. The sea birds were swooping in and out of the ship masts. Sailors and stevedores were moving about the place shifting creates, boxes and parcels. The place was busy and noisy. Neither spoke as they turned and moved away from the harbour and into the town proper.

"So," Heremod began at last as they passed through one of the wooden gates, "you want to know why I left? It is simple really: a friend asked me to."

"You left your home, your family and your place in the Niten dojo because a *friend* asked you to?" repeated Kita, incredulously.

"That's right," he replied. "It is important. He would not have asked this of me if it were not."

"Can you tell me what it is, so I might understand just how important it is?" she enquired.

"I can, yes," he replied simply.

Heremod proceeded to tell her his tale, the story of why he left everything that was important to him to help a friend with an important task. It took an hour or more strolling through the streets of Providentia for him to finish his explanation. When he had finished, Kita took a long moment before she responded.

"By the Seven Hells, that is an exceptional tale, father. I see why you had to leave now. I wish you had taken me with you."

"You were not ready. I wonder if you are now," he replied.

Stopping and taking hold of her father's hands, Kita said, "I want to come with you, to help you complete the task your friend set you."

Heremod looked deep into his daughter's dark brown eyes. "In that case we had best release you from your debt to the Trade Lords," he said. "I think it is time we had a chat with this Captain Ferrand you're working with. I have some information he might find useful."

-Chapter Thirteen-

"So you've been working with the corsairs for six months now, yet you suddenly want to join our side?" asked Reynard of Heremod, suspiciously.

"I'm not on anyone's side," responded Heremod calmly. "I'm here to help out a friend, and as part of that enterprise I found it helpful to ally myself with the corsairs you're hunting, yes. But I'm not on their side – nor yours."

"But you do want to give us information about them?" Reynard continued.

"Indeed. It seems that Kita is in debt to the Trade Lords and in order to get her out of debt, you need to recover the golden armour which Nikolai – Captain Kester – wears. I will help you achieve this, if you want my help."

Reynard took a deep breath and let it out slowly. Of course he wanted the Niten master's help. He just needed to put aside the fact that the warrior from Honshu had only yesterday broken into his ancestral home and killed at least five of his father's personal guard. As far as this man was concerned these were all just steps along the way to his own personal end – whatever that was. He had no remorse, no guilt at the blood he had spilt. He was single minded and focussed on one thing. Reynard decided that if he was presently focussed on helping Kita recover the golden armour then he should use that to his advantage.

"Okay," Reynard agreed. "Tell us what you know."

"I know much," said Heremod. "Let me start with this: Captain Nikolai Kester has been building a band of corsairs for around six months now. He has far more ships in his fleet than you believe. More like around thirty ships. These ships are spread around the whole of the empire, from Ursum in the south to Manabas and Ibini in the north. The corsairs have a base, a central place where they can meet and plan and exchange information. This place is a port called Coruba and it lies on the western coast of Granita, south of the great west promontory."

"Granita?" quizzed Reynard, "But that island is a wasteland. Nothing grows there, no one goes there. It is deserted - save for the strange beasts that are rumoured to roam the wilds there." Granita was a desolate wilderness. Legend had it the island was the location of an ancient magical gate which had let the horrific insect plague known as the Writhing Death into the Rainbow Empire. The gate was destroyed when the High Magi of the Rainbow Empire had gathered to shut the Gate. Now nothing lived there and the place was considered terribly cursed and avoided.

"Exactly. What better place to have a base?" replied Heremod. "No one goes there. The corsairs can plot and scheme in total privacy and they have a place to run to where they consider themselves safe."

"You have been there?" asked Reynard.

"I have, yes. Many times."

"And you can lead us there?"

"I can and I will, if it will help Kita," the warrior replied.

*

The *Javelin* left port the next day and turned west. Reynard had spent many long hours with his father and had convinced him that he needed to finish this. The simple fact of the matter was that the Guild was too powerful, even for the Earl of Providentia to go up against. Reynard needed to recover the armour and to get himself out of their debt.

The team had agreed that their next port of call should be Cansae and a return to face the Trade Lords. They had discovered the location of the corsair base in Granita, but they also had information to the effect that the corsairs numbered over a score of ships, many of which would be in Coruba. The *Javelin* could not hope to simply sail into that port and attack. They were going to need help.

There was no Imperial Navy in Lucarcia – the emperor had never commissioned one. So there was no military force present on the Inner Sea and the oceans surrounding Lucarcia. The closest thing to such a force now was the Guild. They controlled hundreds of merchant vessels. If the Trade Lords wanted their golden armour returned, they would need to organise the attack on Coruba. Reynard would have to convince them to go to war against the corsairs.

The journey west to Cansae was one of just under three hundred nautical miles. They would cover that distance in about four days with reasonable winds. Summer was shrugging off the last remains of spring and the temperatures were rising.

The journey west was mostly uneventful. On the third day a squall hit them from the Southern Ocean. It caused them a great soaking and a little discomfort. There was a small amount of damage as one of the topsails ripped in the high winds, but it was nothing compared to the storm they had experienced when they came through this stretch of water back in the spring.

Each day Kita continued her lessons with the crew. She now had to teach two classes per day so that all the students could be accommodated whilst still enabling men to run the ship. Heremod watched his daughter teach with a look of fierce pride evident on his face.

On the fourth day out of Providentia they turned into the Aper Sound just thirty miles or so from Cansae. Kita was teaching her class and was having trouble trying to explain a concept to them. Finally, she called her father over to her. She explained what she was trying to teach and asked him if he would demonstrate a scenario with her. Of course he agreed.

The two Niten warriors bowed and dropped into stance. Kita told her class that her father was going to perform the attack she was teaching them to defend. He would do it slowly so they could see exactly what they were supposed to be trying. Heremod announced his attack to his daughter, telling her exactly what he was about to do. He paused and then initiated his attack, slowly and precisely. She moved smoothly to intercept him, blocked his attack, taking his arm high and demonstrated the position she would move into to sweep the attacker to the floor.

"Do you see now?" she asked the assembled students.

"Yes, but can we see it done properly please?" asked one of the students. "We get the general idea but it would make more sense if done at full speed."

Kita smiled at her father and raised a questioning eyebrow. He bowed in return, also smiling. The two returned to their stances, but this time they were somehow deeper and stronger, giving off a feeling of great potential energy. The smiles faded, to be replaced by serious, concentrated looks. Heremod was low, centred and poised. Kita was lightly balanced on both feet, weight slightly forward, distributed evenly. Heremod announced his attack, and then waited.

The pause seemed to go on for ages. The crew's attention almost began to wane then suddenly Heremod exploded into action. His strike came out almost too fast to see, a huge eruption of power all focussed into one blow.

Kita appeared not to react. The strike flew in so close to her face that it seemed she was about to be destroyed by it. Then at the very last moment she moved. Dropping sideways and down she deflected the strike just enough to miss her by a hair's breadth. She grabbed her father's wrist and pulled, taking him off balance and then pushing her hip into his she twisted and flipped, pulling his body off balance and whipping his legs around with her thigh.

Heremod flew in the air and landed on his back. Kita still had hold of his wrist, controlling his movement. Her knee shot up in the air and then instantly straight down again, her leg straightening, the edge of her bare foot driving right down into Heremod's exposed neck. A deafening shout split the air and she stopped her kick right in the flesh of her father's neck, just touching the windpipe.

Silence fell. "Like that," she said into the stillness. The crew jumped to their feet clapping and cheering.

Kita looked up to where Reynard was leaning over the rails on the quarterdeck looking down. She smiled up at him and his face split into a grin as she did.

*

The Red City was stunning in the early summer sunshine. Reynard walked up the hill towards the white marble edifice of the Guild Hall with Mosi by his side. They were going to try and convince the Trade Lords to go to war. This could be an interesting exchange. Still, if the Guild wanted the Armour of Lucar back again they would have to provide some help.

"The Light shows his support to our venture," commented Mosi, white robes brushing the cobbled streets as they climbed.

"How do you mean?" asked Reynard, striding along at a fast pace, hand on his rapier to keep it from swinging around too much.

"Look to the skies," said Mosi, "the sun is bringing its warmth to the streets of the city and shining on our path. It is a good sign."

"You don't think this is just what happens in summer?" asked Reynard, smiling his easy smile. He had grown to like the priest, who was usually quiet and reserved. Mosi never usually said much but when he did it was usually a wise or comforting word.

"Summer is the Light's season, for sure," replied Mosi, "but not all days are filled with his blessing. Today, however, he looks down on us."

"That's good to know," smiled Reynard, looking up at the white Guild Hall as they approached its front doors. "Now let's go and convince the Trade Lords of that."

*

It took three days to get a full audience with the leaders of the Guild of Master Merchants and Sea Farers. Reynard was told to come back to the Guild Hall where he would be met by Varus. He was to bring his entire command crew. On the day in question, Reynard decided to bring Heremod too; after all he was the only person who had been to Coruba.

The group entered the huge Guild Hall at the appointed time and there, waiting for them, was Varus. The Guildsman was dressed in a rich looking green silk shirt and had loose fitting brown trousers on over black boots. A fine rapier was at his side and he was stroking his well-trimmed beard between thumb and forefinger as the group entered the hall.

"Well met all," said Varus bowing a courtly bow before them. "I see you have grown in number since last we met," he continued.

Reynard nodded curtly, "This is Heremod of Albion. He has information which is vital to what we are to discuss with your leaders."

"Then he is welcome too. Let us ascend to the audience chambers."

Varus led them up the sweeping marble staircase and into the antechamber adjacent to the audience room. Once again it was laid out with a large spread of foods and drinks. Again Varus bid them sit and refresh themselves and he disappeared through the far door. This time the group were less in fear for their lives and most started to tuck into the fabulous array of sweetmeats, biscuits, breads and fruit arrayed on the tables here. Reynard poured himself a large measure of Pembrose Red, swilled it around the crystal goblet and took a long drink.

Minutes later Varus opened the door and invited them in. The group rose and proceeded in to their second audience with the mysterious Trade Lords.

*

"You have done well," commended the deep voice coming from the depths of the grey cowl in the middle of the table. All twelve of the rulers of the Guild were in session, every seat at the large cedar table taken. Reynard and his crew sat on six small seats facing them and Varus hovered behind them. "In fact, very well," it continued. "But now you want to command a fleet of Guild ships to make an attack on a den of corsairs. This plan has very little chance of making this organization any profit, and a large chance of costing us dearly."

"I suppose," replied Reynard, "that it depends on how much you want the golden armour returned to you." The group had agreed not to mention the armour by name. The Trade Lords probably knew what it was but they felt the less they knew about what Reynard and his friends had discovered the better. "Heremod here tells us that the corsairs have a regular meeting every full moon in Coruba. The *Moray* and Captain Kester are nearly always there. A dozen or more of his captains will be there too. This is the perfect chance to strike at this group, to smash their growing power and to recover the armour at the same time.

"The corsairs are, I'm sure, a growing thorn in your collective sides. They are obviously striking at Guild ships across the empire and their threat is growing each day. I would have thought that information about their hidden base, and a time when they are most likely to be there in numbers, would present a major opportunity to cripple them – and at the same time recover the armour you seek."

The Trade Lords did not answer immediately and silence grew in the room. Reynard let it grow knowing that it added weight to his argument. He wondered idly if the hooded figures arrayed before them were somehow able to communicate together and were even now discussing the possibilities.

"Do you have a plan?" came back the light, high pitched voice from the left end of the table.

"I do," said Reynard. "You send a fleet of ships in to Coruba at night to blockade the port. Do not let any corsairs escape. On those ships you place a force of mercenaries. I'm sure you employ them or can hire them for this venture. That force puts ashore and attacks the town.

"Meanwhile the *Javelin* will have split from the fleet and will drop anchor down the coast a short way. Our team will disembark and make the short journey to Coruba across land from the south. We will enter the town on foot about the same time as the fleet strikes. We will make the most of the chaos inspired by the attack, find Kester, kill him and return the armour to you. "

Again there was a long pause. "That is an ambitious plan," commented the deep voice from the central figure. "You must leave us to consider it. Please wait in the adjoining room."

Reynard and his friends rose and made their way back to the antechambers where they sat and waited the decision.

*

"So why are the Guild so intent on getting their hands on this armour?" asked Mosi, tightening his rope belt around his white robes before picking up a small pasty and dropping it into his mouth.

"It is enchanted," commented Tanithil from his position on a low sofa near the window. "The wearer is imbued with great powers of persuasion and leadership. There is a lot to be gained from owning such an artefact."

"To say nothing of the fact that it must be worth a fortune," said Okoth smiling his white smile.

"Agreed, the Guild could make a lot of money from selling this armour, but I think it is more than that," speculated Reynard. "This is the Armour of Lucar. It is a relic from a bygone age – a symbol of power and of past glories. If the Guild were to possess it they could push one of their own men into the forefront of Imperial politics."

"And with the emperor in his last days, now would be the right time to be gaining an interest in politics," said Tanithil pointedly, "Especially in light of what the Ebon and Ruby Houses have been getting up to recently."

"Which raises the other question," said Reynard, sipping his second glass of red. "What are the corsairs doing in attacking a training camp of Pyromancers and trying to assassinate my brother?"

"We know that your brother was in league with the Ebon House," said Tanithil, pulling his silver hair back from his face. "And obviously the Pyromancers are sponsored by House Ruby. So the corsairs appear to be attacking the covert interests of the major Houses. But why and to what end?"

"They are doing the same thing everyone else is doing," observed Heremod from where he was stood by the door, "Preparing for war."

All eyes turned to the Niten master. Reynard addressed him. "You have spent six months with them, Heremod. What do you think their agenda is?"

"I have no idea, I'm afraid. Nikolai keeps his cards close to his chest. I'm not sure that even his favoured lieutenants know what he is up to. Maybe his first mate, Baku, but actually I suspect not even him."

"Baku? The giant man who wears the bulls headed helm?" asked Reynard.

"That's him," confirmed Heremod, "but be warned: he is not a man."

"What do you mean?"

"Baku does not wear a bull's head helmet. He is a giant man with the head of a bull. He is some sort of strange aberration."

"Really?" said Mosi, brushing some crumbs off his goatee, "That sounds like something out of a children's tale."

"Well he is real enough," said Heremod. "Kester uses him as muscle and as his enforcer. Baku has no qualms. I have seen him literally rip a man's head from his shoulders. The crew on the *Moray* is very disciplined as a result. From what I could gather from the crew, Kester found Baku on Granita and impressed the beast enough to get him to join up with them. I have no idea what Baku was doing in the wastelands of Granita, or how he survived there. No one ever explained that to me. I was under the impression that nothing could survive on Granita."

Reynard raised his eyebrows in surprise, "Quite the character, this Kester. He steals the legendary Armour of Lucar and blithely wears it around the capital city for all to see. He employs a creature from children's tales to be his first mate. And he is the first captain in who knows how many years to form an alliance of the corsairs. But why attack the major political houses?"

"We know he has attacked the Ebon and Ruby houses. Perhaps he has attacked the others; perhaps not – yet. I suggest we simply don't know enough," replied Tanithil.

"In which case we have more to find out when we get to Coruba," said Reynard as the door to the Trade Lord's audience room opened and Varus entered.

"The Trade Lords will see you now," he said.

*

"It is agreed," said the Trade Lord with the deep, commanding voice. "We will send a fleet of ships to attack Coruba as you have proposed. Varus here will command the fleet. The *Javelin* will be part of it and will deploy a strike team to hit the town on foot. You will find and kill Captain Kester and bring the golden armour back to us here in Cansae. Any questions?"

"Only one," said Reynard. "When do we consider ourselves freed from your debt?"

"You will be free when the golden armour is here in Cansae, safe in our hands. Until that moment you are ours."

"You can hand it over to me when the deed is done," said Varus from his position at the side. "I'll bring it back here."

"No, Varus," contradicted the deep voice. "Captain Ferrand and his friends will bring the armour here themselves."

"As you wish," Varus replied, bowing his courtly bow to the row of hooded figures behind the table.

"Then we are in accord," said Reynard. "We will deliver the armour to you before the end of summer."

"As soon as you have it, Ferrand," commanded the deep voice. "You will bring it straight back here immediately."

"Of course," agreed Reynard, rising from his seat, "Immediately."

-Chapter Fourteen-

The *Javelin* moved out into the Southern Ocean on a south easterly heading. Before them the crew could see a large island rising from the crashing surf. They were some fifty nautical miles south of Tail of Ursum and looking upon the island of Tenos. It was an uninhabited rock of great size. About forty miles across, by a little over twenty wide, it would make for a pretty inhospitable place to live but Reynard was not sure why it had never been settled.

"Four times this rock has been settled," observed Birgen, as if reading Reynard's mind, from beside him on the forecastle. "Every time the inhabitants have built up a small community, trying to escape from the rule of the empire I guess. Every time the settlement has simply been destroyed with no survivors. No one knows who - or what - has obliterated the settlers, but now the place is simply considered cursed and no one in their right mind comes here to try and live. You can still see the ruins of the houses when you sail close by," he observed.

Reynard studied the rock as they approached. It rose on sheer cliffs some fifty feet high on this side, but the tops of them looked grassy and safe enough from what he could see. There was little or no shelter and the strong south westerly blowing from the deep ocean bent the long grass sideways. It looked cold and inhospitable.

The *Javelin* sailed around the eastern side of Tenos and as it passed around a jutting headland a flotilla of ships came into view. There were a score or so carracks and caravels all anchored off the north-eastern side of the island, taking shelter from the gale coming out of the Southern Ocean to the south west. Flags of every sort flew from the masts but the Fox and Scales of the Guild was prevalent.

Reynard had Okoth take the ship in close to the edge of the fleet and raised a hand in greeting as he sighted Varus on the prow of a large carrack called the *Dragonet*. Varus signalled for Reynard to join him on the command ship and so Reynard had the ship's boat lowered and Florus rowed him across.

An hour later the battle plan had been laid out by Varus to the assembled ship captains. They were to sail east from here to Granita and follow the coastline around to the north once they reached the desolate shore. A little distance short of Coruba the *Javelin* would split from the flotilla and would drop anchor. A small band of men – Reynard and his command crew – would row the ship's boat into shore and make the trip across land to the port on foot. Meanwhile the rest of the flotilla would approach Coruba with all running lights off. They would blockade the port, ensuring no ships could escape, and would deploy mercenaries into the town on foot to fight the corsairs there. Reynard and his band would enter the town under cover of this chaos, find Kester and kill him.

It was a simple plan and Reynard liked it. After all, he had come up with most of it himself.

*

The *Javelin* reached the coast of Granita around noon the next day. The low beaches rose gently to rocky wasteland. Sands covered much of the lands adjacent to the shore here and the winds off the Southern Ocean whipped them up into a cloud, making it impossible to see too far inland. The place was notably bereft of any plant life whatsoever. The crew could see no birds in the skies – they had seen the last seabird hours ago. It was a desolate, barren place, devoid of any life at all.

The flotilla was still together, all twenty two ships moving in a group as they skipped along on a following wind. As they reached the shore of Granita they seemed to huddle closer together, something about the island making the ship captains feel nervous and in need of close support. They turned north and followed the barren coastline towards Coruba.

The journey north along the coastline of the desolate island was entirely depressing. Waves rolled into shore and crashed into the reefs and sandy beaches as on any other stretch of the empire, but beyond the initial beach line, all the usual things one would expect to see were missing. No small settlements, no grasslands, no animals grazing, no dark forests or light woodlands. Everywhere was just wasteland, with the perpetual sandstorms restricting vision to tens of yards beyond the beaches.

As night fell the flotilla had almost reached the location Heremod had identified as the site of Coruba, the corsair base. At the agreed signal the *Javelin* broke ranks and turned to starboard and into shore. Reynard noticed many of the crew making the sign to ward off evil as they approached. Okoth brought the ship in close as he dared and then they dropped anchor. The *Javelin* rose and fell on a strong swell and the sails snapped in the onshore breeze. The sound of big waves crashing on the shore was all they could hear from the island.

The crew lowered the ship's boat. Reynard handed over control of the ship to the boatswain, Birgen and then himself, Mosi, Tanithil, Okoth, Kita and Heremod climbed down into the boat. Okoth and Reynard took up the oars and the boat moved away from the *Javelin*, turning into shore and the sound of crashing waves.

"It feels like we've been here before, little man," smiled Okoth as the two sat side by side on a bench, pulling on the oars together.

"Yes," but let's hope the guards are less brutal on this boat," replied Reynard grinning.

The small rowing boat picked up speed, pushed into shore by the swell and the powerful rowing. Okoth and Reynard, both tall and strong, were able to propel the boat quickly through the surf and they rapidly closed the distance to the shore. Overhead clouds scudded past and a full moon shone down through the gaps, illuminating the crashing waves on the shore.

Suddenly a large wave picked the small boat up and launched it shoreward. The craft was travelling at great speed now and hurtling into the beach. At that moment the clouds obscured the moon and the night grew dark. Reynard could hardly see the beach now, but he could definitely hear it. The waves were even more violent this close in. "Reverse the stroke!" he shouted to Okoth next to him, struggling to be heard above the breakers. "We need to slow this boat down!"

Too late Reynard and Okoth tried to halt the rapid movement of the small boat to shore. They tried to dig their oars in deep but the large wave had caught them. The wave grew as it drew closer to shore, the angle building as it did. The front of the boat dipped as the back rose and the passengers had to hold on to stay in their seats.

Suddenly the shore was visible, right in front of them. Reynard saw the sea rushing underneath him. The boat rose on the building wave as more water was pulled under it. The craft reached a vertical position and he felt himself about to fall out.

Then the wave broke.

The next few seconds were terrifying. Reynard was thrown from the boat. He smashed into the few inches of water under him, and then hit the sand directly underneath it. The impact forced all the air from his lungs. He was about to grab a quick breath when the breaking wave crashed into the back of him and he was underwater. He felt himself pulled back then thrown upwards and then rolled across and down, all the time not breaking the surface, still underwater. Something hard smacked into his leg. He lost all sense of direction and had no idea what was up and what was down. His lungs were starting to complain, needing fresh air.

Still being spun around by the force of the wave, Reynard was rolled forward along the sandy floor, like a rag doll, arms and legs flailing. He was getting dizzy now and his lungs were on fire. The rolling slowed and he put feet and hands out trying to figure out where the ground was. A hand touched sand and he realised he was upside down. Quickly orienting himself he placed his feet on the ground, pushing upwards. His head broke the surface and he gasped in a lifesaving gulp of air.

Then the next wave crashed into his back, smashing him back under again.

*

The group dragged themselves up on to the beach. All of them had suffered badly in the crash, but Okoth had had the presence of mind to grab the boat and pull it onto the shore before it got washed away. One of the oars was missing but amazingly enough the boat itself was still intact.

Looking around most of the party were sporting bruises of one sort or another. Reynard himself had a large welt on his leg where something had battered into him in the crash. Then Reynard heard a groan and turning saw Heremod still lying face down in the sand. Rushing over, he reached the Niten master just after Kita. Instantly Reynard could see it was bad.

"Father?" Kita said, a note of real concern breaking into her usually calm voice. "Can you hear me?" She put her hand to her mouth and closed her eyes as she saw what was wrong with him.

"Let me look at him," broke in Mosi arriving next to them and kneeling in the sand. The priest quickly examined the Niten master. Heremod's face was covered in bright red, fresh blood. His cheek was caved in and a few teeth were missing. But worse was his leg. The shin had snapped half way down and was bent at a right angle. "It is bad," he reported. "The leg is catastrophically broken."

"Can you fix it?" asked Kita looking into the priest's dark brown eyes.

"I will try, but this is a very serious injury. Quick, find me some wood – a long, straight bit. Hurry." As Kita set off along the beach looking for driftwood, Mosi withdrew his golden sun disk from inside his white robes. Looking up at the dark clouds and moonlit night he shook his head. "This is going to be difficult," he confided to Reynard. "The conditions are far from perfect for me to call on the Light's aid, but this injury will not wait till morning to fix. I need to do it now. Will you help me?" he asked.

"Of course," Reynard answered without hesitation. "What do you need me to do?"

"When I nod, I need you to straighten his leg. It will be an unpleasant experience."

"I can do that," said Reynard, looking down at the broken shin and swallowing.

"I am going to help him with the pain. Then you will straighten the leg. I will then set it in the right place and then we will lash it in place using the wood which Kita will hopefully bring. Are you ready?"

"Yes," nodded Reynard. "Let's do it."

Mosi took his sun disk in hand and began to chant softly. The disk seemed to glow slightly, as if moonlight had fallen on it, but looking up Reynard could see the moon still hiding behind dark clouds. Mosi held his other hand open, palm down, over Heremod's broken body. Slowly a soft glowing nimbus appeared to surround the fallen warrior. Reynard saw the man's crumpled face seem to relax as if the pain was lifting.

Mosi nodded and Reynard swallowed hard again. He took hold of both parts of the fractured shin and straightened them. No expert, he put the two parts of the leg together as best he could. It made him feel quite light headed.

Mosi, still chanting, moved down to the leg and indicated with his head that Reynard should give him space. The priest then released the sun disk from his hand, took hold of both parts of the shin and adjusted them slightly, bringing bone and tissue into line. His chanting increased in volume and intensity, and the sun disk, now hanging down from the priest's neck, began to glow notably brighter.

Reynard watched as the tissues and muscles in the leg slowly knitted together. Looking at the man's face he could see the bones in Heremod's cheek slowly pushing back into shape, the cut to his face healing before his eyes. Heremod seemed to relax even more and perhaps had fallen asleep.

Mosi continued to chant for a few minutes and then Kita returned with a short plank and some strips of cloth she had salvaged from the ship's boat. Mosi nodded at her and, still chanting, took the splint and cloth from her and strapped it to Heremod's leg. Finally, he stopped chanting and sunk to sit on the floor, exhausted. The soft glow in the sun disk subsided.

Heremod opened his eyes and looked up. "That was a nasty ride in," he commented.

"Are you okay, father?" queried Kita, obviously very concerned.

"Of course," he replied. "Why would I not be?" Starting to rise he noticed the splint on his leg. "Where did this come from?" he asked, looking confused.

"You have been unconscious for a little while," answered Mosi from his seat in the sand. "You broke your leg, but I have fixed it as best I can. You will need the help of the splint for a little while."

Heremod stood gingerly, testing his leg. He winched in pain unable to stop himself before anyone noticed. Kita looked on, concerned.

"You're in no fit state to fight, father."

"I'm fine," he replied, shifting his weight to his good leg.

"You need to stay here. There is no way you can be part of this raid."

"I'm coming and that is an end to it. After all I'm the only one who even knows Coruba. You need me on this one."

"He has a point," agreed Reynard. "But, sir, please allow us to help you move. We need to get going and can't afford to waste more time if we are to arrive at the port on time.

"Let's go then, and stop wasting time," said Heremod, limping off north along the beach.

*

The group nestled down in a small bowl in the rocks, looking down on the makeshift port of Coruba. The cove itself was deep, sheltered and circular, the perfect place to build a secret base. Sheer cliffs rose on all sides, rising to a height of between fifty and one hundred feet above the settlement. The angle of the entrance to the cove was such that it was protected from the worst of the incoming waves and the waters of the bay were dark and still.

The corsair port itself was a ramshackle affair. A series of wooden jetties had been constructed around the base of the cliffs in a circle, making the streets of Coruba. Wooden beams set deep into the harbour waters supported the jetties. The few wooden buildings in the settlement had been constructed on top of the jetties.

The port was dominated by a huge wooden hall, roughly in the centre of the jetties. To either side of it three or four smaller buildings had been erected. The main building was the meeting hall and centre point for the port. It was where the corsairs would be meeting this full moon. From this distance it was hard to make out quite what the purpose of any of the side buildings was. The jetties were lit by the occasional lantern and lights could be seen coming from the large central hall, which was clearly occupied. The other buildings all appeared dark in the moonlight. A few people were moving about the jetties, but for the most part it was quiet.

Nearly a dozen ships were anchored in the port and even from this distance up on the cliffs Reynard could make out the distinctive outline of one of the carracks: The *Moray* was here. A few sailors were working on various tasks on some of the ships but most were settled and still. The majority of the corsairs were clearly in the great hall involved in whatever meeting was typical for them each full moon.

Looking out to sea Reynard could just make out the silhouettes of the Guild fleet as it approached the cove. Reynard could see the *Dragonet* in the moonlight, heading the group. None of the approaching ships had any running lights showing. They were doing their utmost to come in unnoticed by those in the port, to maximize their surprise.

"Look, what's that?" asked Mosi, pointing down at the darkened Guild ships. "Some sort of light is flashing." Looking back at the ships it was just possible to make out a small light going on and off at the prow of one of the ships. As they looked closer it was clear that the light was coming from the *Dragonet*. The light would be impossible to see from any of the ships in the Guild fleet but visible to anyone in the port. Reynard and his companions could only see it because of their vantage point looking down on the town.

"Someone is signalling the port," observed Tanithil. "They are alerting the corsairs."

Seconds later a cry echoed up from the cove. Crewmen on one of the ships at anchor had spotted the light and were calling out. In the dark of night it would be hard for the men down in the port to be able to see the ships out to sea. People were straining to look out and obviously it was not yet clear to everyone in Coruba what was happening.

The light on the *Dragonet* went out and the fleet closed in on the small bay. As men began to shout and rush about in the port the Guild ships slowly closed the trap. Sailing right into the slim entrance to the cove they dropped anchor in lines, packed tightly together. The port was closed, the blockade in place.

In Coruba, the port was now fully alerted. Sailors on the docked ships were grabbing weapons. Someone ran into the huge hall at the centre of the town, shouting at the top of their voice, alerting the assembled corsairs that their settlement was under attack.

The battle for Coruba had begun.

-Chapter Fifteen-

Reynard and his companions began the climb down the cliff face into the port of Coruba. It was a fifty foot drop and they had to get Heremod to the bottom with his broken leg. They had discussed leaving him up on the cliff face, but he'd insisted on coming and Kita would not leave him behind.

As they started to pick their route down, sailors on the Guild ships lowered their boats into the sea. Armed mercenaries filled them, bristling with weapons. The men readied swords, axes, daggers and cudgels. These men were not a unified fighting force, but rather individuals and small teams who had signed up for the job because the pay was good. Their role was simply to cause chaos in the port in order to provide enough of a distraction to allow Reynard and friends to slip into the settlement unnoticed.

Reynard was trying to pick out the next section of the climb in the moonlight. They had made it nearly halfway down without incident. Now he was at the top of a tricky section. About ten feet of sheer cliff dropped down to a small ledge. The drop below that was a further twenty feet. A slip here would be fatal. He was trying to pick out holds in the darkness.

"I'll go first," said Kita, from next to him on the cliff face. She moved carefully past him on the ledge, forced to brush closely against him to do so. She smiled up at him as she moved past, her face just inches from his.

He blinked and looked down into her deep brown eyes. "Be careful," he whispered.

"Always," she smiled back.

Kita crouched down and lowered her feet over the edge. Quickly she located two foot holds and began to move slowly down, three points of her body in contact with the wall at all times. She was forced to feel her way in places, unable to see anything beneath her. Then, as she was searching for a new foothold for her right foot, her left hand slipped.

She fell away from the rock face, her left arm swinging backwards. The shift in weight caused her left leg to fall out of its small foothold and she was left hanging by the fingertips of her right hand.

Kita winced as pain flashed down her strained right arm. She could feel her fingertips begin to slip on the rock as she flailed her left arm, trying to change her momentum and get her body to swing back into the wall. Time seemed to slow as her body eventually changed direction and moved back towards the cliff. Quickly she reached out and found a handhold with her left hand. This enabled her to reposition her slipping right hand and get better purchase. She brought her feet in and planted them safely. Taking a deep breath she looked up.

Reynard was staring down at her. From this angle it looked like his face had drained of colour. He forced a smile onto his face and she returned it, feeling relief wash over her. Another half a second and she would have fallen.

She took a few more deep breaths and steadied her racing heart. From her new position she scanned the rock face. To her left she could see a large crack in the cliff which would provide a much easier route down. From Reynard's position above it was impossible to see, so they hadn't noticed it before. It looked like the overhang would be easy enough to traverse.

"Reynard," she called up to him, "there's an easy route down over there," she said indicating it with her head. "Everyone should be fine descending that, if I just point out the holds from here."

"What about your father?" he asked.

"Yes, he should be alright. Once over the small lip it's a simple traverse."

"Okay, I'll start sending them down," he replied. "I'm glad you're safe," he added so only she could hear.

They exchanged a lingering look. "Me too," she replied, smiling.

*

Down in the port the ships' boats had reached the jetties and the mercenaries were pouring out onto the wooden planking. As they climbed up from the boats the few corsairs from the anchored ships came to engage them, cutlasses and knives flashing in the light of the full moon. The superior numbers of mercenary warriors swiftly overwhelmed the corsairs and the jetties were soon swarming with Guild-paid fighters.

Suddenly the doors to the great hall burst open and out rushed a huge figure. Easily two feet taller than all those around him, and with moonlight glinting off his horns, Baku took in the scene. Seeing the jetties packed with Guild mercenaries and the row of ships blockading the harbour he bellowed an inhuman roar. He grasped his great axe in two hands, dipped his head and charged. Rushing out of the doors behind Baku came a flood of corsairs, the bulk of the men from the dozen ships at anchor. Armed with a variety of weapons from knives to axes and swords, they followed their talisman Baku out onto the jetty and crashed into the oncoming mercenaries.

Impaling two men on his horns Baku flicked his head, flinging their bodies high into the night sky to land among their companions. Swinging his huge axe with both hands he began to carve a huge swath in the ranks of the mercenary warriors swarming the decking. Men dropped back before his rage. Behind him the corsairs surged forward.

One group of mercenaries, a small band of experienced ex-soldiers who now earned their money as men-for-hire, decided to tackle the great bull. Splitting into a rough military formation they moved to flank him, swords driving and axes slashing at the giant man-thing. Baku took many wounds from their attacks but each swing of his axe felled two or three opponents and within seconds the whole mercenary band was dead. Baku was covered in blood – most of it not his own.

Everywhere on the jetty the battle raged. The mercenaries were better equipped, better trained and had better numbers. The corsairs had Baku. It looked like it would be a close fight.

*

At the base of the cliff, hidden behind a small rock fall, Reynard watched as the giant bull-man smashed into the ranks of mercenaries. Ahead the whole port of Coruba was a battle ground. Reynard and his friends were just taking a quick breather as he observed the fight.

As yet there was no sign of Kester. Assuming he was here, he must still be in the large hall in the centre of the village. As Reynard scanned the crowd he spotted a dark figure creeping towards the hall. Moving carefully from shadow to shadow, avoiding the mass melee, was an auburn haired man with a trimmed beard: Varus.

As Reynard watched, Varus reached the door to the great hall and slipped inside. What was he doing? Was he trying to kill Kester himself and take the glory? Or worse still, steal the golden armour? There was no time to consider what this meant now, it was time to move.

"Let's go," commanded Reynard to the group around him. Setting off he moved quickly into the shadows of one of the dark buildings near the cliff face. Seconds later the others joined him, Okoth helping Heremod along. The Niten master looked drawn and pale, but had not muttered a single word of complaint on the whole arduous climb down the cliff.

Reynard timed his move and rushed from one dark building to the next. The group followed in his wake. Rounding the corner of the next building Reynard almost bumped into a corsair who was heading the opposite direction, away from the battle. Fastest to react, Reynard smashed the surprised man in the face with his fist and he crumpled to the floor, unconscious. "Teach you to run from a fight," he commented as he stepped over the prone form.

Moments later they reached the door to the great hall. It was open and a corridor led inside with a few doors leading off it. Reynard drew his rapier and stepped inside, the others close on his heels. Tanithil quickly checked they were not being followed, and then closed the door behind them.

*

Moving down the hallway the group proceeded as quietly as possible. Reynard could just make out the sounds of the battle out on the waterfront. Expecting to find one big room inside the hall they were surprised to find a series of short corridors with a set of small rooms leading off them. Heremod directed them through the maze.

Soon they reached a shut door. "Behind this door is the main hall where the corsairs meet for their full moon gathering," Heremod told them, holding onto the wall for support. "If we don't find Kester in there then he has a private office in a small room behind it."

Deciding the time for stealth was over Reynard kicked the door open and rushed in.

He found himself in a large room. The floor and walls were all of the same hardwood as the rest of the building. There were no windows in the chamber. Two lanterns hanging from the walls lit the room. A few sparse wall hangings here and there broke up the uniformity and a single plant stood in a pot near one corner, looking entirely out of place. Rows of rough tables and a large scattering of chairs dotted the room, filling the space in the middle. The room looked a lot like one of the many tavern common rooms Reynard used to frequent.

Stood at the far side of the large room was Kester, in full golden armour. He was talking animatedly with Varus and a group of half a dozen or so thuggish corsairs stood nearby. All looked up as Reynard burst in.

"Did I interrupt anything important?" Reynard asked, moving into the room and behind a table.

"Ah, Captain Ferrand, so good of you to join us," smiled Kester. "Varus here was just telling me all about your plans. Cunning, very cunning," he congratulated.

"Varus you bastard, why did you turn against us?" asked Reynard, moving around the first table. "You're the one who signalled from the *Dragonet* aren't you?" Behind him the others filed into the room, spreading out. As they did so the thugs began to move forward slowly, fanning out to make a protective wall around Kester and Varus.

"Oh, don't blame poor Varus, captain," admonished Kester. "He has always just been a lackey – but a damn fine swordsman." Kester turned to the short auburn haired man beside him, "Now be a good lackey and kill Captain Reynard for me won't you, Varus?"

Varus bowed his theatrical bow, drew a razor sharp rapier and moved towards Reynard.

Reynard waited until Varus was within range then grabbed one of the chairs next to him and threw it at the advancing swordsman. Varus stepped nimbly sideways, judging the flight of the chair perfectly, letting it smash onto the floor behind him. He had not even slowed at all.

"I suggest you try using a sword, Ferrand," he mocked.

Reynard dropped into a defensive stance and waited.

As Varus reached the other side of the table nearest Reynard the auburn man suddenly sprang up onto a chair and on to the table top in two quick strides. Then he was jumping down at Reynard from a position of unexpected advantage, blade thrashing down. It was all Reynard could do to parry, stumbling backwards. Blocking a follow up strike Reynard retreated a few steps.

Behind Varus, Kita and Okoth moved to engage the half dozen thugs defending Kester. These men were well trained warriors and the pick of Kester's crew. Facing three men apiece would normally be very dangerous odds. Facing three well trained fighters would mean death for most people. But Kita was a Niten student and one of the best that school had seen in generations. And Okoth was the Champion Gladiator of Nubia. The corsairs never stood a chance.

"Your friends are being butchered," pointed out Reynard as Varus advanced.

"They are neither my friends, nor my concern," replied the shorter man. "All I care about is your death. And that is coming soon," he continued, launching into a wicked series of strikes, thrusts and slashes. Many swordsmen used known combinations when fighting. If you were well trained and experienced you could often anticipate their moves. Varus, however, simply improvised. He was unpredictable, wild and seemed to lack any care for his own safety. As such he was lethal.

Reynard fell back before the onslaught, desperately parrying each thrust and lunge. He didn't have time for a single riposte; such was the speed and ferocity of the assault. Varus was like a man possessed. He seemed to care nothing for his own safety, leaving gaping holes in his defence. However, to take advantage of such a hole would mean coming in range of his flashing blade. It would mean death.

Reynard moved rapidly backwards, trusting to his good footwork to keep him out of range; to keep him safe. He worked his mind frantically trying to come up with an angle, some advantage whereby he could turn the tables. But he could think of none. It was taking all his attention just staying alive. And he wasn't sure how long he could keep that up.

*

Kita slashed downwards, the blade of her *katana* cutting the last man from shoulder to hip. He collapsed to the hardwood floor, guts and entrails spilling everywhere. Looking up she saw Okoth was lifting the last of his opponents off the floor with his spear. He had thrust it right into the man's belly and out of his back. Swinging the spear sideways Okoth slid the dead corsair off the end and into a pair of chairs nearby smashing one and knocking the other flying.

Kita looked at Okoth, nodded and turned to face Kester. Okoth did the same. There was no one between them and the man in gold. A few tables and some chairs separated them.

"Varus, to me – now!" commanded Kester.

Glancing back to look over at Reynard, Kita saw him pinned back against a table. As Varus pressed his advantage, Reynard was desperately parrying thrust after thrust. He had nowhere to go and was bent back across the table, his shoulders almost on the table top. Varus knocked Reynard's blade sideways and was about to skewer the tall Lucarcian when he heard Kester's call.

Ignoring Reynard totally, Varus spun on his heel and prepared to rush back to Kester's side. Reynard had a moment of doubt at what he was about to do, then pushed it aside and drove his rapier right into Varus' unprotected back. The auburn haired man staggered, looked down at his chest where the point of Reynard's sword was sticking out, and dropped dead.

*

With Kester's crew defeated it appeared the fight was over. Mosi helped Heremod forward, putting his arm around the injured man's shoulder. He was amazed at the warrior's constitution. Only an hour or two earlier he had suffered a terrible fracture of his shin, yet here he was, still hobbling around on it. Of course the Light's power had helped – fusing the bone and mending some of the tissue around it – but Mosi knew his connection to his god was weakest at night so the healing was incomplete. An injury like the one Heremod had sustained would have stopped most men for weeks.

The two moved forward into the large hall, Tanithil at their side. Ahead Kita, Okoth and Reynard were surrounding the golden armoured man. He was making no efforts to run, nor did he look like he was about to fight. His rapier remained in its gem-studded scabbard.

"It's over, Kester. There is nowhere to run and you're outnumbered," said Reynard, standing at the front of the group, his family rapier in hand. "It's time to surrender."

"Hardly, old man," smiled Kester, appearing unperturbed by the developments. "After all, I have you surrounded," he continued, indicating the doorway behind them.

Turning to look, Mosi saw the huge hulking form of Baku ducking through the wooden doorway into the hall. "Time to make ourselves scarce," he said to Tanithil, grabbing the silver haired man and dragging him to the side and safety. Kita and Okoth exchanged a single glance and turned to face Baku, heading off in the bull's direction, drawing weapons as they went. Heremod limped after them.

"Alone at last, Reynard," said Kester smiling again, slowly drawing his jewelled rapier. The lantern light glinted off the razor sharp blade.

"So it would seem," Reynard replied, launching a lightning fast lunge, trying to catch the golden armoured man off guard.

"You'll have to be quicker than that, my friend," said Kester, rapier slashing down and to the side, easily deflecting the attack.

"I intend to be," said Reynard.

The two fencers went through an opening exchange. From his position at the side of the hall, Tanithil watched in awe at the speed of the blades. The two swords flashed in the dim light, sparks occasionally flashing as they touched and parted. Tani had trained with some of the best in his time in the Thought Guard, and although he had never been a very good swordsman, he knew skill levels when he saw them, and the two men before him now were both masters.

Reynard was never one to show all his cards in a duel. He believed in always keeping something in hand, ready to draw on if the need arose, but he quickly realized he would have to hold nothing back if he was to survive this encounter. Reynard prided himself on his quick feet. His opponent was wearing a full set of plate armour, made from heavy gold. Kester should have been slow – very slow – but his footwork was even better than Reynard's. He moved as if he was wearing an outfit of the lightest Honshu silks, not a lump of heavy metal. Reynard upped the attack, going full on the offensive. Determined to finish this quickly, he took Kester through a short series of attacks and parries, finishing by manoeuvring

Kester's blade out wide and then struck a solid, direct thrust into the corsair's midriff. The blade struck home.

*

Kita and Okoth moved across the hall, splitting up. They weaved their way through the tables, heading for the door and their new opponent. Baku stepped into the room and rose to his full height. He was well over seven feet tall and just as wide. The great axe he carried was almost as big as he was. Close up and personal, they could see that Baku was a fearsome beast. He had the head of a huge bull, with massive horns and red eyes, and the body of an enormously muscled man. He wore nothing save a loin cloth. Kita and Okoth glanced at each other and a look of worry passed between them. This was no normal enemy.

Okoth moved in, jabbing his spear for the giant's belly. Baku moved quickly for such a huge beast, blocked easily with his axe haft and swung mightily at the Nubian. Okoth parried in turn but such was the force of the aberration's blow that the warrior was smashed back, falling to the floor. He landed on his back and Baku took a step forward over him, raising his axe.

*

Reynard's rapier, an heirloom forged in the fires of the Iron Fortress, and one of the strongest blades in the empire, simply bounced off the breastplate of the golden armour. The armour didn't even have a scratch.

"Good armour, eh?" smiled Kester as Reynard's strike was thwarted. Taking the offensive, the corsair pressed forward, his rapier a blur. Reynard worked furiously to fend him off, moving backwards and away. Kester pushed hard, giving Reynard no space or room to breathe.

Reynard was dancing backwards, making full use of his good footwork, wending his way through the tables. He toppled a chair into Kester's way as he passed it, but Kester merely kicked it aside, continuing to advance. The chase took them to the corner of the room near the door where the others battled.

Suddenly Reynard found himself by the lone plant pot and stepped behind it, seeking a moment's respite from the attack. Kester's rapier flashed out horizontally at Reynard, who didn't see it coming from behind the leaves.

At the last possible moment Reynard saw the glint of lantern light flash off the rapier. He ducked and the blade missed him by a hair's breadth, cutting the plant in half. Reynard raised an eyebrow at Kester, rising slowly behind the shortened shrub.

"I never liked that plant." Kester kicked out and the plant pot toppled, rolling across the wooden floorboards towards the nearby door. Kester renewed his attack, nothing between him and Reynard any longer. The young noble backed away again, parrying and blocking for his life.

*

Kita darted in and attacked the aberration from behind as he stood over Okoth. Sensing her at the last moment Baku whirled quickly and blocked her *katana* with his axe, but Kita's *wakizashi* scored a minor gash in the giant's thigh. Baku roared in pain and threw out a backhand which caught Kita across the cheek and sent her flying backwards. She landed hard and struck her head on the wooden floor, seeing stars.

Okoth pushed himself up from the floor and screamed to get Baku's attention. He charged forward, spear lashing out. Baku spun back to Okoth and easily blocked the Nubian's thrust with the thick haft of his axe. Tossing his head the bull tried to gore the Nubian with his horns. Okoth ducked quickly and stepped back, spear poised.

Kita stood up, shook her head to clear it, and moved warily back into position, swords ready. The two warriors circled Baku and looked for an opening.

Kita and Okoth nodded to each other. Okoth launched another attack, swinging his spear around in an arc. As he did so Kita struck out, driving both her swords in, timed to coincide with Okoth's attack. Baku moved with great speed for one so big, spinning in place, hands whirling as he somehow blocked all three attacks with the haft of his axe. He followed up with a huge two handed sweep of his axe, spinning on his heel. The axe travelled in a full circle and both his opponents had to leap back to avoid getting struck.

Dropping his shoulder, Baku drove into Okoth, striking him full in the chest, sending the big man sprawling. Okoth flew backwards, landed heavily on his back and crashed into the toppled plant pot, his head striking the porcelain hard. The pot cracked open, spilling earth and the remains of the plant onto the floorboards. Next to it, Okoth blinked twice and collapsed unconscious.

*

Reynard was breathing heavily now. Kester was driving him across the hall and it was taking all his skill and dexterity to stay alive. The corsair was a master fencer and even when Reynard was able to breach his defences he had solid armour to protect him. Reynard had no such luxury and was relying on his ability to keep him safe. So far it had not let him down but it was just a matter of time.

Kester began a combination of attacks which Reynard didn't recognise. Relying on his skill and reactions, Reynard parried as best he could, trying to keep a safe distance from Kester's flashing blade. The corsair backed Reynard right into the corner. Reynard's back hit the wall and he realised he had nowhere to go.

"There's nowhere to run, Reynard. This time, you die," taunted Kester.

Reynard had to agree.

Kester pressed the attack. "Time to end this I think, Reynard," he said, lunging at the noble.

With nowhere to go, Reynard gambled. Tumbling forward under Kester's lunge, he rolled past the corsair's side and came up behind him. "Couldn't agree more," said Reynard striking Kester in the back with his blade. The corsair stumbled slightly forward, off balance and Reynard moved back out of range. Kester spun and lunged at the retreating noble but Reynard leapt, going over a table and scrambling down the other side. Kester kicked out at the table and sent it toppling into Reynard who caught it and propped it up on its side between them.

"You had best come up with a good plan, Reynard," said Kester, "as I can't see how you can possibly beat me. You're a competent fencer, for sure, but I'm better. And I wear the golden Armour of Lucar. Any ideas how this can end well for you?"

"I'm working on it, trust me"

*

From behind Baku, Kita rushed in and struck. Her *wakizashi* plunged into the giant's back. Baku screamed in agony and spun, axe levelled at Kita's neck, aiming to decapitate her. Only Kita's exceptional reflexes saved her life. She was able to get her two blades up into the line of the attack. There was no way she could block the sheer power of the blow, but she was able to deflect the axe head so that the shaft, rather than the blade, hit her. It was still enough to smash her backwards, off her feet and into the wall behind her. She slumped down into a sitting position, the wind knocked from her body, her head spinning.

Baku took a step forwards and, looming over Kita, brought his huge two handed axe high above his bestial head ready to finish her.

Baku's axe fell with all the strength and leverage the seven foot tall monster could bring to bear, straight down towards Kita's head.

The axe deflected off Heremod's razor sharp *katana*.

The Niten master stepped between Baku and his daughter, fingers stinging from the blow of the giant's axe. "If you want her, you will have to go through me," he said, looking up at the huge aberration.

"No, father! You're too badly hurt!" shouted Kita, trying to get to her feet. She propped herself up on one arm, then slumped over again. Her head was spinning and her ears were ringing terribly. Trying again she got to her feet this time, but her legs were not her own to control. She wanted to step forward, to come alongside her father and to stand beside him against the enemy, but her legs would not obey and she fell back into the wall again, struggling for balance.

Baku once again raised his huge axe, both hands high above his head. Again he brought the entire force of his power to bear and clove the axe downwards at Heremod, who stood defiantly before him, his *daisho* raised in defence.

Reynard stepped out from behind the table. Planting his feet into a comfortable stance be began an attacking sequence. This sequence was the same one he had used to defeat Captain Waverley on the *Hammerhead* all those weeks ago at the beginning of this mad adventure. Now he hoped it would save his life, at the end.

Kester smiled as he recognised the pattern. "You know how this ends, don't you, Reynard? You force my defence low and then strike down, hoping that I'm not good enough to parry the opening your pattern creates for you. Sadly for you," he continued, blocking and moving as directed by the combination, "I know this pattern and I know the correct block. Furthermore, I know the deadly counter. Twenty seconds from now your guts will be spilling out across the floor."

"That's what you think," said Reynard, bursting into action. Instead of following the pattern Kester was expecting, Reynard grabbed the corsair's weapon wrist with his left hand. Twisting Kester's right arm sharply the noble stepped in next to Kester and drove his right hip into the corsair's midriff. Pulling Kester's right hand forward across his chest, Reynard flicked his hip and threw Kester over and onto his back. As he did so Reynard twisted Kester's grip and prized the corsair's rapier from his grasp. Kester crashed onto the floor and Reynard stepped over him, the points of two rapiers pushed into the small gap in the neck of the golden armour.

"I learnt that move watching Kita teach my crew to fight," said Reynard, triumphant.

*

Baku's axe crashed down onto the Niten master. Heremod brought both his swords up to block the blow. The phenomenal power of the monster drove the swordsman down into the floor. The Niten master's broken leg simply snapped under the immense force and any chance Heremod had to support his parry was gone. His arms buckled and the axe smashed into his head, splitting it in half like a ripe melon.

"No!" A long and agonized scream came from Kita and she staggered to her feet and rushed to her father's side, her own danger forgotten.

Baku stepped back, somehow happy to let the young woman go to her dead father. The aberration looked over to where Kester was lying on his back, defeated. Nearby Okoth had come conscious again and was dragging himself to his feet. Baku was bleeding from multiple wounds and was more tired and hurt than he could ever remember being. Nodding in respect to the three warriors he had faced; he turned on his heel, ducked out of the doorway and headed back out onto the wharf.

*

"Well done, old chap," praised Kester. "Nice move. She taught you well. But, come now," he continued, looking deep into Reynard's eyes, "you and I should never have been enemies in the first place. We are so alike. In another life, you and I would have been firm friends – brothers even. I would never treat you as your true brother has. That was disgusting. I would stand beside you through thick and thin," he continued, eyes boring into Reynard's.

Reynard's mind flicked to his brother, Maynard – his scheming, plotting and cowardly brother. How much better would it have been to have had an honourable, brave and adventurous brother like Kester? He withdrew the two rapiers from Kester's throat.

"Thank you old man," said Kester, propping himself up onto his elbows. "And why not now, in fact? We could still work together against the Trade Lords."

By this time, Mosi and Tanithil had approached, listening to what Kester was saying. Behind them Okoth was carrying Heremod's body. He had draped a cloth over the warrior's head to hide the terrible damage. Kita, her face a mask, was walking along beside him.

"Kita, my dear," Kester said, eyes moving to the young woman's. "I am so sorry for your loss. Heremod was a good man. A great man. The six months we spent working together were wonderful times. He would speak of you constantly. You were a great source of pride to him. Perhaps, now, you and I should work side by side as your father and I did? I know he had some sort of goal driving him forward. No doubt you will want to continue his work. I can help you. Let us work together to finish what he started, in tribute to a great man and a wonderful father." Kester's eyes held Kita's for a long moment, not letting them go. Finally, she nodded almost imperceptibly.

Kester looked to the priest. "Mosi, the great and humble priest, I am honoured to be in your presence. I have heard so much about the fantastical healing your faith brings to those around you and in your care. My men have no one to care for them. They have no one to teach them the ways of the Light; no one to help them grow emotionally and expand their faith. Would you consider becoming the spiritual leader for this retched band of souls?"

Mosi considered the offer. His Haji had sent him here across the sea, to find out about life and faith in Lucarcia. What better way than to offer his services to this heroic figure who spoke so eloquently? These men needed guidance. They would gain so much from the Light's knowledge and warmth. How could he refuse? "I would be honoured," he said.

"And Tanithil," Kester continued, his deep blue eyes flicking to Tani's violet ones and holding him long in his gaze. "You need stability, solid ground on which to thrive. I know of your addiction and your brave fight to resist the evil temptations you face every single day. I admire your courage. Not the courage of the tall, strong warriors around you, but a silent courage; courage of defiance. I can offer you consistency, a safe harbour, a steady environment. Working with me you need not worry. We can work through it, you and me. I have been there and know what it is like to face yourself every day, to steel yourself for the coming battle each and every sunrise. We can face it together. What do you say?" asked Kester, his face still staring intently into Tanithil's.

Tanithil looked around him at the others in the group, and simply nodded, his face impassive.

"Excellent. And finally, Okoth," he said, eyes flicking to the tall black-skinned Nubian. "You are a runaway, far from home, and know you can never return. The Rodinians made sure of that when they put a bounty on your head. The best gladiator to ever come out of your country and they hunt you like a wild animal. I can offer you a family. You will be welcome in our brotherhood as an equal. You will never be a slave again. You will have a new family, here among the salt of the earth. People like you; people like those you grew up with. What could be better than a life free from slavery and in the bosom of a new family? Perhaps we could even organize to bring your family here to Lucarcia, away from the terrible conditions they face at home?"

Okoth thought back to his family at home, to his wife and daughter. He missed them terribly. He wondered what they were doing right now. It would be wonderful indeed if the golden man was able to bring his family here. And even if he could not, Okoth knew he longed for freedom and family life again. Why not with these sailors? As the golden man had said, these were his kind of people. He smiled his straight white smile and nodded.

"We have a common enemy. The Trade Lords are the real evil here, after all," Kester continued, looking intently from face to face, staring each of them in the eye. Okoth laid Heremod reverently down on the floor as Kester spoke. "They made slaves of you all and you are *still* their slaves. Why not rise up against them? Join with me and my men. Set yourselves free!" he urged.

Reynard looked around at his friends and saw that they were all nodding at Kester's suggestion. He offered the corsair a hand and Kester took it. "You make a lot of sense, Kester," he said, smiling his easy smile and pulling the corsair to his feet.

"Let's go and take the fight to the evil Trade Lords!" encouraged Kester. "The mercenaries out there on the wharf are Guildsmen. Let's get out there and do something about it. Destroy the evil mercenaries fighting my men and we will have struck our first blow against their tyrannical masters! Are you with me?"

"Yes!" the group cried in unison, drawing their weapons.

*

Mosi drew his *kopesh*. He had hardly used the weapon in anger since his Haji had sent him across the seas to the Empire of Lucarcia. Now he felt it was time to fight – to stand up for what was right. The golden man was right. The Trade Lords and their evil slavery was the real enemy. This was a cause Mosi could get behind. The golden man was a man Mosi could follow. He felt the blood rise in his veins and his temples throbbed. Beside him he saw the others stirred to action, all drawing their weapons and heading for the door back out to the port.

Mosi saw Tanithil quickly search a nearby table. He wondered what Tani was doing. Why choose now to search a table when there was a holy fight to be fought? He saw Tanithil pick up a silver letter opener. Ah, of course. Tani was unarmed – now he had a weapon. Not a great weapon maybe but with the Light's aid, even a humble letter opener could make a difference. A silver letter opener for the silver haired man. It was poetic somehow.

The group followed Kester to the door of the long room. He led them on through the short series of corridors back to the main door which led out into the port. Kester put his hand on the handle and prepared to open it. "Are you ready my warriors?" he asked them.

"Yes!" they cried together, weapons drawn, preparing to rush out into the town and fight off the Guild invaders.

Suddenly Tanithil loomed up behind Kester. Mosi saw his arm rise and fall quickly, the silver letter opener in hand. Kester cried out in shock and pain as the tiny improvised knife drove deep into his neck, finding a small gap in the heavy golden armour. Kester clutched at his wound as blood flowed freely through his fingers. He slumped to his knees.

"Mosi... Help me..." the corsair implored.

Mosi was about to rush to the golden man, to call upon the Light's aid to heal the stricken hero. He took a step forward. Tani put out a hand, grasping Mosi's arm as it reached inside his robes to withdraw his holy sun disk.

"Not this one," said Tanithil intently. "This one you let die."

Mosi wanted to argue, wanted to explain that the golden man was a hero; that he was leading them to battle against the evil Guild. But of course, they had come here with the Guild to attack this place. In fact, they had come here with the sole purpose of finding the man in the golden armour. Moreover their goal was simply to kill Captain Kester and recover the armour to return to the Trade Lords, so they could win their freedom.

Looking down Mosi saw the sun disk in his hand and the body of Captain Nikolai Kester at his feet, dead. Now he understood how Kester had managed to enthral so many corsairs and inspire such unswerving loyalty in them.

The Armour of Lucar was truly an artefact of stunning power. And now it was theirs.

-Chapter Sixteen-

Out in the fresh night air, stood on a jetty in Coruba the group gathered around Tanithil. "How did you know what Kester was up to, Tani?" asked Reynard.

"I didn't at first," said the silver haired man. "But then I heard some of the rubbish he was spouting and saw your reactions and I quickly realised he had ensorcelled you somehow. As I told you before, the Armour of Lucar was rumoured to have powers of leadership. I think we have seen for ourselves that it is far more than that."

"How come you were not affected?" asked Reynard, embarrassed that he had fallen for the glamour, arcane or otherwise.

"Simple training," shrugged Tanithil. "One of the first things they teach you in the Thought Guard is how to keep your mind defended. Never let anyone or anything in. It is so ingrained I hardly even noticed I was doing it."

"Well, I knew the emperor's guards' loss was our gain Tani. You would make your teachers proud," congratulated Reynard.

Tanithil smiled in thanks. "So, what now?" he asked uncomfortable with all the attention and trying to change the subject.

Reynard looked about him. Coruba was theirs. The corsairs were defeated, most killed but many surrendered. The Guild mercenaries had corralled the survivors and had them penned up in one of the outbuildings under guard. With Varus dead the Guildsmen had turned to Reynard as their leader.

"We need to search this place and find out what we can about the corsairs and their purpose. They had an agenda and I still don't understand what it was. Kester had an office back in the hall, perhaps there will be some information there."

"And we need to deal with Kita," said Mosi, putting a hand on Reynard's shoulder. "I think you are best suited for the task."

Reynard looked over to where the young Niten warrior was sitting, legs dangling over the wharf side, staring into the dark depths of the harbour. She had not said a word since her father's death and had refused to speak to anyone, not even the priest, Mosi.

"That may take some time," said Reynard. "I think for now she needs to be given space and time, and left to herself. Let's get on and search the office."

"One more thing," added Okoth, "Baku is missing."

"Not exactly," corrected Tanithil, pointing up at the cliff at the back of the port. All eyes turned to look. High above the great hall at the top of the cliff, silhouetted in the light of the full moon, was a huge figure. The bull-headed man shook his axe down at the assembled Guildsmen, turned and strode off into the wastes of Granita.

*

"Look here," said Tani, picking up a thick leather-bound book. "This looks like it could have something interesting in it." He handed the tome to Reynard and returned to searching through the papers on the desk.

The group – all bar Kita – were in the room at the back of the hall in Coruba. This was Nikolai Kester's personal office and there were lots of books and papers to sort through. Most of the books were studies on sailing, ship warfare and geography. A few were notably about the collapse of the Rainbow Empire and the formation of the Lucarcian Empire. The papers were cargo ledgers and various messages and missives to and from the captains in Kester's fleet.

From what they could discern Kester had thirty ships in his fleet of which only a dozen had been present when they blockaded the harbour here. So they had killed the leader of the corsair fleet and killed or captured perhaps a third of his men. But had they completely destroyed the corsair threat? And what was Kester's true purpose in forming his fleet? This they were yet to determine.

Reynard flipped the book Tani had passed him over in his hand. It was well worn leather, soft and brown and felt well cared for. Opening the cover he discovered a folded piece of paper placed carefully inside the front sleeve. He opened it and scanned it. It was a short letter.

My Dearest Nikolai,

I hope this letter finds you in good health. It has been such a long time since I have seen you. You have not visited us in many

long months. It would please us greatly to speak to you in person again after all this time. Please do come as soon as you are able. Your loving aunt,
Lily.

Reynard wondered if there was any significance to the letter but decided not to worry about it too much at that time. Turning the paper he read the first page of the leather bound book. It was clearly a personal journal. Curiously the very first entry in the diary described going to the palace in Ibini and visiting the Verdant Queen, Lily Jade. The date was some twelve months ago. Was it possible that the Aunt Lily from the letter was actually the Verdant Queen, ruler of the island of Ibini and head of the noble Jade House?

Reynard wracked his brains. There was no Kester family on Ibini that he could think of. Did Lily Jade have any nephews? If his memory served him well there was an obscure family related to the Verdant Queen by marriage. They were the Terkes family, Reynard seemed to remember, and there was a young man in that family by the name of Nikki.

Nikki Terkes. Nikolai Kester. Swap the two syllables and Terkes became Kester. It was too much to be a coincidence. Captain Nikolai Kester, commander of the corsair fleet, was the Verdant Queen's nephew.

Reynard scanned more of the journal. Following on immediately after his visit to see the Verdant Queen, Kester had written pages describing how he had begun to put together a fleet of ships. It had taken him months to do so, travelling around the empire, speaking to certain captains who he knew or suspected of being corsairs, bribing, coercing and generally convincing them to form a loose band together for mutual profit and gain.

Reynard kept reading. Later in the journal he found an entry describing how the *Moray* had been blown off course in a fierce storm and ended up discovering the natural harbour of Coruba almost by chance. Kester had then encouraged the corsairs to build a small settlement there and use it as a meeting point.

Reynard flipped some more pages talking of normal raids and attacks on small villages and a few Guild ships or privateers. Then he saw mention of Baku and flipped back until he found the passage where Kester and Baku had met. According to the journal, the *Moray* had sailed into

Coruba one day only to find the huge aberration sitting on the wharf, seemingly waiting for them. Kester had approached warily, and after a strange conversation – it appeared Baku spoke no languages but did understand Kester – Baku had joined the corsairs on their ship. He had shown unswerving loyalty to Kester and was an excellent bodyguard so Kester had eventually promoted Baku to first mate.

Further pages went on to describe the day-to-day activities of the *Moray* and the fleet in general. Then another page took Reynard's interest. It described a meeting between a warrior from across the sea who had approached them and asked to be taken on board. Kester had spoken to the man at length asking why he should be taken on. The man had said he would work for free, just requiring food and lodgings. In return he said he would work as a soldier for the corsair leader, fighting his fights and killing whoever he was asked to kill. Kester had tested the man – had sent 6 of his men against him – and the man had bested them all in seconds. Kester had hired him on right away. His name was Heremod.

The next section of the journal was very interesting. It talked about getting some instructions from Aunt Lily and about planning an attack on a specific Guild ship. The target: a suit of golden armour. According to the diary the plan had gone perfectly and the armour, and a sizable amount of Guild money, had been recovered. So it seemed that if the Verdant Queen was behind this corsair fleet, she had also directed Kester to recover the Armour of Lucar.

The entries following began to be more familiar now as Reynard read about the raid on the Pyromancer School in Tunis, followed by a description of the attack on Providentia. Reynard was amused to read about himself in the journal, finding himself described as "the earl's youngest brat." That entry mentioned Heremod's loss and assumed death at the hands of the Iron House. Clearly Kester had been too busy diving through a three hundred year old stained glass window to notice that Heremod and his daughter were reuniting, not fighting to the death.

Reynard was reaching the end of the journal now and was interested to find some notes towards the back where Kester had been musing on his plans for the future. According to the diary, Kester's next plan was to send men to scour the island of Manabas, the seat of the Ice King, in an effort to find the Ice King's heir, Darian Snow. Darian had gone missing years ago, and no one really knew where he had gone or what he was up to. Kester had made notes that he wanted to track down the Ice King's heir and discover what he was doing. The plans seemed fairly vague and weren't of great interest to Reynard anyway.

Reynard turned to the final entry in the journal. He read it carefully twice, not really sure what it meant.

Something is going on here. The supposedly lifeless island of Granita is proving to be anything but. I am noticing an increasing number of weird beasts and aberrations appearing on the edge of the cliff face. Last week a giant insectoid thing scuttled right into town and it devoured four men before we could kill it. I have never seen it's like before and hope I never do again. The increase in this strange activity is making me wonder if the hideaway of Coruba is really as safe as we once thought. It might be time to find a new base.

Granita was supposed to be a deserted and lifeless wasteland. After the Magi destroyed the gate at the time of the Writhing Death and the tidal wave washed everything from the island, nothing could grow. There had been nothing at all living on this island for five hundred years. Or so people had assumed. Now, with the corsairs beginning to settle there they had seen signs of strange creatures. As Kester had put it, something was definitely going on.

*

Later the same night, the group were back on board the *Javelin* in the comfort of the captain's lounge. Once again Kita had refused to join them, instead going off to her cabin and solitude. They had finished their investigations of Kester's office in the settlement. They had found nothing more detailed than the journal, but that information was proving very useful.

In another room behind the main hall they had found four large chests stuffed full of corsair treasures. Coins from all across the empire, jewellery, paintings, sculptures and bags stuffed full of valuable gemstones made up the collection. One of the things Reynard had to decide was what to do with the hoard.

"So you think the Verdant Queen is behind the corsair threat?" asked Tanithil sipping at his glass of red wine.

"Yes, that is my reading of the situation," replied Reynard. "Captain Nikolai Kester is almost certainly Nikki Terkes, the Verdant Queen's nephew. And there are too many references to Aunt Lily and a visit to the Verdant Palace in his diary. It's too much to be a coincidence."

"Yes, I think you're right," mused Tani. "In fact, if you think about it, the corsairs attacked the interests of the Ruby House when they attacked the Pyromancers. They struck at the interests of the Ebon House when they tried to kill your brother. And the diary mentions trying to track down the whereabouts of the Ice King's heir. So the corsairs have been striking at the interests of all the major noble houses, apart from the Jade House. That is another indication they are in league."

"Yes, good point," agreed Reynard, stroking his chin. "So, what do we do next?"

"I'm going to try and find Baku," answered Kita unexpectedly from the doorway.

"Kita? What? Why?" asked Reynard, rising to his feet. "Your father would not want you to risk your life for revenge, Kita."

"Not for revenge, but because my father would have done so, had he been here," she said solemnly, stepping into the room. Taking a deep breath she continued. "About a year ago father was approached by an old friend of his, a man named Camero. This man is a *wu-jen*, an arcanist, a worker of magic. He is a very powerful and well educated man." Tani and Reynard looked at each other. Study of the arcane had been forbidden in the Empire of Lucarcia for five hundred years. Of course Kita and Heremod came from another part of the world, far across the seas, and there were rumoured to be some powerful practitioners of the mystic arts in those distant places.

They looked back to Kita who was continuing. "He belongs to a cadre of like-minded, powerful people from across the world that has made it their business to look into any potential threats to the safety of the planet. Camero came to my father and told him the story of the Writhing Death which emanated from this very island some five hundred years ago, telling him that it was the greatest threat to the safety of this continent in all the known ages.

"Camero told him that he had reason to believe something had occurred on this island recently and that the ancient Gate, which history said had been broken at the collapse of the Rainbow Empire, had not perhaps been completely destroyed as was told. He was concerned that the Gate has now somehow opened again and that the threat of the Writhing Death is not entirely gone."

Kita moved over to the desk and poured herself a glass of wine. Reynard offered her the seat he had been in, but she declined. The others waited patiently for her to continue. "Camero bid my father to leave home and travel to this continent," said Kita from her new position by the desk. "He asked him to find a way to get onto this island and determine the truth behind the things he had heard. He wants facts. That is why my father came here."

Taking a deep draw from her wine glass Kita finished, "It is clear from the journal that something is indeed afoot on this island. I'm going to see if I can track Baku and find out what it is for myself, first hand, so I can report back to Camero."

"What?" exclaimed Reynard, amazed. "You can't do that. We have to get this armour back to the Trade Lords in order to win our freedom," he said, pointing to the suit of golden armour which stood on an armour stand near the middle of the room. "We have chased Kester half way around the empire searching for this artefact and now we have found it you want to wander off into the middle of a deserted wasteland, rather than heading back to the empire and handing it over to its true owners?"

"Actually, the Trade Lords are not its true owners," contradicted Tanithil. "The armour belongs to the emperor. It is an heirloom from his ancestor the Emperor Lucar. The corsairs may have stolen it from a Guild ship but the Guild should not have had it in their possession in the first place."

"That's probably true," agreed Reynard, "but we have an agreement to return it to the Trade Lords in order to get out of their debt. I'm not sure I care if it is truthfully theirs or not. But that is beside the point. The point is why are we talking about exploring this wasteland of an island and not about heading back to Cansae and winning our freedom?"

"I'm choosing to continue my father's quest. I will deal with the consequences later. This is far more important."

Reynard considered. The last thing he wanted to do was to leave Kita behind. She was part of their team and he knew he cared for her, but he wasn't sure quite how deep his feelings ran. She wanted to complete her father's task to find out what was going on here on Granita. And Reynard did not want to abandon her here.

"How long will you need on the island?" Reynard asked.

"A few days, a week at most," replied the Niten warrior, shrugging. "All I need to do is track Baku and see where he goes. I suspect he is somehow important in all this. The trouble is I was never a good hunter. My skills are with the blade, not the wilderness."

"I will track Baku for you," came in Okoth. "In my country I am considered an expert hunter and the dry, dusty wilds of the Nubian plains are not so different to the lands of this island. He won't be that hard to follow."

Kita nodded her thanks to the big man.

"And I will come. I wish to find out what is going on here," said Mosi, sipping at his glass. Again Kita nodded her thanks to the priest.

"I'll join you," said Tanithil, simply.

"I suppose it is a good way to pay our respects to your father's memory," said Reynard. "I'll come too." He smiled at Kita but there was no joy in her eyes.

*

"May their souls soar to the Light," finished Mosi, concluding the ritual. The five ex-slaves gathered around a roaring pyre, heads bowed. Heremod's body lay on the top, his *daisho* alongside him. They stood on a cliff top overlooking Coruba in the dawn light. Nearby many more pyres burned. The Guildsmen were burning their dead, honouring them in the traditional ways of the men of Lucarcia. There was little wind now and the oily smoke of the burning bodies rose directly into the dawn sky above.

As Reynard watched Heremod's body burn he felt a small hand entwine with his. Looking down he saw Kita stood next to him. She was staring directly into the fire. "I'm so sorry, Kita," Reynard whispered so only she could hear, squeezing her hand gently.

"I know," he heard her murmur back. A single tear slid down her cheek and onto the ground at her feet.

*

"That's the last of the hoard," Reynard told Miles, captain of the *Hussar*, as the crew swung the last chest, supported by thick hessian ropes, onto the main deck of the four-masted carrack. The crew of the *Hussar* hustled into action, removing the ropes and dropping the chest down into the gaping hole which was the entrance to the main cargo deck.

The *Hussar* was to lead the fleet on their journey home to Cansae. Captain Miles was a tall blond Lucarcian with an easy manner and a friendly disposition. Importantly, he was also trustworthy. Reynard had selected him to lead the fleet home and carry the spoils they had recovered from the settlement of Coruba. Miles was to take the fleet back to the Trade Lord's headquarters and hand all the money over in person.

All, except the golden armour. The Armour of Lucar was staying on the *Javelin*.

"Okay then, I believe we are all set, sir," Miles reported to Reynard. "We will get this lot back to Cansae; inform the Trade Lords of our success at smashing the corsair threat and hand over the spoils we have recovered. We will inform them of Varus' treachery and will give them Kester's body as proof," he finished.

"And...?" Reynard prompted.

"Oh, yes, sorry. And we will tell them that you have found the golden armour and will be bringing it back to them presently."

"Very good," Reynard said, patting Miles on the back. "I suggest you cast off right away whilst the tides are still favourable," he offered.

"Yes, I agree," replied Captain Miles. Holding out his hand he shook Reynard's. "Good luck Captain and hurry home."

"You too captain. May you find the winds favourable," he finished.

With that Miles turned on his heel and strode off to where he could walk up a gang plank onto the *Hussar*. Minutes later the Guild fleet set sail and headed off into the west, bound for Ursum.

Later, Kita was on the wharf of Coruba going through some Niten forms. From the way she was moving through her steps, it appeared that she was on the edge of control. Okoth was down in the crew quarters packing his gear ready for the trip into the wastelands of Granita. Mosi was on the deck watching Kita go through her paces and Reynard and Tani were down in the captain's lounge arguing.

"It's simply not safe, Reynard," insisted Tanithil, keeping his voice characteristically calm but with an intense look in his violet eyes.

"You can't know that," countered Reynard, annoyed in spite of himself. Reynard wanted to put the Armour of Lucar on, to try it out, to see how it fitted. He had seen Kester wear it and move as if it was made of silk, yet the armour was made of pure gold and weighed the best part of one hundred pounds when picked up. Reynard wanted to know how it felt to wear.

"Agreed," said Tanithil, "but it's not worth the risk. We know Kester was a dangerous and evil man. He was manipulative, driven, ambitious and without morals. What we don't know was what sort of a person he was like before he put the armour on. Was he already like that or did the power of the armour itself somehow corrupt him?"

"From his journal he sounded pretty full of himself even before he had heard of the armour," pointed out Reynard. "Did you read some of the personal stuff?"

Tanithil laughed, "I did, yes but that is beside the point. I simply want to do some more research into this strange item before you start wearing it. That's all. Let me look into the history of the armour. Let's see what the legends can tell us."

"Okay Tani," accepted Reynard. "I guess you're right. It is the sensible option. But I'd still love to feel what it's like to wear it."

"Maybe one day," replied Tanithil.

Picking up his backpack, Reynard slung it over one shoulder. "We should get going. Baku already has twelve hours head start on us."

"Okoth seems confident he can track him, all the same," said Tanithil, rising from his seat and picking up his own, lighter pack.

Up on deck many of the crew were resting in the early summer sunshine. Birgen was in charge of the ship and had instructions to give the men some well-earned time off. They were nervous about spending this much time anchored off the cursed island of Granita but being given time to lounge about in the warm sunshine and have a few days off work seemed to be keeping them happy.

Reynard gathered the command group together. They each had a pack with various useful items of gear and enough rations for ten days in the wilderness. There would be no game to hunt, nor roots or vegetables to be foraged for the next week or so. They would have to rely on carrying their food and drink with them. Each person carried as much water as he or she could. Okoth and Reynard, the strongest in the team, both carried extra water for the weaker members.

"So, the plan is to track Baku down and find where he has headed off to, right?" Reynard asked Kita.

"Yes, in essence. We need to find out what is happening on this island. We'll start by tracking Baku and seeing where that leads us. If we see or find anything which trumps that move then we might change plan. I'm afraid I can't be much more specific than that. We just have to head out there and see what we find."

"Okay. So we walk out into the middle of an inhospitable wilderness on the trail of an unlikely aberration of a man with no plan about what we are going to do when we catch up with him, and no idea what we are really looking for," summed up Reynard. "That's my kind of a plan."

He was rewarded with a slight smile from Kita, and his heart soared.

-Chapter Seventeen-

The group set out from Coruba that afternoon. There was some discussion on whether they should wait till the next morning, but Okoth pointed out they were already twelve hours behind Baku and more time would only make his job of tracking the aberration that much harder.

The Nubian took the lead, taking a winding path from the cove the settlement nestled in, up on to the cliff face where they had last seen Baku, the night before. Once up there he cast around for sign and soon located some obvious foot prints in the dust. Baku was a huge creature and weighed a lot which could only help in following him.

From the top of the cliff Reynard looked out across the wastes of Granita. It was a desolate scene. Dusty ground stretched off across the land as far as the eye could see. There was no vegetation whatsoever and only different sets of craggy rock formations broke the vista at various points. Far off to the east a high ridge could be seen – perhaps a row of low hills – and that was the direction that Okoth led them.

The sun beat down on the wilderness scene and a mild wind blew in from behind them, pushing them gently along. The wind whipped occasional dust devils up as it swirled around the odd rock formation. Okoth often lost the trail as the constant mini dust clouds obscured the sign, which was already fairly minimal given the hard rocky ground they were traversing.

As night began to fall the group reached the bottom of the ridge they had spotted earlier. Okoth suggested they stop for the night as tracking in the dark would be next to impossible on this ground.

"I estimate we are now about fifteen to twenty hours behind Baku," the big Nubian told them as they sat around their small fire. "And we will drop even further behind over night of course, although, wherever Baku is, he is probably also resting now."

"You say that," came in Kita, sat with her back against a low rock, "but father told me he never saw Baku sleep in all the time he was aboard the *Moray* with him. I'm not sure he does."

"Well, either way, we can't push on at night – we will lose him," finished Okoth, pulling a blanket over himself and settling down to sleep.

*

The night passed quietly, in fact eerily so. There were none of the usual animal sounds to be heard. Reynard slept fitfully. Around midnight he woke with a start. A terrible keening sound echoed off the rocks around him. The others were also waking. Okoth grabbed his spear in alarm.

"It's been going on for some time now," said Tanithil's calm voice, coming from the darkness nearby. Reynard squinted in his direction and could just make out the silhouette of the telepath, sat on a rock just outside the firelight. Tani was taking his turn on watch. Reynard rolled out of his blanket and moved next to the silver haired man.

"What do you think it is?" he asked.

"Absolutely no idea, but it doesn't sound friendly," replied Tanithil.

"It must be about my turn on watch now," continued Reynard, "Why don't you try and get some sleep."

"Okay, thanks," came back Tanithil, getting up off the rock. "Enjoy the show."

"Show?" enquired Reynard.

Tani pointed to the brow of the ridge above them. "Yes, just keep an eye on that skyline. Good night." With that the Lucarcian returned to camp and nestled back into his blanket.

Reynard yawned, stretched and tried to get comfortable sat with his back against a rough granite rock. The others had all returned to their bedrolls and were settling down. Occasionally a keening howl, which set his teeth on edge, split the silence of the night, but it seemed very far away. It was hard to tell which direction it was coming from as it echoed around the rocks.

Suddenly a vibrant purple glow lit up the dark eastern sky. Occasional orange flashes split the darkness and there was a sense of positive energy crackling on the horizon. Reynard stared at the light show as it continued. Whatever it was, the source of it was far across the landscape, beyond the ridge at the edge of the horizon, probably some fifteen or so miles away. From what Okoth had said that was the direction that Baku's tracks led off. Perhaps they would be heading that way tomorrow.

The light show lasted about ten minutes and then calmed down and the darkness returned to the eastern skyline. The keening sound echoed off the rocks again and Reynard thought perhaps that it was getting closer but it was very hard to tell.

Reynard sat out the next two hours, listening to the occasional sounds bouncing around him and watching in fascination as every thirty minutes or so the light show restarted. After his watch was over he woke Okoth, shaking him gently from his sleep. Reynard settled back down under his blanket, his head on his pack and tried to get off to sleep. But sleep came fitfully for the noble as he pondered on the significance of the sounds and sights of the night.

*

Reynard woke to the smell of bacon frying. Getting up he found Kita cooking a light breakfast for the group. Mosi was down in a natural dip nearby, saying his morning prayers to his god. Okoth was missing.

"Where is Okoth?" asked Reynard, looking around the camp. The big Nubian's kit was all still in place, his bedroll packed up and his backpack sorted ready to travel, leaning up against a rock.

"He has gone off to look for the trail before we head out," replied Kita, not looking up from the pan where the bacon was sizzling.

"How did you start a fire?" asked Reynard, yawning and moving over to her and squatting by her side. "There is no wood in this accursed place."

"I brought some," she said, looking up at him, "just in case. And I grabbed some bacon rashers and some bread from the ship's locker too." Looking back to the pan she flipped the bacon over to start cooking on the other side.

"Good job," congratulated Reynard. "There is nothing like a bacon breakfast to set you up for the day," he continued, feeling his mouth salivating. "Only thing is, we are on rationed water and bacon always makes me thirsty."

"Well, you don't have to eat it, if you would rather cook up more oats?" Kita came back.

"Bacon in bread sounds perfect," replied Reynard. "Thank you." Rising he moved off to sit beside Tanithil who was perched on a rock outcropping looking down on where Mosi was praying. "He's very devout, isn't he?" Reynard said to Tanithil.

"What? Oh, him, yes. Very impressive," came back the distracted reply.

"You weren't actually watching him, were you?"

"No, not really. I was just thinking."

"What about?" asked Reynard, watching as Mosi gathered his robes about him and began the climb back up to the group.

"About the Armour of Lucar," said Tani.

"Go on."

"Well, we have to return it to Cansae and the Trade Lords or we risk incurring the wrath of one of the most powerful organizations in the empire. But the armour isn't really theirs. It belongs to the emperor and, upon his death, to the emperor's House. The empire is on the brink of civil war and this armour is a huge symbol. Possession of this armour could have a huge impact on the course that a civil war could take," said Tanithil.

"Agreed," said Reynard.

"What will the Trade Lords do with the armour if we return it to them, I wonder?" posed Tani.

"It's a good question and one I have been giving a lot of thought to over the last couple of days," replied Reynard, scratching at the stubble which was beginning to show on his face. "As you say, possession of the Armour of Lucar could be critical in the coming months."

"So what do you intend to do about it?" queried Tani.

"I have no idea," said Reynard, standing and turning back to the camp, "but the bacon is ready."

*

A couple of hours later the group were trudging along following Okoth. The ground was hard and dusty and they were amazed at the Nubian's ability to pick out the tiniest trace of the passage of the big creature, Baku. They had come to a steep rise and Okoth was double checking the sign.

"This Baku is a tough customer," noted Tanithil. "It seems he just waltzed right up that almost sheer cliff face ahead of us."

"So it appears, from where Okoth is checking," agreed Reynard. "And his pace doesn't seem to have dropped off at all either. Does he ever stop?"

"As I said before," came in Kita from where she was sitting, drawing deeply from her water bottle, "Father was with him for months and never once actually saw him sleep," she said. "Or eat or drink come to that."

"Definitely a strange and unusual creature," said Tanithil. "I wonder where he came from."

"Well, according to his journal, Kester picked him up on this island, back at Coruba one day," said Reynard. "But what he was doing here is anyone's guess."

"I think we will have to go around," said Okoth, returning to the group. "The sign shows that Baku climbed up this rise but I think it will be easier for us to move around it and pick up the trail on the far side. He seems to have been heading pretty much due east solidly since leaving Coruba so unless he chose this rise to deviate from his course it should be quick enough to pick it back up again."

"Okay, lead on then," said Reynard standing and shouldering his pack.

Okoth moved off to the north, circling around the outcrop of rock that Baku had apparently simply scaled. The group followed him. The sun was high in the sky and the scenery around them was shimmering in a heat haze, caused by the combination of the warm summer heat and the constant dust in the air. As the group rounded the promontory they could see the high hills on the eastern horizon, now considerably closer and growing taller by the hour.

"Are those the same hills all those lights came from last night?" enquired Tani. "I'm a bit disoriented here with all the dust and heat haze."

"Yes, I believe so," replied Reynard, squinting into the middle distance.

"How long to reach them do you think?" came back Tanithil.

"Three, maybe four more hours," replied Okoth from the front of the group. "We should reach them before the sun sets. Hopefully we'll get to the top and be able to see what lies beyond whilst there is still light. If we keep up a good pace, that is."

"Best press on, then," advised Reynard.

Okoth soon picked up the trail of the giant Baku and it was still continuing in a generally easterly direction. Occasionally he varied his course slightly left or right but the overall direction he was heading was still easterly and still towards the hills. Reynard couldn't help notice his heading was also still towards where the strange lights had been coming from in the night.

The group travelled on into the afternoon. It was early evening when they reached the bottom of the high ridge which they had been heading for all day. A simple switch back trail climbed up the side of the rock face and Okoth indicated that Baku had gone this way many hours previously.

"We are getting slowly further and further behind," warned Okoth, looking up from his position squatting down by the trail. "I would say he is now nearly a full day ahead. I'm losing his trail regularly, and only pick it up again due to the fact that he is travelling in a pretty predictable direction. In fact I think it is safe to say that most of the time I'm guessing as to his route and occasionally I pick up sign to show that my guesses have been right."

"Well, it certainly looks like our option now is to press on up this ridge, following the trail – if that's where he went. I suggest we get to the top of the rise and see what we can see from there, and then decide on our next move," said Reynard.

"Agreed," said Okoth. "That was what I was about to suggest anyway. But I don't like the look of those dust clouds in the west," he said, standing and pointing back the way they had come.

Reynard turned and looked over his shoulder. Far off in the west he could see a large dark cloud. It was funnel shaped and seemed to be moving at speed across the wasteland. And it was coming their way. "How long till that gets here?" he queried.

"If it is anything like the dust storms which ravage the north of my country," said Okoth, "then I would guess it will be here before dark. I would say we have an hour, maybe two, to climb up into these hills and find some shelter. Either that or we hunker down here and wait till it gets here."

"But the storm might pass us by of course," reasoned Reynard, "and we are wasting time not following Baku. Plus if it does pass by here it is going to destroy any remaining sign and we'll be blind. I think we need to press on."

"Makes sense to me, little man," smiled Okoth.

"Let's go then."

They began the steep climb up the path in single file. Okoth took the lead, stopping to check for any signs that Baku had passed by every hundred yards or so. Everything he saw seemed to show that the huge man had come this way so he reduced the frequency of his checks and concentrated on the climb, trusting to pick up the trail when they reached the top or if the track split.

As they rose higher into the hills the winds began to pick up and the dust started to swirl. Soon Okoth stopped them and warned them all to wrap a scarf around their faces, telling them that the grit and dust would get into their throats and noses and be very painful, to say nothing of making them need more of the precious water they were carrying.

Once they were all suitably protected they resumed the climb. Reynard could feel the sweat dripping down his back as he toiled. The evening heat was still present and the climb was steep and relentless. Okoth was setting a fierce pace – trying to get to some sort of shelter before the dust storm hit them.

Looking back over his shoulder Reynard could see that the cloud was much closer now and was coming unerringly their way. He had no idea how long they had but it certainly looked like the storm would hit the hillside soon. Trusting in Okoth to judge when they should stop, he pulled out his canteen and drank deeply. He pulled his scarf back over his face, returned his water bottle to his pack and set off up the trail again.

The dust continued to swirl around them as the winds rose. It was getting increasingly harder to see any distance. Reynard could tell they must be nearly at the top of the ridge of hills now as the ground appeared to be levelling out, but they seemed to go over one false summit after another. Far behind them the sun had just set and the night was setting in. The dust storm now filled up most of the sky behind them and it looked very dark.

The group pushed on for another fifteen minutes, following the indomitable Okoth as he drove on up the trail. The dust storm was now almost fully upon them. The light had swiftly died as the thick swirling dust cloud enveloped them. Reynard, who was second on the trail, could only just make out the hulking form of the Nubian ahead of him. He took his scarf from his face and called out, "Okoth! Okoth! Stop a minute!" Dust and grit filled his mouth and he retched and spat to get as much out as he could. Ahead he could see the big man stop and turn back to him.

When Okoth reached him the Nubian took his cloak from his shoulders and draped it over Reynard to shelter them both from the storm as much as possible – at least enough for them to be able to speak together.

"We need to stop, Okoth. This is too dangerous. One of us could wander off the trail and get lost – or fall over a cliff and be injured or worse," Reynard shouted into the Nubian's ear.

"Okay, little man," agreed Okoth, trying to be heard above the whipping of the cloak around their heads. "You all stay here. I will find shelter and return soon."

Before Reynard could voice his opinion of the Nubian tracker's plan he was off, plunging on up the trail. By now the others had all reached Reynard's position. He signalled to them to join him and then he sat on the floor, trying to keep low and out of the winds. The others huddled down around him and Reynard passed on the general plan to them as best he could.

Minutes passed as the group waited on the trail side. The swirling winds battered and blasted them with grit and dust. Reynard began to fear for the great Nubian's safety but then a dark silhouette appeared through the swirling dust. Okoth was back.

"There is a cave," he told them. "Another hundred yards up the trail. It looks to me like Baku spent the night in there last night, or at least visited it around that time," he continued. "It is the perfect place to wait out the storm – and the night," he finished.

"Okay, everyone holds hands with the person in front and behind you," instructed Reynard. "Don't get split up. Stick together. We move at the speed of the slowest."

The group stood and made a human chain. Okoth led them up the trail, into the full onslaught of the biting winds. It was very hard work and

Reynard could feel the grit slipping into every fold of his clothing. Any part of his skin which was exposed was getting flayed now and the experience was turning from unpleasant to painful.

Eventually Okoth turned them off the trail. It was impossible to see more than a few feet ahead, but soon through the dust storm Reynard could just make out a darker area in the gloom of the dust and deepening night.

As he passed into the dark spot Reynard felt instant relief. The winds died and the grit and dust ceased flying. It was pitch black in here, but the wind and dust storm was gone. Reynard continued holding onto Okoth's hand ahead of him and Kita's behind him and trudged slowly onwards at the speed Okoth set.

Soon the big warrior stopped and let go of Reynard's hand. A few moments passed and then Reynard saw a spark fly and seconds later Okoth had a torch going. It lit up their immediate surroundings.

They were in a large round cave about thirty feet in diameter. The small side passage they had walked in was the only exit Reynard could see. It was pretty much the perfect spot to hide out the storm.

"Let's hunker down here and rest for the night," Reynard told the others. "There is no way we are going back out there in this storm and once it passes it will be too dark to follow a trail anyway. Let's take what we have and make the most of what looks like a comfortable place to spend a relaxing evening," he smiled.

The group happily dropped their packs to the floor and began to set out their bedrolls. Reynard tried to get the dirt and grit out of his clothes but found it was everywhere. He even had a nearly full boot when he took off his footwear to empty them. Worse still was the chaffed skin.

Mosi moved among the group, sitting with each one in turn and looking at the damage their skin had taken. He took some healing salves from his pack and applied them to each person's face and any other exposed skin where they had been damaged by the storm. His skills as a healer were not restricted to calling upon his god's power; he clearly was a talented herbalist too. The entire group thanked him for his help as his salve provided instant relief from the pain of sand burn.

Kita got a fire going – using the last of her fire wood she had carried with her – and they cooked up the last of the bacon. They decided they wanted a heart-warming dinner after the battle with the storm, and bacon and bread seemed to be just the medicine.

After a pleasant if dusty meal the group settled down to sleep out the rest of the storm and the night. Reynard posted a guard and each person wrapped themselves up in their bedrolls and tried to get some sleep.

*

Reynard was on last watch. He placed himself in the small passage which lead in and out of the cave and sat down with his back to the wall. He didn't bother with any light, preferring to let his eyes adjust naturally to the gloom and use his ears. His ears could not help but pick up the echoing sounds of the terrible keening wail they kept hearing. It was definitely nearer and louder now but he had no idea what it came from. Outside the dust storm must have passed because he could now see the occasional flicker of purple and orange glow lighting up the tunnel.

A couple of hours later Reynard became aware of a subtle lifting of the light. He knew dawn had broken outside the cave and he stood, stretched out his back and headed out into the morning light. Emerging from the cave into the morning sunshine Reynard realised that in their struggle to the top of the rise they had crested the summit. From the cave mouth it was a short distance to a small outcropping which overlooked the eastern landscape below them. Reynard moved across to it and sat down. Shielding his eyes against the early morning sunrise he struggled to make out what he was seeing. When he fully comprehended it he swore loudly.

The ridge dropped away from his vantage point, a few hundred feet or so, down to a large desolate plain. The plain stretched far off into the distance, east, north and south beyond the ridge. About five miles away down on the valley floor was a massive abnormality. A huge pulsing circle of energy floated in mid-air above the ground. The circle was purple and orange with flashes of crackling power fizzing across its surface.

As Reynard struggled to take in the strange view he noticed that the ground in front of the abnormality was moving. He strained his eyes, trying to focus, and slowly realised that the ground was not moving, rather it was covered with a giant swarm of tiny creatures, crawling over one another. As his brain started to make sense of the vista before him he realised that more and more of these tiny creatures were crawling out of the strange purple and orange vortex in the valley.

His mind flashed back to his history lessons. The island of Granita where he now sat was the site of the legendary Gate to the Void accidentally created by experiments of the most powerful High Magi of the Rainbow Empire five hundred years ago. It was the location where the Writhing Death had come into existence. According to legend a cadre of High Magi had travelled to Granita and had used ancient and powerful rituals to close the Gate, stopping the Writhing Death.

Now the Gate was open again and slowly and inexorably, the Writhing Death was returning.

As Reynard watched a creature popped out of the Void. It was large – the size of an average family dwelling – and hideously malformed. With legs and arms in strange places on its body, it had all of its internal organs on the outside and in weird places. The creature screamed in agony as its body expired, unable to cope with living in this environment. As it fell to the ground the swarm of tiny creatures covering the floor enveloped it and within seconds it was completely devoured.

Unable to tear his eyes away Reynard watched longer as more of these large creatures popped out of the Gate. Each was slightly different from the last, as if some deity was rolling dice to determine where each body part should be stuck. As each one was exhumed the Gate pulsed with the flash of purple and orange light which had been lighting the sky through the night. Most of these giant aberrations could not survive here and fell with a keening wail to earth where the Writhing Death simply devoured them. But as Reynard watched one came out which was suitably structured, the arms and legs mostly in the right places and with its organs on the inside. This one let out an enormous wail and an echoing bellow from a nearby hillside answered it. The giant beast strode off on wobbly legs to the hillside, where it joined a throng of hideous, misshapen aberrations which were aligned in ranks in front of a huge rock formation.

The rock formation was shaped in the rough form of a giant throne. The ranks of creatures were arrayed before the throne in fairly straight lines which seemed strangely incongruous, given the chaotic and hideous nature of the beasts. Sat on the throne was a giant hulking creature which seemed to be in charge of the host of aberrations and was organising and ordering them about.

Reynard strained closer to see the creature who sat upon the throne and who appeared to have control of this massive army of aberrations which were coming into this world from the Void. He strained to make out who it was that had control of the newly formed Writhing Death.

It was Baku.

-Epilogue-

The fire was burning low in the hearth and Reynard moved to throw another log onto it. It was midsummer but still his old quarters high in the eastern tower of the Iron Fortress were chilly. A low whistle sounded from the shutters opposite the hearth as the wind found its way through the ill-fitting wooden barriers. The flames in the hearth flickered and licked up the outside of the new log and started to consume it.

After warming his hands before the fire, Reynard moved to a nearby table, selected a sweet pastry from it and popped it into his mouth. He looked around the room. Tapestries hung from each wall, depicting various scenes of blacksmithing – the traditional craft of his House. Woollen rugs from across the empire were scattered across the floor, keeping the warmth in. Two torches spluttered in their sconces casting flickering shadows across the room. One stout wooden door led to the spiral staircase down to the rest of the fortress and another led to his bedroom. Both were closed.

Three comfortable couches were arrayed around the room and beside each was a set of low tables. The tables were festooned with plates of cold cooked meats, potatoes, salads, pastries and the like. Three carafes of wine and five wine glasses completed the ensemble. Seated on the couches were his friends. Six months ago he didn't know a single one of these people. Now he would trust each with his life.

"Civil war is coming," Reynard said as he looked into the faces of the four people arrayed around the room. "I have to consider my position as heir to the Iron House. With the emperor dead and the Azure House crumbling House Ferrand no longer has the protection it once had. I must put the future of my House and the safety of the people we protect first."

The group had been back in Providentia for only a few days. The first thing they had learnt upon their return to the empire was that the ancient emperor, Jovius II, last in the line of Lucar, had died. The line of Lucar had died with him and the Azure House had no heir. Currently there was no emperor and a huge power vacuum had formed. Rumour was rife and no one knew what would happen next, but everyone agreed civil war was inevitable.

"It doesn't matter what happens in the aftermath of your emperor's death," said Kita, putting her wine glass down. "If the Writhing Death is not stopped, you have no empire to argue over."

"The empire is in chaos," countered Reynard. "House Snow sits in their stronghold high in the mountains of Manabas and has taken no part in politics in many years. Who knows what they have been plotting all this time? House Ruby has been training Pyromancers, against the age-old decree banning any practice of arcane arts. House Ebon has been making efforts to bring our house under their control – who knows how many other minor houses they have gathered under their banner in secret? And the Jade House has spent the last six months building a corsair fleet to attack the other Houses and the interests of the powerful Guild of Master Merchants and Sea Farers. The Guild itself has set us the task of retrieving the lost Armour of Lucar – an ancient artefact with the power to enable its wearer to inspire fanatical loyalty in all those around him. I cannot, in good faith, leave my father to deal with this alone. I have to put my family first."

Kita nodded her understanding. "Yes, I can see why you feel that way," she said.

"What is your plan then?" asked Reynard.

"I will travel back to my homeland as quickly as possible and find Camero – the *wu-jen* who sent my father on his mission to find out what was going on in Granita. He will tell me what he wants me to do next. I think that he will ask me to help him try and close the Gate."

"That sounds dangerous."

"Yes, possibly. But I know it is the right thing to do. I cannot sit idly by and watch devastation come to this land – even if it is not my land. Not only is the Writhing Death forming again, but also this time it has an army of champions at its head. And that army is led by Baku. It has not escaped my attention that Baku has been all over this empire and learnt much about how it works. He knows your strengths and your weaknesses. He knows something of your politics and is almost certainly aware that the empire is about to collapse into civil war – where it will be extremely vulnerable. I cannot let this go unchallenged."

"What about the rest of you?" asked Reynard, looking about the room.

"I think I will also go with Kita," said Mosi. "The creation of a Gate to the Void here is of huge significance and I would like to lend my talents to the efforts to close it."

"What about you two?" Reynard asked Okoth and Tanithil, aware that everyone seemed to be about to set off and leave him in the middle of a civil war.

"I will stay with you little man," replied Okoth, though the customary smile was missing from his face. "You're the reason I have my freedom and if I can help you and your family then it is a chance to repay the debt I owe you."

"Thank you, Okoth. That means a lot to me. What about you, Tani?"

"It depends," replied the violet eyed Lucarcian. "As you say, the empire we belong to is on the brink of war. The noble Houses are all working hard against each other behind the scenes. Soon that will spill into open warfare. Alongside that, the powerful Guild are plotting and scheming. Everything looks grim indeed for the empire. What I want to know is: do you intend to take the Armour of Lucar back to the Trade Lords?"

"No," said Reynard, "I intend to wear it."